OLD NEWS

NEWS

A Piper Hampton Adventure

Jenean McBrearty

Jenean McBrearty is a graduate of San Diego State University, who taught Political Science and Sociology. Her fiction, poetry, and photographs have been published in over two-hundred print and on-line journals. She won the Eastern Kentucky English Department Award for Graduate Creative Non-fiction in 2011, and a Silver Pen Award in 2015 for her noir short story: *Red's Not Your Color.* She lives in Kentucky and writes full time —when she's not watching classic movies and eating chocolate.

Cover Design: Pepper Jones

ISBN: 9798655470163

Other Titles by Jenean McBrearty

Raphael Redcloak: Guardian of the Arts
Parker Hunt: A Man of Deeds
Helmut Wolf: A Good Engineer
The 9th Circle
Kill the Beautiful Bastards
Tales from the German Mind
Wanted Ones: Published Stories Vol. 1-8

Table of Contents

Chapter I

It was 92°. The desert wind crept over the foothills and descended on a Friday San Diego night. Patricia "Piper" Hampton, 17-year-old retro X-Files fan, had driven through the City College Jack-in-the-Box two minutes to closing time, and was looking for a place to devour her tacos before they got cold.

"You might want to turn down the air conditioner a few degrees if your goal's is to keep those *peros* edible," Josh, the psych major and older brother who blew his Nissan's engine, suggested.

Piper pulled over and stopped under the halo of the street lamp. "I hate Santa Anas," she said. She switched off the AC and rolled her window down halfway. Like bubbles escaping from a shaken Coke, the cool air squirted outside into a dry blast furnace. Josh had already finished his Jumbo Jack and started on his fries when Piper tore into her tacos.

"I can't believe mom and dad left you on your own for a week." Josh was always saying he couldn't believe something or the other. Terminal naiveté at twenty-one.

"I've got my GPA up to 3.6. What's not to love about a girl willing to kick her own butt into scholarship high gear?" The truth was, she refused to go back to Atlanta so soon after her Grandfather's funeral. Rummaging around in his three-story rickety Victorian to 'get his things cleared out' wasn't something she wanted to participate in. Grandpa should have cleared all the junk when Grandma Hampton passed. Everybody knew he wasn't going to last long without her. Sure enough, six months after Piper watched him wiping his eyes at Gussie Hampton's internment, they got another call from St. Elizabeth's Hospital. Winfield Scott Hampton was in the ER complaining of feeling tired. By the time a doctor got to him thirty minutes later, he was permanently asleep.

"Who'll weep for him?" Josh said when she demanded to know why he was flying back for the second funeral. She couldn't bear seeing her father cry a second time. She'd made the first flight only on the condition she wouldn't have to go to the gravesite.

Josh finished off his chocolate shake with a long, loud slurp. "When I was seventeen, they treated me like I was a delinquent."

"You were a delinquent."

"And an entrepreneur who made enough money waxing surfboards at Belmont Park to buy my first car," Josh reminded her.

Piper winced. Josh may have spent most of his junior and senior year at the beach, but he knew how to bust butt too. "Boys are trouble prone. They get into all kinds of crap."

"This coming from a girl who got her first speeding ticket on the way home from the DMV."

"I'm taking you home now, Josh Hampton." She blotted her tee-shirt with a napkin and wondered if taco sauce left a stain. She'd give it a good spray of Shout Out. "When's your Nissan going to be ready?"

"*Mañana.* Shelley's taking me to get it after school so you don't have pick me up."

Lithe and lovely, Shelley-the-girlfriend had long hair and more curves than Palomar Mountain Road. She came out to the car to say, "Hi. I just got home a minute ago, Babe," and smile. "Thanks for retrieving my handsome hulk from the hallowed halls of City College."

"No problem." But there *was* a problem with giddy girlfriend's constant alliterations. Poetry majors. Ha!

"She fed me too," Josh said as he grabbed his back pack.

Shelley slipped a ten into Pipers tee-shirt pocket and whispered, "Bless your heart. It's his last semester before he becomes an Aztec."

Piper stopped herself from rolling her eyes, and said just as sweetly, "Gonna wear SDSU red and black at long last." Josh was way past the preppy-fan stage, but he bounced with every step.

She watched them do a hug-walk all the way to their quaint WW II bungalow. She never did like couples who were a perfect match, but here was her brother and his soul mate right before her eyes. Josh would call tomorrow to check on her and ask if she wanted to go jogging with them in the park Saturday before the flight Sunday morning. It might stay 92 degrees Saturday, but he and Shelley would still pound the path. Josh always did have a macabre sense of fun. She'd beg off. Use the "I have cholera" excuse.

She headed back towards 395, and might have turned right onto the freeway, but turned left instead. What a great night to take pictures of the demolition site before the wrecking crew imploded the old gray Tribune Building.

She turned down Broadway, and then cut over to Market, past the Gaslight Quarter. Maybe someday, someone would pay good money for her photos of San Diego's old buildings. Her art teacher, *Mizz* King, said she had a natural eye for composition. Did people have unnatural eyes?

Before she reached Seaport Village, she made another left onto a dark street, and wondered if there was enough moonlight to get pictures at all. But she needn't have worried. From two blocks away, she saw the wrecking crew had already erected a chain-link fence around the quarter city block site and installed security flood lights that, for now, were dimmed to a glow. They'd probably go bright white if they sensed movement.

She parked across the street and assessed the likelihood of a camera and alarm system that would rouse the dead as well as the cops. She'd have to pass tonight. Tomorrow she could get past the fence. She could tell the guard the truth. Just a few close ups for her art class. Grown men never work weekends, but young guys who loved to flirt and feel important stood guard on Saturdays. She'd come back wearing a dress, with her prettiest smile and cold cans of Mountain Dew to soothe the savage beast.

***

"Piper? It's Mom. Josh said you gave him a lift last night. Thanks. Call me later. Love."

Mom's message went straight to voice mail. Piper checked

herself in the mirror, convinced she looked at least twenty and pleased she'd pulled off a *no-sleaze fatale* with nary a fashion *faux pas*. She loaded her supplies —a backpack full of junk food and bottled water —in her Rav 4 and headed downtown at three in the afternoon. She hung out at Seaport's Upstart Crow after an hour of street photography, indulging in a mocha latte and macaroons. At ten to five, she drove to the Trib Building and waited as a middle-aged loser-guy with the pot-belly traded places with a skinny twenty-something wearing pants two sizes too big. This was one well deserved mental pat on the back. She'd called it right.

"Hi. My name's Becky Thatcher," she said with a beaming smile when she stopped at the gate.

"Sure, it is. And I'm Robin Hood." His name patch had JIM embroidered in red script. "Wha'dya want?"

She looked through the thick lenses of his prescription sunglasses. "I've got an art assignment due Monday and if I don't do better than a C, I'm toast come finals. *Comprende?*" She held up her cell phone and waved to him. "Something old, something new, something borrowed, something sad. Nothing older or sadder than a condemned building." She put her cell in her purse and handed him a Mountain Dew. "I can pay for a guided tour."

"You go to City College?"

"Nope. UCSD." She gave him her best *faux*-flirty smile. It worked, sometimes.

"So, you're down town slumming, hunh?"

"Not at all. I just got through handing out sandwiches in the park with the St. Vincent de Paul people..."

"Is your real name Becky Thatcher?"

"People tease me about that all the time. I'd blame my parents, but they pay my tuition."

"You're a lousy liar. Leave your car outside the gate. It's time I made my rounds anyway." She parked behind the train-car-sized dumpster —out of sight, out of mind —and grabbed her purse.

The tour lasted half an hour. Piper took five good outside shots, but what she wanted was inside stuff. "This place isn't falling apart, is it? It looks like it was built to last a hundred years."

"Longer. It was built in nineteen ten."

"It's safe then. Why the demolition?"

She saw his chest expand and his face change from friendly to I'm-an-expert. "The City wants to add hotel space for the convention center. You know, follow the money. Too bad, too. They renovated the place in the nineteen thirties, and of course they've removed all the valuable art deco stuff, the wall lights, the chandeliers. But the mahogany banister and the marble stairs in the office foyer are still there. And the carved molding."

Piper sighed. "I'd love to get pictures of that. Couldn't we go inside so I can see the first floor? It seems to me you'd wouldn't mind preserving some of the other, not so valuable stuff, Jim, even if it's just in photos. You know a lot about this place, don't you?"

"I surf the internet on my phone, but not on company time. Hell, no. I'm all about following the rules."

"I'd give you a shout-out in the acknowledgements section of my presentation ... Jim ..?"

"Crenshaw. C-r-e-n-s-h-a-w. And you are?"

"P-i-p-e-r. Piper."

They piled into a golf cart covered with a red striped canopy and drove to the front door. Jim unlocked it and led her into the foyer. Piper could feel her eyes run dry as she fought not to blink. The sight might disappear. They were in a paneled room lined with office doors, with an enormous staircase front and center, still shiny with lacquer. And sealing the walls to the ceiling was intricately carved molding. Some of the octagon floor tiles were cracked, probably by careless dismantling crews, and on either side of the elevators were two fading but striking murals. One depicting agriculture of California, the other industry. She inspected them closely. Had the artist used real models for the faces of farmers, and pilots?

"Was Cecil Beatty a famous artist?" she asked.

"Some Depression-era artist commissioned by the Trib but paid by FDR's WPA to decorate."

She started snapping photos one after another. "They couldn't save the murals?"

"Didn't think they were any good, I guess. I like 'em, but what do I know about art?" Jim said.

"You know enough to want to save Mr. Beatty's work. Do the elevators work?"

"When there's electricity. It's shut off now."

"But there's security lights," Piper said.

"They run on generators and stay off unless there's an emergency. The plumbing still works, though."

"That's a plus." She took a photo of the wall-mounted directory between the elevators, noting that one half of the building only had two floors.

"The other side of the building is the original building where the presses are. Big ol' things. This side is the newer side that was added in '20s." Jim glanced at his watch. He withdrew his cell phone, hit his automatic connect, and said, "Badge 451 reports. All clear," then gave her a nod. "Piper, we gotta get back. I gotta check into the system and cruise the perimeter."

"Couldn't I stay here while you do that? I know my way out. Just let me get a few more shots. I promise I'll *vamoose* as soon as I finish. Please. Please."

Jim pulled off his sun glasses. "I'll be back in fifteen minutes. You better be gone."

"Wait," she said, and snapped a photo of Jim Crenshaw, ordinary citizen and art lover.

***

The first thing she noticed was how cool it was. Probably because closed windows and doors not only kept the hot air out, but kept the cooler air in. She went up the stairs and got some downward shots, all the while thinking she wouldn't be surprised to see Scarlet O'Hara and Rhett Butler coming towards her.

At the top, she saw three hallways, each with a sign identifying business offices, reporters, and presses. She headed down the hall marked offices.

"How wonderful to have worked in a place like this," she said as she gazed at a row of three by five-foot photos of old San Diego. The first was a street scene that seemed to move. She drew closer. Maybe it was ants moving across the paper —but no —the crowd of tiny people was bustling about and the tiny carriages and wagons and the horse-drawn trolley were hauling people and goods up and down Highland Avenue right in front of the Trib building. Piper rubbed her eyes. When she opened them again, everything was frozen again.

Imagination is a funny thing. She moved to the next photo dated 1925. The street was still busy, but the clothes had changed. Skirts were shorter. Hats were smaller. Girls looked thinner in their lighter colored dresses.

By the time she reached the end of the hallway, she'd traveled through eleven decades of history captured by photography. And in each picture, the crowds had diminished, and the commerce vehicles had turned to automobiles driving down the deserted street. But such wonderful pictures! They belonged in the Museum of Photographic Arts in Balboa Park, not abandoned to time with Mr. Beatty's murals. She turned to head back to the staircase and stared at the now barren walls. Nothing was there except for large square patches of faded paint.

Maybe it wasn't fear making her throat dry, but the stuffy, dusty air of disturbed antiquity. She took a bottle of water from her backpack and took a gulp, then another. She tested the floor with her foot. If pictures could disappear, maybe wood and marble could too. Silly. She needed to catch her breath, and somewhere in this place there had to be a lounge. Every big building had a lunch area or a cafeteria. A hundred-year-old building probably had a place for women with the vapors to lay down too. A bed would sure be nice. She reached for the handle of the door that had Managing Editor Seymour Vance stenciled on it. Important people usually had amenities no one else had.

"What are you doing standing around?" a voice boomed behind her. She spun around and saw a ruddy-faced giant in a grey suit and wire-rimmed spectacles grimacing down at her. "Well? You think I'd be in my office when we're getting out a late edition?"

"I ...I was just taking a few pictures, Sir," she stammered.

"Get those pictures over to the reporters. Move!"

She sidled past him, scrambled down the hall, and turned left, bumping into a tall, thin, man with a pencil behind one ear, rolled up sleeves and a row of cigars in his chest pocket. "Come on." He grabbed her arm and pulled her through the Reporter doorway.

"What'cha got, Honey?" He sat on the edge of one of twenty desks that filled a room alive with the sounds of ticker-tapes and typewriters running full blast.

"I'm just taking pictures of the building..."

He sobered. "Oh. Oh. You must be with the architects and the decorators. Always underfoot. But you seem like a nice kid. We're waiting for pictures of the Hindenburg tragedy. You know, explosion stuff. Human suffering. Human interest. Sells papers and makes the world go 'round." He unwrapped a cigar and struck a match with his thumb. "Our damn wire service ain't workin' and we're hurtin' for news, you know? Can't have a front page without a photo."

"The Hindenburg?"

A woman wearing a white shirt and tweed slacks came in and shoved a stack of photos at him. "Choose one of these, Mitch. They don't call me Hot-shot McKnight for nothing."

He perused the photos, handed one back to her and put the rest on his desk. "This one, and get it downstairs. This one here!" he yelled to the room as he waved the photo around in the air. "Full half, page one!"

"Oxymoron, Mitch," the woman said.

"I'll give you three bucks for it, McKnight."

"Sold!"

She scurried away, and Piper noticed him looking at her rear. "Where's she going," she said. Had she awakened in an urban Oz?

"To lay-out. Calls herself a photojournalist now that Daddy

bought her a camera. She's damn good too."

"How did she get a picture from New Jersey? I thought you said…"

Mitch laughed. "She didn't take it. She got it off the wire service and delivered it." He winked at her, and whispered, "Her Daddy's with ONI in Long Beach, Office of Naval Intelligence to you. She probably drove up last night."

"Mitch! Copy ready!" someone yelled, and he took off in the direction of a bald man sitting at the biggest desk in the room. Piper picked up one photo in the stack of pictures he'd left, and eyed a Zeppelin engulfed in flames. She'd seen a film clip of the airship disaster in history class. She noticed the calendar on Mitch's desk: May 7, 1937.

He walked back to her. "What's your name, Honey?"

"Piper Hampton." She preferred her nickname to the vintage Patricia.

"Oh, Johnny's cousin? I thought he said your name was Nancy. But knowing Johnny Hampton, he couldn't have a cousin named Nancy. It's too respectable. Okay, Piper, what say we get some dinner?"

A silver Oldsmobile Coupe waited in the parking lot. When Mitch walked to the driver's side, she snapped pictures of the car, the parking lot, anything and everything she saw to record the dream that seemed to be more real than her life.

He said they'd drive to Rudy's, a small cafe on 5th Avenue three doors down from the Dalton's Department Store at the corner of

Broadway. Mitch gabbed the entire way, mostly about the Hindenburg incident that signaled the end of the Zeppelin era and how he wished it would put an end to the Versailles era as well. "That ain't gonna happen though. The Germans sent the Condor Legion of the Luftwaffe to Spain to help Franco's fascists. Your nose is shiny, Honey," he said, and it gave Piper an idea. He expected her to be vain.

She took out her cell phone and pretended it was a compact. It gave her a chance to take close-ups of Mitch and the inside of the car. Maybe she'd wake up in the next few minutes and the pictures would be gone, but the memory of taking them wouldn't disappear.

"Where do you know Johnny from?" she asked. They dined on hamburgers and milk shakes that were little more than softened ice cream.

"The rails in '33. We're both Georgia boys. Met up outside of Wichita at a squatter's camp. Somebody yelled Mitch and I thought they were callin' me, but it was some guy named Bob Mitchum they were wanting. Johnny thought it was funny because my name's Mitch Roberts. We decided we'd become newspapermen and write about the Depression like Steinbeck's doing, you know? But when the war broke out in Spain, Johnny decided he wanted to be a war correspondent like Hemingway. You go to the front, Johnny, and send me dispatches, I told him." Then Mitch got quiet. Not that he just stopping talking, but in the way he ate, too. Slow. He didn't look at her directly when he finally said. "I haven't heard from him in weeks. Your family must be worried sick about you, too."

Piper took out her compact again. She didn't know exactly what he was talking about. Maybe she looked like a rail rider. "They're worried alright." Through her lens, she could see that many people looked worried. A sailor sitting at the counter ate with his arm around the waist of his girlfriend. A mother dawdled over a banana split she shared with her six-year-old son. And an old man sitting alone in the booth next to them rubbed his chin and then his forehead as he pored over a copy of *Life Magazine*. She thought about what her parents must be going through in Atlanta, sleeping in the house of a dead man. "I think I need a place to stay, Mitch."

He smiled. "I figured you're working on spec. I'll talk to Hot-shot."

Chapter II

Hot-shot —real name Carole McKnight —lived on the first floor of a rooming house near the Grey Castle. That's what they called San Diego High School built at the edge of Balboa Park. Piper had driven by it a thousand times on her way home from Josh's place. The rooming house was at the bottom of a hill, on a side street off Park Boulevard. Mitch called it an apartment, but it was more like a hotel room with a hot plate below a sign that read No Cooking in Rooms. It did have a separate bathroom. "A blessing when I have to take a shower at two AM," Hot-shot said. "It ain't much, but you're welcome to the sofa."

Piper saw Mitch slip her a fiver. She saw the fiver again the next morning when Hot-shot took her across the street to a hole-in-the-wall coffee shop that would eventually become the Jack-in-the-Box she'd ordered from the night before. Next door was a filling station where Hot-shot topped off her tank for a dollar, and that's where she got her first sight of the special edition on the Hindenburg tragedy. Hot-shot bought three copies —one to read, one to save, and one to send to her Dad in Long Beach.

"It's wonderful to be part of something like this," Piper said as she perused the paper while Hot-shot drove her back to the Trib Building. She must have looked silly rubbing the paper between her fingers; it had an odd feeling to it, like toilet paper odd.

"What are you going to do for money, Kid?" Hot-shot had pulled into the parking lot and was giving her the once over.

Piper thought about the debit card in her wallet and the two-hundred dollars sitting in the Bank of America branch in Kensington that might as well be Fort Knox. "I gotta get a job somewhere. You know anyone who's hiring?" Her computer skills were useless but she could sweep floors or wash windows.

"Can you make change?"

"Sure."

"The Bay Theater's looking for a box office girl. I know the manager there. He's one of the good guys. Try to look older and you might pass for nineteen. He likes to hire pretty faces but doesn't want minors working there 'cause of all the sailors and Marines. They'll try to pick you up. That never works out."

"I'd be grateful if you'd talk to him," Piper said. The reality of being destitute was beginning to sink in. What if she never woke up from this dream? She felt a tear come out of nowhere and meander down her cheek. Was she dead?

"You wait here. I'll tell Mitch I need to talk to old man Goldstein."

Piper held on to her hand. "Ms. McKnight, I ... don't know what to say. I thought I would, but ..."

"Don't worry kid. I've been where you are. Whatever happened at home, well, lots of families need one less mouth to feed. It's not that that they don't love you. Times are hard is all."

***

Marvin Goldstein was a short, dark, fierce looking man. Hot-shot said his parents were Cossacks who emigrated from Russia after the '17 Revolution.

"When we go in his office, notice the picture of Czar Nicholas hanging on the wall by the file cabinets. The autograph is genuine, he says. But I don't know if anybody believes him. I mean, Czars aren't like movie stars." Piper did glance at the picture when Goldstein went to the file cabinet to get an employment application. Sure enough, there was an illegible signature scrawled near the bottom. It could have read Kanye West for all she knew.

"You like movies?" Goldstein asked as he handed her the application. "The greatest invention since electricity, eh? Them damn Nazis make good use of them. Them and their propaganda. Who's your favorite movie star? Bogart? Stewart? I tell you who I like. The Marx Brothers. Saw them in vaudeville in New York. Funnier guys you never saw. All the time with the jokes. Can you start work this afternoon? Saturday's always busy."

Piper left with a maroon uniform that made her look like a hotel bell-boy and promised to come back after lunch. She'd work one to nine for minimum wage, forty-three cents an hour, and Hot-shot would pick her up. "Make sure you go to the bathroom before you start work, and don't drink water," Goldstein instructed. "I got nobody to relieve you and I don't want my customers waiting in line so they can change their mind. Let's go bowling, they might say. Get 'em in quick so they buy lots of popcorn. You got that? Push the popcorn so it doesn't waste. Nothin' worse than day old popcorn."

Piper nodded. "Thank you, Mr. Goldstein. I appreciate this."

"Sure. Sure. Show up and don't steal. And don't let nobody

sweet talk you into letting them in for free. I fired the last girl because she let people in for free. Can you run a business like that?"

"No, Sir."

Goldstein was right. By one-fifteen, people were lined up down the block to see The *Awful Truth* with Cary Grant and Irene Dunne and *Charlie Chan at the Olympics* with Warner Oland. She had to get used to selling tickets off the roll, but making change wasn't a problem. Admission was a nickel for kids and a dime for adults. Piper thought about paying twelve-fifty for a matinee showing of *The Avengers VI*. It's the technological effects, she knew, but still ...

At four, Goldstein came out to the window. "Take a break. Get a coke. I take the money." She ran to the bathroom, grabbed a coke, and was back in ten minutes. "The navy will be here in a few minutes. Smile. Flirt. As soon as they get a ticket, yell, next! Anybody gives you guff, you come get me."

He waddled off. One of the good guys.

***

The program changed after nine. Hot-shot picked her up at five after and told her not to pay any attention to the clientele that would be queuing up. "After nine, Goldstein shows girlie movies. No one under eighteen allowed."

"Some of those guys don't look eighteen to me," Piper said when she got in the car.

"If they're old enough to join the service, their old enough to see peep shows, Goldstein says."

They drove up Broadway, and Piper watched the night crowd

take over the downtown streets. Was that a cop she saw walking among the people? Yes, and there were SPs and MPs —Shore Patrol and the Military Police.

"Tomorrow you can catch the bus at the stop across from the high school at noon. Tell the driver you want off at Fifth, and you'll have time to walk the two blocks to work." Hot-shot handed her three dollars. "Mitch said I should give you this for bus fare and a sandwich."

"He's good people. I think he likes you," Piper said.

"Lots of guys are good people and lots of guys will like you. You just can't like them back if you know what's good for you."

As friends go, Mitch and Hot-shot McKnight were the best ones she ever had. Hot-shot was saving her money to move to Los Angeles when and if the Times ever called her for an interview because LA is where the real money is. San Diego's just a small military town compared to Hollywood-land, she said. Mitch was saving for a house. He had an apartment on Front Street. One with a separate bedroom and a real kitchen. He called it a mansion compared to the house where he grew up in Georgia. Yet, they both seemed to feel it was their responsibility to look after her —the stranger in their midst —without question.

She spent her third night in '37 at the Young Women's Christian Association at 10th and C street. McKnight talked to Director Stevens, who put her name at the top of the list because of her age. "You're a hard-ship case," McKnight explained.

"Miss McKnight tells me going home isn't an option for you,

Miss Hampton. You're not in the family way, are you? If so, the Salvation Army runs a home for such cases."

"No, Ma'am. I'm very careful."

Stevens raised an eyebrow. "I can make a referral."

"I'm okay, really. And I have a job."

"Miss McKnight told me. Maybe we can find something more suitable later." Stevens handed her a Resident's Handbook. "We charge $2.00 a month, $2.50 for a room with a bath. No cooking in the rooms, but you can have candy or fruit. The cafeteria closes promptly at eight o'clock, but I'll have one of the cooks set aside a plate for you. We lock the front door at ten. You can receive visitors in the lounge, but, of course, no gentlemen callers allowed upstairs. No smoking. No drinking. If you break the rules, we'll ask you to leave."

"Yes, Ma'am, I understand."

"You can walk to work in the daytime, but I wouldn't advise it at night. Miss McKnight said she'd fetch you after work."

"She's been very kind." Piper handed her $2.50 and wondered if she could survive till payday on fifty cents.

"She stayed here until she found her place. Always neat. Always followed the rules."

Piper followed her up two flights of stairs and down a long, white hallway to a room. Hot-shot had brought her a toothbrush, a towel, a change of clothes, and a promise: "Tomorrow, I'll take you over to the Salvation Army for something to wear on your days off. Can you drive a car?"

"Only an automatic."

"Wow. My Dad said they were developing automatic transmissions. I didn't know they were available already. Your folks own a Cadillac or something?"

Her Dad drove a Lexus and her Mom a Prius, the cars meant to impress other architects and other government HR Specialists. "They've test driven one. But I'm a quick study! You just show me how to shift and I'll get used to it."

Much as she valued privacy, the reality of aloneness hit her hard that night as she lay on the bed listening to the unfamiliar sounds of downtown. The jumble of juke box music from the bars and eateries on Broadway. The sirens. The chatter-banter of the sailors heading back to the pier. It'd been a long day sitting alone in the ticket booth. Goldstein said weekday afternoons would be tough. "Hope you enjoy reading because that's all there is to do Monday and Tuesday."

Wednesday and Thursday were her days off. If Mitch could take time off, maybe it was time she told him the truth and beg him to help. The Dorothy Gale thing had lost its excitement. She'd clicked her heels and repeated there's no place like home a hundred times in the ticket booth, but, with no ruby slippers, it wasn't going to work. She'd have to try something else.

***

"Take me to lunch?" Piper gave Mitch a smile and looked over his shoulder. "Hot-shot around?"

"She's out taking pictures of the Padres. But I can pop for a hot dog at Bernie's." Mitch grabbed his tweed sport coat and steered her out the reporter's room door. "Heard you got a room at the Y. Good. How's the job?" They descended the marble staircase and went to the parking lot. "Feel like walking?"

"Sure. The job is fine. I wanted to say thank-you. And other stuff."

"Knock it off. You'd do the same if I was in a jam." He tried to sound as gruff as Editor Vance. Practicing being a curmudgeon. Instead of turning toward the street, he led her to the parking lot and his silver coupe. "On second thought, let's go to the beach."

Ten minutes later they were eating hot dogs at the Ocean Beach Boardwalk Piper hardly recognized. "We can talk private here," Mitch said.

From his attitude so far, Piper figured he didn't go in for small talk. "I'm not from around here."

Mitch interrupted. "I know. Muller said you wouldn't be."

"Muller?"

"You probably know him as Anatole Bauer. I figured you'd want to make contact as soon as you were settled in. Welcome." He handed her a business card that read: German-American Bund. In the corners were embossed U.S. and Nazi flags. "Bauer's house is in Point Loma where he can keep tabs on ship and personnel movements. You want to meet him and Honnolore tonight?"

Piper finished a bite of hot dog. "Uh. Not tonight. I have an ice cream date with Hot-shot."

"Perfect! Already infiltrating. Bauer had his reservations when I told him how young you are, but I said New York knows what it's doing. How soon do you think you'll be meeting Daddy Navy Guy?"

Her mind raced through her McKnight file, and found his reference to Carole's father, the naval intelligence guy. "Sooner than I thought," she said.

Mitch gave her an admiring glance. "I'm impressed. Shall I tell Bauer we'll come tomorrow? We can have dinner before the Bund meeting." He handed her another five. "Buy something nice. Sweet and sexy. Something that says it's okay to flirt with you. It's all about donations, right? You've heard the Bund is getting flak from D.C. Anatole says Kuhn's headed for legal trouble even if he doesn't know it."

She didn't recognize the names but she knew enough to keep her mouth shut. "Okay. I'll see you at five-thirty, then. But, you'll have to pick me up."

"You need a car. What's your favorite color?"

Was he serious? "I like yellow." She slid the card into her wallet.

"Yellow it is." He gave her a poke in the ribs. "The Bund's gonna take real good care of you. You're a natural. We'd better get back."

***

Mitch dropped her off at the Y with a reminder of their date. Alone in her room again, Piper laid on the bed staring at the ceiling fan, wracking her brain for a memory of history class. When did the

Second World War start? She tried her cell phone to do a little research, but, of course, it couldn't deliver. Nine-teen thirty something. August. No that was the first war. December 7, 1941. Yeah, that was it. Something about infamy.

***

"What do you think, honestly?" she said to Carole when she'd finished relating her conversation with Mitch. Bernie's would be empty until four when the sailors came ashore. The pier-side restaurant was new, according to Carole. Piper and Josh went there often because it was a landmark.

"What do you think?" Carole was staring at Mitch's business card that now bore a chocolate ice-cream fingerprint.

"I think they think I'm a spy."

"Are you?"

"Oh God, no. I could barely remember the date the war begins."

"Which war?"

"Ahhh…the last one," Piper said. It's embarrassing when you realize you sound stupid.

Carole signaled the waitress and ordered two coffees when she came to the table. "Even if they're in the espionage business, why would they believe you're a contact?"

Piper took advantage of the opening. "Maybe because of this." She turned on her cell phone and gave it to Carole, who examined it intently. "Just touch the screen."

Carole peered at one picture after another. "Where's the film?"

"There isn't any. It's digital."

"Digital? Is that a scientific term?"

"A top-secret scientific term. I was taking pictures when I got here."

Carole tried to hide a grin. "And where would a young run-away like you get a top-secret scientific camera?"

Piper wasn't prepared for the question. "You can see it's not a toy." Suddenly sober, Carole looked closer at the photographs before handing the camera back to Piper. "And tomorrow I'm supposed to tell Mitch and Bauer when I can meet your dad. Bauer's interested in naval operations. You've got to listen, Carole. There's going to be another war."

Carole laughed nervously. "Not in this century! Hitler talks a good game, but he's all carnival and no star."

"You're wrong. Dead wrong. I think you know it. Your dad has to know it too." The tears of this afternoon's bout with loneliness were threatening to return. Wednesdays were lattes-at-Starbucks days with her mom. Thursdays were gym day to sweat them off.

"Look, kid," Carole said. "Things are tough. I know. The depression is hurting all of us nobodies. But the Bund is only one organizations. Lots of people support Hitler, although they won't admit it. Germany's economy is roaring along while millions of our people are still out of work. There's no reason why Hitler would go to war and throw all that prosperity away. It doesn't make any sense."

"Then why does he have spies in a Navy town? Answer me that."

"You say they're spies, but I've met the Bauers. They came here after the war because of the way things were in Germany. Starving people. Communist agitators. Violence in the streets. They've got Old Country manners and think Hitler's the Second Coming, but they're harmless."

"They take peoples' money."

"Like every other preacher in town. Look, Piper, there are government spies and there are industrial spies. I'd want to know which they are before I'd report a guy like Mitch for sedition ...or anybody." It was Carole's turn to look away now. She scanned the juke box list of tunes and pretended she hadn't given away her feelings. "I couldn't have made it without his help, and neither could you."

Piper had hoped Carole returned Mitch's feelings for her, but now their relationship seemed all wrong. Dangerous even. "Maybe there's a reason Mitch helps damsels in distress. Damsels who have navy dads and small cameras."

She was truly alone. If Carole didn't believe her about possible espionage, she sure wouldn't believe a story about a lost-in-time traveler. She put the camera back in her purse and held it tightly in her lap. If something bad happened to her, there was no way to notify her family anyway. With no way to call or text, or recharge her camera, her cell phone would be useless very soon. "I'm going to meet with Bauer so I can snoop" she said.

Chapter III

Mitch picked her up at quarter to six. She expected sauerkraut not spaghetti from her obviously pro-Hitler hosts. Adolph's picture was prominently displayed over the fireplace mantel, to the left hung a portrait Fritz Kuhn —identified as the American Fuehrer by a banner underneath —to the left was a Nazi flag. Honnolore, a model-thin woman of forty-something, dragged her into the kitchen to help cut Italian bread into slices and slather them with butter, while she fussed over the sauce and chattered about what a good guy Mitch is. "He's a catch," seemed to be her favorite words in her rave review. She uttered them every five minutes.

"I think Carole McKnight knows that. She's in love with him," was Piper's contribution to the discussion.

The remark caused a long pause in Honnolore's soliloquy. "Trust me, she's not his type," she said after adding another half cup of wine to the simmering tomato sauce.

"She's been a life-saver to me," Piper said.

"It's good you're friends. The closer the better. Wait until you see the car Anatole found. A yellow coupe. Fred Gunderson just happened to have one sitting on his lot. He's bringing it to the hall. Such a pretty dress. Shows off your bosom."

The dress was thirty-five-cents worth of pretty from the used store on Market Street. A light white cotton with blue polka-dots with a white belt to match her new dollar-fifty shoes. She and Carole had shopped all afternoon.

"You *are* a delight," Mitch said when he saw her.

"I scrub up well." She wondered who these people really thought she was.

The Bund met in an Ocean Beach hall rented from the Sacred Heart Catholic Church two blocks away. It wasn't fancy, but Bauer had done it up right with bunting, flags and a podium. Piper expected tattooed skin-heads, but the audience was mostly middle-aged couples who mostly ignored her after Mitch introduced her as the Bund's newest member. He yielded the floor to Anatole Bauer, and from then on Piper felt like she was in church.

He led them in a prayer thanking God for the *Fuhrer*, and a chorus of *Deutschland Uber Alles*. He read a passage from *Mein Kampf* and spoke about how the Jewish bankers were monopolizing the world's currencies. Piper understood little of what he said, but it was clear he wasn't happy about unemployment, homelessness and the birth rates of undesirables. The enthusiastic applause made it clear his listeners agreed with him. Twice they stood up and yelled, "Truth! Truth!" when Bauer assured them Hitler would put a stop to it.

Honnolore spoke too, urging every woman to have at least three children. One to replace your husband. One to replace yourself. And one for the Fatherland. From the way the women nodded their heads in agreement, Piper concluded they thought it was a good idea.

And, just like church, Bauer passed the plate. People dropped in checks, and bills, and envelopes. Bauer made a special mention of Gunderson's donation of a car for the 'East Coast runaway' and winked at the crowd. The Treasurer made her report and announced the Bund had a thousand-fifteen-dollars in the coffers after expenses, and was sure more would be coming. That got a round of applause too, and Piper was invited to stand. Suddenly, they were paying attention to her. By the time school started in September, the Treasurer noted, the Bund would have enough to restart week-end German language classes at the hall despite last year's difficulty finding friendly facilities.

At nine sharp, the meeting ended. "Wednesday meetings are purposely short because some members have to look for work," Anatole Bauer explained as he walked her outside where the yellow Ford coupe was parked. He handed her a key. "She's all yours."

Piper managed a weak, "Thank-you," What was she expected to do in return? If it had anything to do with donating a windfall or teaching German, they were out of luck. "Is it really mine?"

Bauer laughed. "Check the registration. You'll find Mitch's contribution in the backseat."

It was a jack and a lug wrench with a note that read SPARE IN THE TRUNK. What would she tell Carole? Too bad you had to save your money, I got my car from Hitler. She wouldn't blame the woman if she got pissed —but then again, here was evidence Mitch and the Bund believed she was somebody important.

"The car speaks for itself, doesn't it? They think I'm related to an east coast big-shot. It's crazy."

"Maybe you are related to an eastern family. The Capones of East Chicago. Or the Lucases. Maybe you just don't remember."

Carole ran her fingers lovingly over the soft brown leather upholstery. "Where are you from? Why have you come here? And how? You didn't ride the rails or hitch-hike."

The questions came pouring out. The ones, Piper was sure, that had plagued Carole since the day they met. "Okay. I'm going to tell you, but you have to tell me what Honnolore meant when she said you weren't Mitch's type." She and Carole weren't BFFs, but if they cleared the air, maybe they could be. "Let's play Twenty Questions. I'll go first," Piper said and held up a finger. "I'm from San Diego." She held up another as though she was counting. "I was born here, to Chuck and Sunny Hampton. He's from Atlanta, Georgia. Mom's from Lexington, Kentucky. I have a brother, Josh. He's twenty-one and lives with Shelly-the-girlfriend, in 2018." She took out her cell phone. "This is a phone as well as a camera and a data storage device." She clicked on a picture. "This is Josh and Shelly-the-girl-friend. There, that's eight answers in a row."

Carole looked at the photo. The young couple was standing in front of the El Cid statue in Balboa Park. They were both wearing shorts and printed cotton under shirts that read UK Cats, Undefeated SEC Champs 2015. Behind them were rows of automobiles she'd never seen before. "What kind of cars are these?"

Piper tapped the screen until a picture of her white RAV 4 came up. "This is my Toyota. It's a Japanese car. Twenty-five years after the war, Japan starts importing cars to America. Toyotas. Datsuns. Nissans. This is a Sport Utility Vehicle. SUV. Six cylinders. Automatic transmission. Air conditioning." She showed Carole her key ring, and the key with the Toyota logo. She pulled out her wallet and showed Carole her driver's license, social security card, insurance card, and her plastic debit card. But the biggest piece of evidence was her check book register with three calendars: 2016, 2017, and 2018. "You can believe I'm crazy, but you can't think for a minute I can manufacture stuff like this. In my world, you're ninety-nine, if you're still alive. Okay, now it's your turn. Go!"

But Carole couldn't take her eyes off the cards, keys and cell phone pictures. She kept turning them over, tracing the embossed numbers and the printed names. "I don't understand how this could happen," she said softly. "Or why."

"Neither do I, but it has."

Carole stopped staring at the artifacts, and patted Piper's hand. "You must miss your family terribly."

Piper nodded and stifled a sob rising from the pit of her stomach. "My Dad will keep busy designing his dream house, but my Mom is the emotional type. Cries when she sees pictures of baby bunnies. When I think of the agony she must be going through, you can't imagine how it feels."

"You're wrong there. Mitch found me walking along the beach, six months pregnant. Just fired from Oscar's Drive In. No place to go. I couldn't tell my family. You know how it is. Mitch took me to the Bauers and they took me in. Arranged a private adoption. Mitch got me the job at the Trib. I'm in the typing pool and moonlight as a photojournalist. That, my Dad can handle." It was Carole's turn to share a photo. A baby girl with a face crowned with auburn ringlets.

"My Dad's proud of the photojournalist me. The Hot-Shot part. The unwed mother Carole me is still a deep, dark secret."

"She's beautiful," Piper said. "What's her name?"

"Suzanne Somebody. I never met the people. Honnolore said they had enough money to give her the life I'd want her to have. I'm sure that's true. They know scads of wealthy people."

"How old is she?"

"Over a year, now. This was taken when she was three months old."

"Did Mitch know your father's a Navy big-wig before he helped you?"

"I know what you're thinking, but Mitch doesn't believe in all that Nazi stuff, Piper. Honest."

"He's got me fooled. You should have seen him last night. What does he do for the Bund, anyway?"

"He's sort of a mechanic. Secretary. Security. Gives them good press." She paused. "Recruits."

"How long has it been since you went to a Bund meeting?"

Carole thought for a minute. "I haven't been there for a year at least. Mitch thought that was the best way for me to forget my experience."

"And this picture is supposed to help you forget her and how he helped you, right?" Who knew a photograph could be as heavy as an anchor chain? Mitch had to keep Carole on the string while he was free to recruit new girls. Like her.

"I get crazy with curiosity about her sometimes. Guess that's natural though, right?"

It sounded like Carole expected an answer. "I'd say it was absolutely natural."

Carole put the picture back in wallet. "Maybe I'll tell my parents someday, when I'm married and have a few grandkids to take her place. But, right now, you'll keep my secret, won't you?"

"Absolutely. If you keep mine. I haven't told Mitch anything about myself. He's never asked either." It was too soon after swapping confidences to ask to see her dad, but Piper knew he was the one she needed to talk spy-stuff with. It was also too soon to suggest that Carole lived in fear that Mitch and his spies would tell her father about Suzanne even if it was a foregone conclusion. But, Piper was desperate. "I have to talk to a grown-up about the Bauers. Your dad can tell me what to do —who to talk to." This round of the twenty-questions game had ended in sniffles and sadness. It was time to appeal to sentiment. "He might be able to explain my being here, him being in intelligence. And I can go home."

***

On the deck of a wooden hulled fishing trawler, the *Sea Rover*, Piper zeroed in on two men in white uniforms walking past a row of saluting sailors. She and Carole had driven to the Long Beach's Terminal Island Pier to meet Captain Mike McKnight following his inspection of the ship for possible Navy purchase. He spotted the two young women, whose presence seemed to reinvigorate the snap of the crew's salute and waved as he came down the gangplank.

"There's my favorite brunette," he said, and gave Carole a hug and a kiss. "You must be the photography friend." He shook hands with Piper. "Catch up with you later, George," he said to his companion who was giving them the once-over. "I'm treating my daughter and her friend to lunch."

The man's eyes shifted immediately to the waiting black sedan with the blue and gold flags on its bumpers. "Have a great time, ladies," he said and waved.

Mike was so much like her dad, Piper wondered if there was a secret dad-school in California. "Nice to meet you, Captain McKnight," she said.

"Nice smile. Nice manners. Nice attitude. You'll definitely be a good influence on this wild child of mine." He slid his arm around Carole's shoulders as they walked towards Piper's yellow coupe.

"We're here on a mission, Dad," she said.

"Sounds serious. Is this your car?" he said to Piper.

"Yes, Sir."

"It's a doozy."

Carole gave Piper a quick glance. "It's part of the story."

After rib steaks and baked potatoes at the Harbor House, and plenty of small talk about the Hindenburg accident that ended the Zeppelin era, they drove to the McKnight's house. It was one of those Spanish designs that was all the rage in the 1920's, with a red tiled roof and white stucco walls. Mrs. McKnight kept it immaculate. "Mother doesn't trust the maid service," Carole explained when a thick-set Irish woman opened the door and sent them up-stairs to wash up as though they were children. "She brought Tessie with them from Ireland when I was two. One thing, though, you'd better talk to Dad privately. I'll let Mom try to talk me into moving home, while you share particulars with him."

Captain Mike led her into the den, a sort of home office and smoking room, Piper surmised as she noted the OFF-LIMITS sign on the door. Her Dad's man-cave sign read Welcome to the Jungle. "We won't be disturbed," he said as he closed the door. He settled into an anchor print overstuffed chair with a matching hassock and lit up his pipe. "Why don't you tell me your thoughts about Mitch, and your meeting with the Bauers."

"How do you know about that?"

"The ONI has a mole in the Bund."

"Mitch Roberts?"

"Certainly not!" he blurted, then took a deep breath. "We got word there was a new face in town. Why don't you start from the beginning?"

Once again, her words tumbled out, surprising her with their desperation. "They're happy I'm infiltrating your family, but I know you're not going to give me any secrets. Why would you? Especially if you're important. What should I do?" she pleaded as a way of tying up the whole miserable olio into one big package of unhappiness.

McKnight emptied his pipe bowl. "What do you know about a girl named Edwina Blackledge?"

"Nothing, sir. Never heard of her."

"She's the daughter of Alfred Blackledge who owns At-Pac

Merchant Marine Builders in New Jersey. The Bund headquarters. She was supposed to pick up a hundred thousand dollars of West-region donation money about nine months ago and deliver it to Alfred for recruiting and training German sympathizers in the ship building and airplane industries. Propaganda and lawyers take a lot of money, and they're going to need a boatload of it since Kuhn came back from his visit to Berlin. The Feds are fuming over our inability to crack the case as much as Kuhn."

"Who's this Kuhn guy?"

"Fritz Kuhn, the man behind the Bund," the Captain explained.

"Well, I don't have any money, and Mitch knows I'm broke."

"They all know you're not Edwina either. She's dead. Nobody's sure how she died. The press reported that she was thrown from her horse at her father's Texas ranch. A fabrication, of course. Her body was found in a seedy El Paso hotel, minus the money. The speculation is that she was running off with a lover who loved money more than her or Hitler. Not exactly a patriotic demise for the kid of a true believer in Nazi moral purity."

"So, who do the Bauers think I am?"

"Her replacement, probably. Do you honestly think they'd believe you're a time traveler? You haven't told them, I imagine. My guess is, they think you're here to investigate how the cash went missing. Maybe uncover the facts about Edwina's demise."

"Why don't they just call New York and verify who I am?"

"And let the investigators know they know they're being investigated? They'd lose their plausible deniability in case, well

…in case something happens to you. You're too useful to them now anyway. They know you're friends with Carole and who I am."

"Do they think ONI had something to do with Edwina's murder?" Piper said.

"Maybe. More likely, they think Berlin sent you to find out if the Bauers had had something to do with it, and your stranded young woman role is just a very good cover story. The Nazis are great at using people."

"*Did* Naval Intelligence have anything to do with Edwina's murder?"

Captain Mike shook his head no. "One thing I can tell you about the spy game —real spies play for keeps and they play with a lot of other dangerous people."

Piper slid off her perch on the arm of the sofa and sank into the cushion. She brought out her cell phone and gave it to the Captain. "I think they want this. Although why they don't just take it from me, I don't know. Mitch can't believe my phone is a compact full of face powder."

He examined the phone and gave it back. "Without knowing how it works or who manufactured it, they'd never take it. You might be a genius, and your invention would be worthless to them, especially if it's designed to self-destruct. The Nazis may be politically misguided, but they're not stupid."

"They lose the war," Piper countered.

She saw concern cloud his face. "Many of us believe Herr Hitler's on the road to war. It'd be terrible if we were right."

"It's going to be more than terrible for millions of people," she said. "I know that much."

She looked up and saw Captain Mike staring at her like a freshly dissected frog. "We'll have to talk to the brass."

"Will they believe me?"

"Not about everything, so we're not going to tell them where you came from or about the camera phone. For now, you're just another good citizen who's stumbled on a nest of vipers. But I believe you. There isn't any other explanation of how a young girl possesses an MX12 prototype."

"It's a Samsung cell-phone. If I could get reception, I'd show you proof of everything I've said." She sounded like a kid justifying stolen candy. Captain Mike just gave her a peculiar stare, as though she was a space alien.

"When are you supposed to check in with Mitch?" he said quietly.

"At the next Bund meeting."

"Then we can't waste any time. I never wanted Carole involved in anything to do with the spy game, and what does she do? She falls in love with the newspaper game and meets up with one of the sliest spies in San Diego."

"You know Mitch is a real spy?"

"We know a lot of things we can't do anything about at this point, and we need to know a lot more. Strange that it might be you who's going to get us the information we need. One thing, though … you'll need a different camera if you're going to take pictures for us. We need to put faces with names. Start building dossiers of these guys. I'll send you a Baldina —they'll like that. It's made by a company in Dresden."

Chapter IV

Admiral Bailey didn't look like a high monkey-monk. When he showed up at the McKnights fifteen minutes after Capt. Mike called him, he was wearing a bright blue flowered Hawaiian shirt and white golfing shorts. "I came in camouflage," he said to Piper when he shook her hand.

"He's been at the driving range," Capt. Mike whispered to her loud enough for Bailey to hear.

Mrs. McKnight brought them all iced tea and lemon wedges, and said she had no interest in listening to the men try to persuade the girls to go to nursing school.

"The Navy needs nurses," Bailey said as she waved a so-long and joined housekeeper Tessie in the kitchen for Cribbage. "It needs information too, Miss Hampton. Carole here can't be much help with that," he said when the door closed.

"That doesn't seem fair, Uncle Bailey," Carole said, and turned her attention to a slippery lemon slice.

"But it's accurate," her dad said. "All you can think about is that newspaper and your boss."

"You act like a job and a hobby are bad things." She caught a squirt of juice in the eye.

"Okay, I admit they can be useful in the spy game," Bailey interrupted. He lit a cigar and looked around for an ashtray. Piper pushed one toward him, a heavy crystal octagon-shaped one with an anchor etched on the bottom. "You seem like one smart cookie for somebody so young," he said to her.

"A scared little cookie too," Piper confessed.

Bailey shot Mike a smile. "Good. You'll be careful. Alert. Look ladies, naval intelligence is monitoring the Bund, concentrating on recruitment methods, funding sources, and whether this Mitch fella is using his press credentials to spy." He turned to Piper. "You know why. Hitler's rearming. We want to know his plans for his navy. Anything you can find out…"

"I can try."

"You get what you can. Pass it on to Mike and he'll get it to me. You and I won't have much contact that way. Sometimes we'll give you false information to give to them. The kind you might hear from sailors at the movie house. You have a problem with that, Carole?"

"What if the Bund gets suspicious? If what you say about them is true, this could get dangerous," Carole said.

"You won't be involved with the Bund," Mike said, tersely. "Whoever Mitch thinks Piper is, we want him to keep right on thinking it."

"You want me to leave Piper all on her own?" Piper wasn't sure whether the question sprang from concern or jealousy.

"She won't be alone at the meetings with our mole there. I promise," Bailey said.

"Everybody! It's okay," Piper said. A family squabble was the last thing she wanted to get involved in. "All you have to do is keep an eye on Mitch at work, Carole. He'll be on his best behavior. He won't let you see him for who he really is." She'd made a decision.

If spying was the mission that brought her here, she'd be the best spy she could be —as long as she was alive.

***

The trip back to San Diego was long, and the night quiet, except for the ocean waves and the radio set on low. At Five Points, Piper pulled into a filling station and got out of the car to pump gas. It always sent the attendants into a tizzy to see a girl handle a hose.

But this time the attendant was a grease monkey. He slid out from under a De Soto he was working on, stood and wiped his hands, and watched her from the shadows. She hung up the hose when the meter read eighty-cents, still amazed she could top off the tank for less than ten dollars. She walked over to him and handed him a dollar.

"Becky Thatcher?"

She squinted at the silhouette, straining to identify the voice. "What?"

"Fancy meeting you here. It's me. Robin Hood."

"Oh my god, Jim Crenshaw!" She threw her arms around his neck and clung to him like a barnacle, tears of joy wetting his shirt. "I'm not alone!"

"Looks like we both landed in yesteryear." He was hugging back.

She heard a car door slam and instantly Carole was at her side. "Piper, what on earth? You know this guy?"

She unstuck herself from him, and sputtered, "He's from the newspaper. Jim, this is Carole McKnight." She wiped her eyes with a windshield towel he pulled from the holder on the pump island. "How did you get here?"

"C'mon inside. We've got Coke on ice." He put the dollar in the till and fished in an ice bucket for three curvy bottles. "If I knew that old building was going to swallow us, I never would have taken you inside."

Carole sat on the desk. Piper sat in the swivel office chair that squeaked with her every move. Jim clumsily used the bottle opener bolted to the side of the desk. "Pop-tops are a long way off," he said as he handed each of them a Coke.

"Will one of you enlighten me?" Carole said.

Jim sat on the other end of the desk. "I saw your Toyota parked behind the dumpster, Piper, and thought you might still be in the Trib building, hurt or lost. I tripped going up the stairs and when I looked up —BOOM! Everything had changed. I didn't know how much until some guy tells me the paper's closed for business and points over my shoulder. I turned around and sure enough, there's this huge clock over the front door. He tells me we have to leave, so I start down the stairs."

"What guy? What'd he look like?"

"My height. Black hair. Rolled up sleeves. Carrying a tweed sport coat."

"Sounds Like Mitch," Carole said.

"Then what?" Piper said.

"I asked him to drive me to the police station, and he takes me, guess where. The old station on Market Street. Lucky for me I hit the ATM before my shift, so I had almost three hundred dollars on me. Money goes a long way here. Where'd you get your wheels?"

"It's a long story. Suffice to say I couldn't have made it without Carole's help."

Carole leaned against the door jamb. "Well, I'm dumbfounded. I figured Piper got here by accident, but the both of you? Even Madame Blavatsky would be befuddled. There's gotta be a reason for all this spooky stuff."

Jim and Piper exchanged shrugs and nodded in agreement. "There's a reason. We just don't know what it is yet," Jim said.

"It's insane is what it is," Piper said sadly. Carole reached over and gave her a pat on the shoulder.

"Are you two roomies?" Jim said.

"We were. I stay at the YWCA now. Hot-shot…er... Carole's got a room over by San Diego High School. You?"

"I rented a bungalow in Old Town. You remember the Padre Inn. Ain't it funny? I mean, Mission Valley is nothing but cow pastures. San Diego is so empty. If people only knew what's coming."

"Nobody except Navy intelligence believes there's going to be a war, Jim. Everyone else thinks Hitler's a great guy, and Japan isn't even a threat the radar," Piper said.

"What's radar?" Carole asked.

"The British invent a tracking technology that can monitor moving object like missiles or planes." Carole mumbled an 'oh', and he moved to her side. "Electronic technology is the big woo-hoo where I come from. Here the big woo-hoo seems to be pretty girls.”

Carole looked up at him. Piper hadn't really seen Jim as a man, just a geeky guy she'd never consider dating in a million years, but Carole was giving him an I-think-you're-swell smile. Of course, she'd like him. She could tell he wouldn't mind if she was ambitious and wanted a career in photography. And Jim? He'd be thrilled to win a competition with the likes of Mitch Roberts. Something inside her knew Mitch was destined to become a memory for Carole.

As she lay awake, her thoughts turned to them. She thought about how they talked to each other, how they laughed together, and how Carole was a pro at batting her eyelashes like a woman and not like a teen-ager —she'd have to learn her flirting technique. Carole and Jim were falling in love alright. And wherever you find love, that's where you stay. If she wanted to go home, she'd have to be careful with her heart.

***

“I think we’ve found a mole for Admiral Bailey, if Jim can get on at the shipyards,” Carole said when Piper asked her what she thought of him. She wanted to talk possible romance, but Carole was all business. They were eating peanut butter sandwiches and drinking orange soda pop under one of Balboa Park’s eucalyptus trees near El Cid.

“You talked to him about spying, already?”

“He said he’d talked to you, so I thought it would be okay. He’s committed to preparing for war. Said he was a prepper, whatever that is. Now that I think about it, I shouldn’t have said anything. I’m going to make a lousy spy."

As long as she recognized that, there was no need to rub it in how stupid it was make assumptions. "Jim came to the Y yesterday and we had a long visit in the parlor." It was like lunch in the schoolyard. Jim wanted to know if Carole had a boyfriend? Do you think she likes me? "You believe me now."

"It was that radar thing, Piper," Carole said. "I guess I could take what you said with a grain of salt even though I said I believed you. I did, sort of. But the two of you, well it gets harder and harder to deny that you're really from the future and not just smart people who can put two and two together. Jim says millions of people are going to die and he wants to stop it. Maybe that's why you're here."

Piper couldn't be angry with her for first impression skepticism even if it did sound a little sexist. Jim's presence was irrefutable evidence that *something* paranormal had occurred. She shivered with goose flesh.

"Are you cold?" Carole said.

Piper shook her head no. "I want to believe that we can stop the war, but I know different. Even if we could, it might mean millions of more deaths in the future. Maybe my parents won't be born."

"It's horrible either way. But Jim's brave. I like to think I'm brave too, Piper, but all the stories coming out of Europe about concentration camps and public executions… makes me faint with fear."

It's easy to be brave until you meet danger face to face, Piper wanted to tell her, because she wasn't brave, just determinedly resigned. "Jim talked me into taking him to the Bund tonight. Tell your dad."

***

Jim picked her up at 5:00 PM sharp. It'd be good if she showed them she had recruiting skills, he explained. "Just tell them we met up at the theater and were talking at the popcorn counter. They'll be glad to have another follower. Cults are cults. And I'm sure in this cult young women don't get to talk about important stuff."

"You got that right. Last time, I mostly did kitchen clean-up stuff." If she was going to get Capt. Mike and Admiral Bailey information, it would come through Jim, not her. The first question she asked him when they'd said their good-byes to the Bauers was, "What'd you find out? I got a recipe for strudel."

"They want to get me that job at the Maritime Shipyard in National City. Grooming me for sabotage, I think."

He reached in his wallet and pulled out an I.D. card. "They wanted to know what I can do, so I told them I can weld, and they jumped on that like white on rice."

"Can you weld?"

"I had three years of metal shop in high school. I sort of remember some of it. Anyway, they gave me a government certification card and told me to show up tomorrow. The pay is better than the gas station."

Piper studied the cards. "I need to make a copy of these…oh, crap. Oh, well, a picture will have to do." She snapped a shot with her cell phone. "They look authentic. Wonder where they got them."

"That guy, Mitch? My guess is, he stays late at the newspaper and uses the equipment. How much battery life do you have left?"

"I'm working on one bar. I brought a charger with me. Always keep one in my purse but it doesn't work in my cars cigarette lighter. Can you find a way to recharge it?"

"I can try."

"That's what I need." She was staring at the cards, side by side. "This is interesting. The cards are numbered."

"So? Cards like that always are."

"I mean their sequential. Trackable. Like raffle tickets. How do you work at a company with a phony I.D. unless somebody inside is in on it? Look, this one's a journeyman's certification."

"Ain't no way I qualify for that."

"Shouldn't there be a test? I.D. cards come through HR. My mom taught me that. She approved interns, too."

Jim came to a stop in front of the YWCA. "Now we have news for your contacts. The Bund has infiltrated the shipyard for sure." He gently removed the cards from her fingers and put them back in his wallet.

Piper didn't seem to notice. "The cards, starting work on a Saturday without an interview or a filling out a withholding form. When Josh worked at the surfboard place, he had nine kinds of forms to fill out. I'll bet you're taking somebody's place. The cards are real, but the employee is interchangeable."

"It's possible. Identity theft is common back home, why not here?"

The word 'home' made Piper realize just how far away they were. No copy machines. No cell phone chargers. No instant communications. With Jim's coming, she was no longer alone in exile, but she took little joy in shared misery. They were either pawns of history, or characters in a diabolical novel, and both possibilities were equally terrible.

***

Mrs. McKnight served them homemade cinnamon rolls and hot tea. "A Southern lady's way of saying welcome," she said. In appreciation, Jim helped himself to two gooey hunks of heaven.

Captain Mike gave Piper a smile of approval. "Piper tells me the Bund's taken a liking to you, Jim. You've been hired at Maritimer?"

Jim hauled out the I.D. cards. "It's good work too. Saturday and Sunday, I welded a hull. The foreman said, not bad."

Captain Mike wrote down the cards' numbers. "I'll check with our mole at Maritimer to see if they belong to a corpse."

"That's a grisly thought," Piper said.

"Until I hear something, you two find excuses to stay clear of Bund meetings."

"Are the Nazis that dangerous, Dad?" Carole said and inched closer to Jim on the sofa.

"The Germans we faced in '17 were lightweights compared to this bunch. On the other hand, if 003417 is dead, it doesn't necessarily mean the Bund killed him."

"Yeah, 003417 could have be one of them," Piper said. "He could be in Berlin drinking beer right now."

This was the second of what became weekly visits up the coast until Captain Mike was transferred to San Diego a month later and took command of ONI North Island. Jim was earning twice what he was at the station, and soon gained journeyman-level skills. Carole kept regular company with him and all three of them helped Mrs. McKnight move the delicate objects she didn't trust the Navy to crate and carry. Of her ivory-colored soup tureen, the Confederate Daughter of America remarked that it would be horrible for it to be broken, having survived the Civil War.

"My grandmother felt the same way about her flowered teapot," Piper told her. "It's one of the few family heirlooms my mother treasures. The hair of a dead relative in a tarnished locket, not so much."

The three helpers spent the day carefully wrapping china and family photographs in newspaper, transporting expertly engineered packed boxes to the new house in Point Loma's Rosecrans neighborhood, and then just as carefully unwrapping. Their reward was pot roast and baked potatoes, and a lively game of hearts as Mrs. McKnight put the revered heirlooms in a glass protected cabinet.

Around six, Captain Mike arrived, and breathlessly announced that 003174 had been issued to a guy named Erik Sorenson in 1932 whose last known address was the same as the Bauer's. He'd worked the same week-end shift as Jim when he was hired on and was rated A-1 by his supervisor —a Bund member. "The 00 signifies a floater number used for part-timers, temporaries, and sub-contract employees."

"Sort of like on-site stringers," Carole observed. "How strange."

"Not where I come from," Jim said. "Full-time employees get fewer and fewer. I know people who once worked three jobs to make what people used to make with one."

"But it's convenient for Jim," Piper said. "It means he can move in and out of different departments without anyone keeping an eye on him."

"Convenient for spies, too," Carole observed.

"Is Sorenson still kicking, I wonder?" Jim said.

"He's got a warrant out for failure to appear for a DWI. The San Diego police thinks he's in Yuma," Capt. Mike said.

"Why don't they demand extradition?" Jim said.

"Over a DWI? It's a misdemeanor. Why bother?"

"Oh. *That's* certainly different."

"There's more," Captain Mike said. He sat down and heaved a sigh like a man carrying a hundred-pound sack of cement. "Japan has invaded China —they attacked Peking." He looked at Jim. "Is this the beginning of the second world war?"

"America's got four years before Japan attacks Pearl Harbor," Jim said.

Captain Mike reached for the last cinnamon roll and put in on one of Mrs. McKnight's pink china dessert plates. "Is that what the history books say?"

"There's film. If I could find a relay tower, I'd show you the *USS Arizona* on fire. I could show you the Twin Towers attack too."

"Twin Towers? What are they?" Carole asked.

"Two skyscrapers that were in the way of two jumbo jet airplanes. It's a tragic story too."

Chapter V

"I can flirt with the sailors, but I can't socialize with them, Mitch. Goldstein said I was hired to sell movie tickets, not wolf tickets." They were sitting in her car, looking at the ocean in the moonlight, and sharing little boxes from Sun Li's Chinese Food —a surprise dinner, he said, so she wouldn't have to eat Y cafeteria food. It was appreciated. Without a microwave, reheating the plate Director Stevens set aside took forever.

"Maybe so, but you sure dazzled Crenshaw," Mitch said. "He's all in." Had he not noticed his Hot-shot was always busy in the evening, and no longer spent her off time hanging out in the Trib's employee lounge? Maybe he really believed Crenshaw's willingness to work week-ends was Fascist dedication. "You got a way about you, Piper. It's your big brown eyes, I guess. It's like they've seen everything before, and yet you're so young and … inexperienced?"

Was he talking sex? Piper thought about Manuel Lopez and Junior Prom night. Did it count if she'd had a couple of glasses of pilfered Champagne?

Mitch broke open a fortune cookie and handed her the folded paper. "These young guys fresh off the farm think they're men because they survived boot camp. They need a pretty young girl to admire them, and it's your patriotic duty to boost morale." She'd never heard flirting described as patriotism. It was hard to tell when Mitch was playing and when he was serious. She unfolded the paper strip.

"What's it say? What's your future?" Mitch demanded.

"It says, get your butt back to the Y, dessert is bread pudding tonight," she said.

"You a fan of bread pudding?"

"According to the Chinese fates I am. Not that they're reliable. Peking and all that."

"Is Crenshaw?"

She sensed the answer to the question was important. "Is he what, reliable? Sure. A fan of bread pudding? I've never asked him. But I rarely see him now that he's working in the shipyards."

"Word has it, he's a crackerjack welder."

Captain Mike certainly seemed to think he was a crackerjack. Piper saw the way the older man treated him like an equal. Like his surveillance of the shipyard was crucial, even though so far Crenshaw hadn't seen anything unusual or been approached by a Nazi mole to do anything but weld. She also saw the way Carole regarded him too. "Are you jealous of him, Mitch?" she teased.

"Jealous of Crenshaw? Naw..."

"Pining over Hot-Shot, then? You miss her?"

"Not since I met you." Can you take a man seriously when he makes a declaration of interest with his mouth full of final bites of fried rice? "Softee Freeze is still open. You want a cone?"

She looked out the rear window and saw the old version of the Frosty Freeze that she, Josh, and Shelly-the-girlfriend hit the last time they were at Ocean Beach. "Sure. Yeah."

Mitch gathered the empty cartons, got out of the car, and stuffed them in the trash can before sprinting across the parking lot. He got in line behind three Marines and a nana with two grandkids in tow. He'd be long enough for a quick snoop. She opened the glove box. Nothing but roadmaps. She checked under her seat and felt metal. She wiggled out a box the size of a small lunch pail. Inside was a palomino-colored holster that held a pistol. She didn't know what caliber it was, but the bullets in the magazine that lay beside the holster were real. She took one bullet and put it in her purse. For the first time the possibility of danger hit home. She closed the box and returned it to its hiding place.

Mitch was next in line. She slid her hand under his side of the seat and found his wallet. It only had ten dollars in it, but what she found behind the two fives was worth a million —it was the same picture Carole had shown her of Baby Suzanne. On the back was printed the name Erik Sorenson. She opened the door, so the inside light would come on, and took a photo of the photo with her cell phone. She slammed the door shut and checked the back window. Mitch was hurrying across the parking lot with two cones of vanilla ice-cream. She threw the wallet under the seat and got out with the last of the cartons for the trash. Mitch was smiling.

"Let's not eat these in the car. I don't want to drip on your car seat," she said.

He reached in his pocket. "I remembered napkins."

"I have to hurry. Stevens will have the cops after me if I don't show up before eleven."

"She knows you're with me, right?"

"Yeah, but she hovers like a mom. I don't mind. Makes me feel safe." She told herself to act natural. Not to talk too much or too little. "I could be a little friendlier with the guys, I guess. Goldstein's made me full time. I work until nine-thirty now. Have to, the lines are so long. I met this one guy from Jersey. Cabot Swan. He says Charles Lindbergh has the right idea about Germany."

"Good! Bring him to the Bund this week. Does he have any friends?"

"Sure. Everybody likes Cabot. He talks like a gangster."

Mitch mounted a direct attack. He took her hand in his and looked straight into her eyes. "It's you they like, Piper. You're the magnet."

She felt her face grow hot and was grateful the light from the streetlamp was dim in the night mist. Carole wouldn't be blushing. He kissed her cheek "A guy could get lost in those eyes." Was this why Carole thought she was in love? Silly compliments and a kiss in return for …what? One thing she knew for sure, Carole wasn't pining for his attentions anymore. Carole had Jim Crenshaw, and she had? Cabot maybe. He was everything a girl could want in a Jersey Boy. She found herself humming the theme from the *Godfather* when she saw him in line. A song that wouldn't be written for another thirty-five years for a film that was considered a classic, one of the oldest she'd ever seen.

***

Honnolore Bauer gave Cabot and his four friends a giddy hello. With their boot-camp good manners and military-sized appetites they made short work of her *hor d'oeuvres*. Maybe the Bauers really believed youthful exuberance could be transformed into devotion to a cause invented on the other side of the world, and maybe they were right. Two hours after Bauer began preaching his by now familiar sermon on racial purity and a young man's duty, Cabot and his friends were hauling out their wallets. When the collection plate passed by them, there wasn't a clink of change to be heard. When it was time to clean up, the swabbies donated their muscle too.

"See you next month," Cabot promised, and the others echoed him with firmly spoken yeahs. Maybe those nodding heads and avid applause hadn't been for show. "We'll be going home on leave, Ma'am, but we'll be back," he explained to Honnolore, and she cooled herself with a feathered fan.

"Now that's what they mean by Aryan superiority," she whispered breathlessly to Piper as she passed her on the walk. "See you soon." Her voice was positively melodious.

Piper unloaded Cabot and his crew at the foot of Broadway at the San Diego Bay Launch Pier. "It was wonderful," Cabot said. He leaned into the driver's seat window. Not far enough in to steal a kiss, but it might have looked that way to his friends.

"You don't share Bauer's vision for real, do you?" she asked. Perhaps a little too plaintively.

Cabot's smile disappeared. "He speaks the truth. It's tough to hear, but we're ready to get America under control."

"Good. Good to hear that," she said.

His eyes were like the flashing blue lights on a cop car. He leaned in further and gave her a peck on the cheek. "You'll make somebody a good wife, Piper."

She waved good-bye as his blond haired, slim and hard as steel body walked away, and whispered to herself, "God, please not him." Inside her heart was pounding. Two guys in two days had confirmed that in this world she was a desirable woman. She was growing up quicker than she thought possible. All the way to the Y, thoughts tumbled through her brain, a combination of realizations she half-wished would evaporate. In four short years, these boys, okay, young men, would be aboard ships that would sail in enemy waters. Some of them, maybe all of them, would land in places as foreign to them as San Diego was now to her. Some of them might not come home at all.

Two weeks later she saw Cabot loitering outside the theater in civilian clothes, pretending to look at the movie posters hanging in the glass cases. He'd seen every one of the films at least twice, that she knew of. Around seven, Goldstein came to relieve her. "Your boy-friend's making me tired just watching him," he said, "Go get a soda or something. More than his heels need a cold bath."

"He's not my boyfriend," Piper said. She got her purse from under her chair.

"Well, you better tell him that because he's wearing out my terra cotta tiles. You think I can replace them cheap, maybe?"

She thought she'd get her chance to dampen his ardor when they were sitting at Woolworth's lunch counter, but the moment they slid into the booth, Cabot turned to her and said, "We got orders today."

"That's great … but you're not happy about that."

"Yeah, I am, and no. I mean, I knew they'd be coming, sure, but I thought I'd be stationed here in Dago at the Submarine Warfare School. Turns out, I'm too tall for a sub. Still too short for the basketball team, but too tall for a tin can. Don't that beat all?" He picked up a menu and then put in down quickly because his hands were shaking. "I'll just have a burger. What about you?"

"Turkey on white bread. No mayo."

"So, I open my envelope —all the orders come in these big yellow government envelopes —and it says I'm going to Hawaii! Can you believe that?"

"How … how long are you going to be in the Navy, Cabot?"

"Three years, eight months, and thirteen days. But it's okay because I'm going to train as a machinist's mate on an aircraft carrier. The *Saratoga*. I'm going to fix airplane engines, and by the time I get out, I'll make damn good money, Piper. Flight is the future of travel, believe me."

The Saratoga was a ship name she didn't recognize. The only carriers she knew about were the *Lexington* and the *Enterprise* because Captain Mike mentioned them in a conversation with Jim. She remembered thinking about Star Trek and how funny it was that the names had lasted so long. If only she had internet access, she could get information about what happened to the *Saratoga* in the war. She could look up his family, see if they were on Facebook. "I believe you, and I agree. You'll earn top dollar."

"You could come with me to Hawaii if … if we were married."

He was adorable. With eyelashes so long, they looked feminine. And that smile! "I'm flattered, Cabot, but I can't marry anybody. For one thing, I'd need my parent's permission."

"Oh, well, sure. But you could send them a telegram and they could answer back. I asked around. There's this place called Winterhaven where the Justice of the Peace marries anybody."

"Then there's the fact that I don't love you. I like you very much, but I'm not ready to make a commitment like that to anyone. Right now, at least."

"But you'll write to me? Promise me that."

"Sure. Yeah, but I can't promise I'll write often."

He looked like a little boy who'd just been told he wasn't getting a puppy for Christmas. Behind all that Jersey swagger was regret the size of Texas. Adventure always sounds great until you're living it alone.

"What'll it be kids?" the waitress asked, and Piper wanted so much to say Batman band-aids for two scared and broken hearts.

***

For the third time, Piper called the Trib from a pay phone looking for Carole. The McKnights didn't have their phone yet. It still amazed her it took a week for the phone company to come to their house and connect a bunch of wires to a pole outside. She'd get up early and drive to Point Loma tomorrow, if she couldn't track her down. She'd have to tell Captain Mike about Cabot, too. At least the part about his fascist sympathies. The Navy should keep an eye on him.

"Thanks for spelling me, Mr. Goldstein."

"Unh … where's your boyfriend?" Goldstein was looking over her shoulder.

"He's just a friend, really."

"Too bad. He's a nice boy. You got lots of friends. Carole was here looking for you. Left you this note." He handed Piper a folded piece of theater stationery. "It says you should meet her at the park tomorrow. At eleven. Says she has big news. Maybe she got married. What could be bigger news than that?"

Piper almost laughed. "Maybe so. It would be great, huh?" She put the note in her purse and took her seat in the ticket booth. Goldstein mumbled that all women should get married the day they graduate from high school and ambled back into the theater.

The next two hours flew by as they always did when the sailors lined up for the pin-up movies. Hundreds of guys in white uniforms and square knotted black ties filing into the lobby, constantly teasing and shoving one another as they waited in line to get bags of popcorn so loaded with butter their hands got greasy. The cash registered steadily cha-chinged, and then, suddenly, silence. Two minutes later she heard whoops and hollers, and laughter at predictable intervals during the cartoons. Ticket salesperson wasn't her first career choice, but it was fun. Jim was right when he said people here were nice. There were worse places to be stranded. The newsreels were full of horrendous pictures of thousands of Chinese men, women, and children on the road carrying everything could to escape the artillery fire and the plane strafing. She thought the documentaries her dad watched were straight out of Hollywood, once. Now these people were suffering in real time.

***

The next morning, she met Carole near El Cid, and shared the candy Goldstein forced on her when he cleared out the week-old bars and made room for the next delivery. She'd grown fond of Aba-zaba and Baby Ruth while Carole liked plain ol' Hershey's.

"What's the big news?" She'd let Carole share and hopefully find an opportunity to bring up the photo she'd found in Mitch's wallet. Maybe if she'd been able to tell her right away, she wouldn't be having so many misgivings about telling her at all. "Goldstein thinks you got married."

"Not yet." Carole held up her left hand. "But it's so warm today. I think I'll take off my ring."

"Get out'a town!" Piper held her hand and examined the heart-shaped diamond chip set in gold. "Best wishes and all that, but isn't it a little soon for you and …it better be Jim …?"

"Who else would it be? Isn't it pretty? We bought it yesterday. Jim had the sense to let me go with him. Oh, I know, you think we're rushing things, but you're young, Piper. I'm almost twenty-two, and second-hand goods. Jim's the first guy I've told about jumping the gun, you might say, and he doesn't care."

Piper thought about prom night, and Josh and Shelly-the-girlfriend living together, and all the significant others they each had before the move-in. Carole couldn't even bring herself to say the words, 'I'm not a virgin.' She also realized that by being married and working in crucial war production Jim had probably dodged the draft. A baby was in Carole's future too. Piper felt she'd been thought-strafed: Jim was planning his life like he knew there was no getting back to the 21st century.

"Imagine being lucky enough to have a guy who said he was eight-hand goods." Carole laughed. "I may not get another invite to the dance, you know?" No, she didn't know. She was from a world where women went on TV and had DNA tests of one guy after another to discover who the fathers of their children were.

"Jim's not the promotable Ensign my Dad always expected me to marry, but he likes him. He's trustworthy. I think he loves me too. That's a plus."

"It's a big plus! So, when do we start shopping for a wedding dress?" Piper said. It was settled. She wouldn't spoil Carole's happiness with news of a name on the back of a picture and a gun under a car seat.

"We don't have to worry about a dress until after New Year's. We've reserved the church for May. So, what's your news?" Carole said. Piper had never seen her look so pretty, so happy.

"You know that guy, Cabot Jersey? He got orders for Hawaii and asked me to go with him. Crazy, right?" Gnawing at the back of her mind was the big question: Was it time for her to start a life here too?

***

How do you access a history that hasn't been written yet? It was the question she kept asking herself every time she looked at her cell phone and kept getting the same answer. You don't. Didn't that meet the official definition of insanity? Stop dwelling on the past's future, she told herself again and again. It's your day off. Do something useful. Do your laundry. Maybe get a hair-cut. She checked her savings passbook. Thirty dollars. With gas fifteen cents a gallon, she could afford to take a trip to Yuma, but without air conditioning, Triple A, or her phone?

If she left around four AM, she'd be there by eight thirty. She'd have five hours to sleuth before she'd have to shelter in place. *Siestas* were invented to solve the afternoon brain-bake, Josh said when the family went to Cabo on vacation. Everybody inside from one to four. Maybe Yuma had a YWCA too.

"Is Cabot around? This is Piper." Dial phones were still so old movie timey to her.

"He's in processing getting more shots for overseas travel. Maybe I can help."

"I doubt it."

"Wha'dya mean? It's me, Chris Sanders. Cabot's friend. I went to the Bund meeting with you, remember?"

"Oh … you're Cleveland. No, Sacramento." Maybe this was better than Jersey. No deep conversations.

"That's me. California born, bred and tanned. What'cha need, Piper?"

"Somebody to go to Yuma with me tomorrow. Early."

***

She'd driven Old Highway 8, that was now the only highway

between San Diego and Yuma, but not in the dark. It was spooky, even to Sandy. He put on a brave face, but the s-turns and steep grades had his Chevy riding the white line all the way down the mountain from Jacumba.

"I don't think we're in Kansas anymore, Toto," she said as they reached the bottom of the foothills and were finally on the flat land of the Imperial Valley.

"I ain't never been to Kansas," Sandy said. "Who's Toto?"

"That's right. The Wizard of Oz wasn't released 'til '39."

Sandy smiled. "Cabot said you're a strange one."

He smiled again when she said the first thing she wanted when they got to Yuma was a phone book, then asked the station attendant for directions, and said, "This would be a whole lot easier with GPS." Was he making fun of her?

He bought them each a coke and delivered her to 312 Santa Fe Drive before she finished half of hers. "I got a street map with the cokes," he confessed, "and checked the route while I was in the head. Who lives here? An old flame?"

"Hardly."

After passing the mailbox marked SORENSON, she had Sandy park on the cross street near the corner where they could get a good shot of the second house on the block. She didn't expect to see anyone except Mrs. Sorenson, but at nine-thirty a man exited the house and walked towards an Oldsmobile parked in the driveway. Erik Sorenson was a 40-ish, slightly built man. Sandy estimated 5 feet 7 inches, and a hundred forty pounds. "Not your typical Swede.

Looks more Italian," he said.

"Maybe he favors his mother," Piper said.

"He's favoring his right foot too. Could be a sprained ankle, but it's probably a war injury. Most guys his age served."

"How can you tell?"

"Everywhere I go, I work in the dispensary, and I don't see guys his age playing a lot of sports, except golf. Why are we watching him?"

"I'll tell you later."

A woman carrying a little girl walked over to the car and handed Erik a lunch pail. "It's kind'a late to be leaving for work," Sandy said. "Want to tail him?"

"Yeah."

The Oldsmobile rolled to a stop at the front gate of Sorenson Air Field. "That explains a lot. He's the boss," Sandy said. He drove past the entrance about a quarter mile, stopped, and made a U-turn. "Listen! Hear that?" A small, two-engine prop plane circled the field twice before landing. "Damn, I wish I'd brought my field glasses." He was squinting through the dust rising from the cracked earth. He took off his tee-shirt and doused it with water from his canteen. "Close your door on this and hang it over your open window. The moist air makes it easier to breathe."

"We better start home," Piper said two hours later. She wiped sweat from her face and looked at her watch. "It's almost twelve thirty. If we load up on water and cokes, we might make it to El Centro before it gets too hot."

They didn't make it past the city limits. At a motel with an entrance built to look like a teepee they stopped and spent the next four hours in room seven, listening to the radio compete with the loudest air conditioning unit Piper had ever heard. "It ain't so bad," Sandy said. "You ought to hear ship engines twenty-four-seven." He'd bought a bottle of beer, swearing that nothing tasted so good as a cold beer on a hot day, but had a blanket wrapped around his bare shoulders as his shirt hung drying in the bathroom.

"You've been on a ship already?"

"Like I said, I work in the dispensary. I'm a corpsman. I'm at the Naval Training Center now, but before that I was on the *Arizona*. Enlisted when I was sixteen. I'm startin' my second rodeo."

She figured he was a youngish, older-type guy. He wasn't nervous at all when the desk clerk raised an eyebrow and asked to see his I.D. Sandy had put his arm around her neck and said, "We're newlyweds coming back from Winterhaven." The clerk just grinned and gave him the key.

"Cabot's going to Hawaii," Piper said, as though he didn't know. She was sitting at the table near the AC, her eyes closed, letting the cool air dry the sweat to unstick her clothing.

"He thinks he's in love with you."

"He's wrong. But let's not tell anyone about this little trip we took together. It's better for all of us," Piper said.

"It's okay by me. I don't want to break his heart. We're all going to Hawaii. He'll be on a ship. I'll be at Hickam Field. I probably won't see much of him anymore. But that's the Navy. I haven't seen the world, but I've met a lot of people."

There was a wistfulness in his voice that echoed her own aloneness. "What do you think about the Japanese bombing Nanking?" she said to change the subject.

"I think it's none of our business. Roosevelt thinks all the BS going on in the world is none of our business too. He signed the Neutrality Act, didn't he?" He didn't sound like he meant it. He just closed his eyes and sipped his beer while Guy Lombardo's *Red Sails in the Sunset* played on the radio. Maybe he thought a war was coming too.

Chapter VI

"We have to talk, Jim, and not about the wedding," Piper said. "Meet me at the Softee Freeze."

Over hot fudge sundaes, Piper poured out the story of her first surveillance. "Erik Sorenson probably left the shipyards when he and the Mrs. got the baby. They'd have to. The neighbors would want to know where they got a newborn. They probably weren't the first blackmail-able people snagged by Mitch Roberts, and Carole won't be the last. These Nazis are smart, getting their hooks into people long before they face tough choices."

"You have to hand it to Mitch. It's a smart move on his part." Jim said. He was still uncomfortable with the looks he got when Piper picked up the tab. Yeah, she'd called him, but it didn't fit here.

"I just wonder how many other young women Mitch's gotten his hooks into."

Jim scraped his paper cup one last time, getting every drop of chocolate he could. "Has he ever made a move on you?"

Piper winced. "Why do you think I took Cabot and his pals to the meeting? But it doesn't matter." It did matter. Mitch had maneuvered her into doing something she hadn't wanted to do without so much as a threat. "I have to tell Captain Mike about this, but I can't hurt Carole. I wish to God I hadn't found out what I found out."

"And you want me to tell you what to do."

"Well, sure I do. She's your fiancé."

"Come on, let's walk."

They headed down the beach, stopping every once in awhile to look at the shore line cottages that would be replaced by high-priced apartments. It was Thursday afternoon. Not a college student, soccer mom, or surfer to be seen. An old man sat reading in a striped folding chair and had tied an umbrella to the arm. His dog was chasing sea gulls and barking, the noise being carried out to sea by an off-shore breeze. "Things damn sure aren't what they seem, are they?" Jim said. "I mean, you and I know what's coming, but to these people, what's here is all they know. Weird, isn't it? Different realities being the truth at the same time, and different truths being the same realities at the same time."

Piper weighed his words. "Honestly, do you think we're dead, Jim?"

"Nope. That camera in your phone still works. You still have pictures of your family. Your car. You can't take it with you, remember? Our reality is nothing to them, and to us it's just …over. Yet, they're the dead ones."

She plopped down on the sand, and he sat beside her. "Two realities," she said. "Hmmm. Suppose I tell Captain Mike all about Sorenson and the baby. He doesn't have to know it's Carole's baby. Mitch can say it is, but there aren't any legal papers identifying her as the mother, and there's no DNA testing now."

"True."

"On the other hand, Edwina Blackledge *is* dead, and Captain Mike knows little about her. Hypothetically, who's to say Suzanne isn't her kid? What's to say Mitch didn't kill Edwina for the money but decided to give her kid to the Sorensons?"

"Isn't Suzanne too old to be Edwina's kid?" Jim said.

"So, I'm off by a couple of months. What do I know about babies? If Edwina cheated the Nazis out of a bunch of money, well, maybe she kept her pregnancy hidden, and gave up her baby so she could keep the father hidden too. The important thing is that it's just plausible enough to get Sorenson investigated."

Jim began nodding his head in assent. "If the Sorensons turn out to be Nazis, there's a young couple and a happy Navy Captain willing to give the child a home. No one has to know where the baby came from. The Sorensons probably don't know." He stood up quickly and pulled Piper up by the arm. "C'mon, we're going to see Mike."

"Now?"

"Yep, as soon as we get Carole and bring her up to speed on the alternative reality."

They headed for their cars. "Where's Carole now?" Piper said. She hoped a little more conversation would slow Jim down to a comfortable sprint.

"Her place getting' gussied up for her parents' anniversary dinner tonight."

Piper stopped so quickly, Jim was six paces ahead of her before he realized it. He came back to her. "What'sa matter, Piper? Ice cream make you sick or somethin'? I hear some people are lactose intolerant."

"What does that word mean … gussied?"

"It means to make yourself look pretty. Put on make-up. Do your hair. Carole's mom said she knew right away Carole was fallin' for me by the way she got gussied up every time she was with me." Piper heard an aw-shucks in his voice as he lowered his eyes and shrugged his shoulders. "What of it?"

Before she could answer a crack! rang out.

"Holy crap, somebody's shooting at us!" Jim grabbed her arm again and pulled her to her knees. They crouched by the hood of the car.

Piper was shaking so hard, she could barely get her words out. "Do you know anything about guns?"

"I know they can kill you." He crawled to the driver's door and opened it. "Come on, get inside."

"I can't move, Jim. I'm too scared." The world was spinning. He caught her as she toppled over.

The old reader on the beach ran over to them. "Is she all right?"

"Get down!" Jim ordered. "We've got a shooter."

"A looter, you say?"

The man's dog was licking Piper's face, and Jim was pushing him away gently. "Oh, Christ. Help me get her into the car."

A Softee Freeze employee came running too. "I heard it! I heard it. Is she hit?"

"No, just fainted." Jim took Piper's other arm and between the two of them, they got her into the back seat.

"Poor little girl," the old man said. "Must be from Iowa. Lots of people from Iowa come here, watch the ocean, and get seasick. Darndest thing."

"I'll call the police," the Softee Freeze guy said.

"No, it's okay. Maybe it was just a car backfiring …"

"You sure? I saw her go down so I thought …what you thought."

"Yeah, probably better call it a day. Come on Ginger," the old man said, and ambled off. The dog romped after him. The Softee Freeze guy gave a last look at Piper and hustled back to his shop.

Piper took a few deep breaths and groaned. "Jim? Jim?" She looked up at his upside-down face.

"You fainted."

"I was hoping to wake up in 2018." She struggled to sit up.

"Sorry kid." His hands were shaking now, as he stroked her hair. "I think we were just spooked by a backfire."

She got out of the car and scanned the row of cottages. "Yeah, a backfire name Mitch Roberts."

"If Mitch was the shooter, you'd be dead."

"Then who? Cabot? Damn it. Sandy agreed not to tell him about Yuma!"

"But Mitch didn't …and it was just a backfire. Our cars don't have carburetors, so we're not used to all the noises these old crates make. I'm sorry if got you scared for nothing. It must have been a backfire."

***

Piper sat on her bed, looking at the clothes hanging in her closet.

Two uniforms. Two blouses. One cotton dress, two skirts, and a pill-covered green sweater. "I'm pathetic," she said and hugged her knees. "Poor, pathetic, and living like a grown-up. Who thinks she's been shot at."

A knock at the door interrupted her pity party. Mrs. Stevens handed her a long white box tied with a red ribbon. "Someone has an admirer," she said

Piper felt like she should apologize. She opened the box and inside was a dozen red roses. "Thank you for bringing these up to me, Mrs. Stevens." If this was Cabot's way of making amends for scaring the hell out of her, she wasn't impressed. "But, please, take them, and put them in the foyer. They're so pretty, I want everyone to see them."

Mrs. Stevens put the lid back on the box, put it under one arm, and headed for the door. "Aren't you going to open the card?"

Reluctantly, Piper opened the little envelope. To the prettiest girl in the world, it read. No signature. Maybe they were from Sandy. Or Mitch. "I'm kind'a in a hurry. Got to get gussied up. The McKnights are giving a party." The strong scent of lavender told Piper that Mrs. Stevens had come back to the bed.

"I have a few things some of the girls left behind. I keep them on hand, for job hunting and such. Might be something that'll fit. There's a nice green dress … follow me."

Mrs. Stevens led her to the end of the hall and unlocked the door labeled SUPPLIES. It was really a clothes closet that smelled of rose sachet. On both sides hung dresses, skirts, blouses. Piper even saw three wedding gowns.

"I call it a clothes library. You wear it, you clean it, you return it. Or you buy it for a quarter." Mrs. Stevens held up a green taffeta with a boat neckline, cap sleeves, and a straight skirt. "You look around, though. Close the door when you're done."

She was about to say thank you when Mrs. Stevens glided past her, rose box in arms, and went downstairs. Alone in her private boutique, she perused the racks and found a black and green flowered scarf, and a three-quarter sleeved white bolero jacket. With her black pumps, she'd be smashing. And all for seventy-five cents. Should she add a pair of white wrist gloves? Too late, the door locked as soon as she closed it. So much for channeling her inner Melania Trump. She'd never be a princess, she thought, but then spied the card on the nightstand. In retro-land, she had suitors. Beach Bunnies weren't a thing yet. Maybe her life wasn't so pathetic after all.

***

She arrived at the McKnight house just after Jim and Carole. They were getting out of Jim's Plymouth when she pulled up and was met with a complimentary "Hubba-hubba" from Jim.

"The skirt's a little long for me," Piper said when Carole gave her a 'very nice' nod of approval.

"It's called tea length for a reason. It's after three," Carole said.

"It's an original Stevens YWCA," Piper said.

"I shopped there a few times." Carole took Piper's hand and gave it a squeeze. "Jim told me all about Yuma. That's quite a job of detective work you did. Dad will want to hear all about it."

"It won't bother you to hear the details?"

"With you two in my corner? Not a bit. It's a great story. While you were recovering from your trip to the beach, Jim and I met with a lawyer. Jim's adamant no Nazi is going to raise Suzanne."

"You go on in, I gotta to get my purse."

Piper watched her catch up to Jim who was waiting at the stairs. They could be Josh and Shelly-the-girlfriend perfect for each other —yet, there was something different about them. Carole was more like Mrs. McKnight, and Jim was more like … like Sandy —Sacramento. Damn it! Why wouldn't he and his gentle smile stop popping into her thoughts?

***

Captain Mike ushered the three of them into his den where, unexpectedly, Admiral Bailey was waiting. His Hawaiian shirt and shorts had been replaced by a khaki uniform, and his wide smile had sobered. He stood in front of Mike's desk and waited until Mike had closed the door. "Sit down, kids." Piper eased down on the hassock, and Jim and Carole sat behind her on the sofa. "Mike tells me you've got some information for us."

"I found Sorenson," Piper said. "He runs a private airport on the outskirts of Yuma."

"We know," Bailey said.

"You do?"

"And so far, he doesn't know that we know. That could all change if he spots two half-baked ninnies gawking at him and following him to work."

Piper turned around and looked at Jim with disbelieving eyes.

"Okay. Maybe you did track him down after we gave you my work cards, but there's a helluva lot more to the story. Tell him, Piper," Jim said.

"The Bund gave the Sorensons a daughter. Do you know that?"

Bailey glanced at Mike. "Uhhh. No. What do you mean 'gave'?"

"Just that. There was no adoption. The baby belonged to Edwina Blackledge. That missing one-hundred grand wasn't the only reason she was killed, and …"

Bailey pulled up a chair in front of the hassock and sat down. "How do you know?"

"I snooped around in Mitch's car and found a picture of the little girl with Sorenson's name written on the back. I put two and two together but wanted to make sure it added up to four before I came to you. The only way to do that was to go to Yuma."

Bailey lit up a Camel and Mike fired up his pipe. "You're either very brave or very stupid," Mike said. "It's one thing to keep your ears and eyes open at the Bund meetings, but surveillance in the desert with no backup? No weapon. Nobody knowing where you are …"

"Speaking of weapons." Piper dug into her purse and handed Captain Mike the bullet she'd stolen from Mitch. "Can you tell me what size gun fits this?"

"Where did you get this?" Mike said.

"It belongs to Mitch, and maybe someday, if we find out how

Edwina really died, we can include or exclude Mitch Roberts as a suspect."

"Let's hope he doesn't count his shots," Bailey said. He took the bullet from Mike. "Whatever it is, it's rare. I don't think it's American made. I'll get it to ballistics. Damn, smart-ass kids."

Mike slipped into his dad routine again. "Carole, did you know Piper was gallivanting out to the desert?"

"Not exactly, Daddy."

"There's plenty of space out there to bury a body," Bailey said.

"But it wouldn't surprise me if Sorenson is the guy who killed Edwina," Piper said. "How does a shipyard worker buy an airport in the middle of a depression? Unless Mitch bought it and Sorenson runs it. I haven't had time to check the court records in Yuma to find out who owns the place, but …" She stopped when Mrs. McKnight came in.

"Sorry to interrupt, Admiral, but Senator McAdoo is on the phone."

"Would you all excuse me?" Bailey said.

Mike led them to the kitchen. Over iced tea and cookies, eaten in Mrs. McKnight's breakfast nook, he half apologized. "I know we sound harsh, but we can't afford an incident that might jeopardize our intelligence capability. Everybody in Washington knows Japan's imperialist expansion means a full-scale war with China and it'll eventually spread to the South Pacific. The Soviets have signed a friendship treaty with China, hoping to protect their interests in Inner Mongolia. Moscow's even willing to recognize Mussolini's take-over of Ethiopia if the Axis will back off."

"So, you want us to stop spying?" Jim said.

Mike sighed. "We want you to be safe when there's no way you can be safe. We need every scrap of information you can get us. We just didn't expect you'd do such a good job so quickly. You're probably right about Mitch and Sorenson being mixed up in the Blackledge killing, Piper, but we'll have to put that on the back burner to find out what —or who —they're flying in and out of that airport."

"What about the baby?" Jim said. "We don't know anything about Mrs. Sorenson. We have to find out if the baby's being taken care of."

"And we don't know what they might do if the Bund puts pressure on them," Carole added. "If there's no papers on the baby, they can get rid of her as easily as they got her."

Mike went to the kitchen window that overlooked the backyard. "That's thrown me a curve, I admit. Especially since the government is technically neutral and the Bund is legal. God knows how badly the German nationals were treated during the Great War. Registration. Confiscations."

Piper knew the Japanese had been interned during the second war, but the information about German tribulations in the first one took her by surprise. "Did they get their stuff back?"

"What Washington taketh away, Washington keepeth," Mike said.

Mrs. McKnight seemed to appear out of nowhere, so quickly,

she startled all of them. "Michael McKnight, you know I don't interfere with military affairs. It's how I've kept my sanity for the last twenty-five years. But, I have to speak up about this. Neutral doesn't mean hamstrung. You have to figure out a way to get that baby out of there. It doesn't take a genius to know these people aren't above violence if they get desperate." Now, four pairs of eyes looked to Captain Mike for action. "It's not like there aren't people here who will gladly take care of her."

Mike returned to his seat. "Okay," he said slowly. "I want a plan, and a promise you won't carry it out until you've run it by me first. Agreed?"

"Agreed," Jim said. Carole and Piper nodded yes.

Just as Mrs. McKnight said, "Agreed," Admiral Bailey came in with news.

"The *Augusta* took a stray Japanese shell in Shanghai harbor. A seaman was killed and seventeen were wounded," he said, and eyed them all suspiciously. "What have you agreed to?"

"To forego an anniversary dinner out and have hot-dogs at home"' Captain Mike said.

Bailey looked directly at Piper. "I'd order you all to back off but how can I do that when you're filling in the blanks for us? I'll tell our Bund mole to contact you when he thinks you're ready. Washington says there's a rumor Mussolini and Hitler are going to leave the U.N. You're going to have to give them something to build their trust, Piper, so tell 'em that and tell 'em where you heard it."

***

When she got back to the Y, Sandy was waiting. Carole and Jim had been appreciative of her new look, but he was agog. "Must have been some kind of date. Mrs. Stevens said the roses are yours. I was tempted to take credit for them," he said from the parlor doorway.

Piper walked towards him. "I don't know who they're from. It's silly to send anonymous gifts. Defeats the purpose. Have you been here long?"

"Depends on what the purpose of the gift is. About a half an hour." He held up a copy *of National Geographic*. "I learned all about the Zulu War, though. If you ever want to talk about 1879, I'm your guy."

She followed him inside. "I like information. So, spill."

He tossed the magazine gently on the coffee table. "Naw, we've got other things to talk about," he said half-playfully. "Can we close the doors?"

"Against the rules. You might have bad intentions."

He hung his head, as if guilty. "Fun intentions," he corrected. "But, at least we're alone." He sat down on a gray wool settee. Piper took the chair opposite.

"What's on your mind, sailor?"

He picked up his hat and rolled the edge. "The guys told Cabot they overheard me say your name and know I was with you yesterday. I told Cabot I changed a flat tire for you. Thought I'd better tell you."

"Aw, geez. I'm sorry. I shouldn't have put you in that position. I'd never want you to lie to your friend."

He stopped fidgeting. "I'm no fool, Piper. You had a good reason. I just don't know what it is. Who is this guy Sorenson?"

"A friend asked me to track him down. He jumped bail on a DWI."

Sandy laughed. "Really? You moonlight as a bounty hunter?"

"Not a popular enterprise in hard times."

"That's a relief!" She realized he was laughing at himself, not her. "I thought it might have something to do with that Nazi crew. That guy, Mitch? He can't take his eyes off of you." He nodded towards the flowers that Mrs. Stevens had put in a crystal vase and set on the front counter. "Maybe the roses are from him."

"Maybe."

Mrs. Stevens came to the doorway. "Nine o'clock Miss Hampton."

Piper jumped up. "I have to work tomorrow, but we could get dinner at six."

Sandy nodded a yes. "Do I have to leave now? Oh, okay. You're on." Halfway to the door, he turned around. "What do I tell Cabot and the guys if they tell me to meet them at Bernie's?"

"Tell them …I asked you to dinner and you don't know why."

"Tell them I got asked out on a date by a girl? You really think I can tell them that? They'll think I'm a Nancy-boy." Piper felt her face get hot and knew she was turning red. His smile was back. Was she suddenly naked? "But I know why you asked me. You're going to tell me the truth about Yuma." He put on his Dixie cup and gave her a two-finger salute.

Was one of the girls playing her hi-fi too loud, or was that her heart beat she heard pounding in her head? She was a good liar. A great liar, according to Josh. A bad one, according to Jim. Maybe she'd been lying to herself.

She took seventy-five cents to the counter where Mrs. Stevens was standing watch. "Thank-you," she said as she offered her three quarters. "It's nice to have a pretty dress to wear. I never worried about clothes before." Her words surprised her. They were absolutely true.

Surprising too were Mrs. Stevens' kindly eyes that belied the stern demeanor of a commander of the Y's thirty displaced young women. Mrs. Stevens gave a quarter back to her. "Accessories are only twelve and a half cents each."

She put the quarter in her change purse, and a memory of her grandmother opening a needlepoint coin bag popped into her head. She always carried two quarters, two dimes, a nickel and three pennies. "Did Sandy really wait a half hour for me?"

"No, he waited and hour and forty-five minutes. He's a nice young man. You could do worse."

She wasn't sure if Mrs. Stevens' remark was an evaluation of her or of Sandy's prospects, but the thought made her grin as she took off her make-up. All this interest in getting people paired and married was so funny. She figured she marry someday, but why all the hurry here? It wasn't quite *Pride and Prejudice*, but people here were definitely on the lookout for a good match.

Chapter VII

With pen, paper, and determination, Piper met Carole at her apartment at eight o'clock a.m. as planned. "I know this is going to be painful," Piper prefaced her questioning, but Carole wasn't in consolation mode. She'd bought doughnuts on the way home from her parents' house, and there was fresh coffee brewing on the hotplate.

"I'll do what I have to do to get Suzanne back. Dad said we needed a plan, so let's give him a doozy. Fire away. Jim and I have appointed you lead investigator."

"Tell me where you had the baby. Was it a hospital, somebody's guest room or basement?"

"I stayed at this house in the back-country, a place called The Grove for my last three months ...way out in Harbison Canyon. There were two other girls there. It's run by the Bund as part of its charity work, Mitch said."

"Charity work, my ass. They're running a black-market baby scam. I wonder ..."

"Mitch would take me to see a doctor in Imperial Beach. Dr. Chapman or Chartman ...yes, Chartman. Once week. Finally, he said I was due in two weeks, and in two weeks Mitch took me back to his office and Chartman induced me. He had a labor room in the back and a delivery room. Afterwards, a Hispanic couple took me to a hotel downtown. I slept for a long time. I know because I remember the clock read 9:00 p.m. when I got there, and when I woke up, it was noon the next day and I was really hungry.”

“What kind of place is The Grove? A ranch house? Split level? Did it have a swimming pool?”

“It looks like an old-fashioned mansion. Spanish style. White washed. And clean inside. Sort of like the Y.” She reached under the sofa and brought up a shoe box, opened it, and handed Piper a stack of photos. “These will help. The journalist in me couldn’t resist.”

“Does Mitch know you took these?”

“Nope. I’d forgotten what was on the roll of film until I had it developed when we first talked about Suzanne. I figured someday I might be able to stand remembering, you know?”

Piper knew all too well how it hurt to be reminded of how much you’d lost. She went through the pictures one by one, her eyes devouring the images of a pristine San Diego back county. Without familiar landmarks, though, it was going to be a challenge. “Did you get to know the other girls? Remember any of their names?”

“We worked together in the kitchen and the laundry, but we all kept to ourselves. Nobody can tell what they don’t know, right? And we all knew why we were there.”

Piper returned to the photos. “This car in the driveway …looks like there’s someone sitting in the driver’s seat. Do you remember any of the staff? The cook? The head *honcho*?”

Carole took the photo and stared at it. “Supplies were delivered in a truck. Once a week. I never spoke with the delivery guy. Too ashamed. The woman in charge was introduced to me as Sister Rita.

No last name. I asked Mitch if she was nun or something, but he said no. Then there was the housekeeper, Maria, and her husband Enrique, who took care of the property. It could be him."

"Was Sister Rita nice to you?"

"I suppose so. Nice, but not friendly. No late-night chats or anything like that."

Piper was scribbling notes. "Did Mitch ever come to visit you at the house. Just to keep you company, or maybe visit any of the other girls?"

"Never to visit. He did take me to the doctor even though Maria took the other girls."

"Did it seem like he knew Chartman well? Did they talk at all about you or the baby?"

"You're driving at something, what?"

Piper got herself a cup of java and grabbed a chocolate covered cake doughnut. "I'm trying to figure out how deep Mitch is into the baby selling business. This isn't just about Suzanne or you and Jim. It's about the missing hundred thousand dollars and Edwina's murder. Where would the Bund get a hundred thousand dollars? Certainly not from sailors no matter how generous they are. To support all the charity work they do, they need serious money. We know Mitch runs the baby scam, so he might know how the money changes hands —and he'd have a motive for murder." She nodded towards the photos. "Backcountry visits and car trips into the city would certainly give someone opportunity. You got another napkin?"

"I'll get it," Carole said. Engaged or not, maybe she still had feelings for Mitch, Piper thought, and scrawled 'sensitivity' on the note pad. "You're so different from me and my parents. You're so young and yet you know so much about police work. How?" she said as she handed Piper the pack.

"When you grow up watching *Law and Order* and *Forensic Files*, you learn about stuff."

"Watching?"

"Television shows about fingerprints. DNA testing. Fancy machines that can analyze chemicals in paint, poisons, and potions." Carole was looking at her with the same incredulous eyes Piper had seen when she first told her about her cell phone. "I don't know much history, but I do know crime solving takes learning a lot of facts. Even the not so nice ones."

"Like Mitch being a killer and posing as my friend?" Carole had loaded her coffee with milk from an ice-box that depended on an ice block to keep it cold.

"Like mistaking gratitude for love."

"I don't love Mitch Roberts." Piper saw that Carole's hands were steady and she didn't hesitate to reply. Maybe she was telling the truth. She used a folded napkin as a coaster for her coffee cup. She was like her mother. Tidy.

"I was talking about Jim."

Carole caressed her ring with her fingers. "Love will be different when you've got a few years and experiences behind you. It's still wonderful. Just … more practical. You'll see."

"I do see! Oh, this is so terrible." Before she could stop them, tears spilled down her cheeks and Piper grabbed a napkin to stem the tide before the sobs came with them. It didn't work. "Carole, I'm falling in love with Sandy Sacramento and if he falls in love back, Glinda won't let me go home and I don't know what to do!"

Carole slid closer to her and put her arm around Piper's shoulder. "Good heavens, what are you talking about? I thought you were seeing Cabot. Sandy's last name is Sacramento? And who's Glinda?"

"Sandy's from Sacramento. I keep track of the all the guys by their geography. He was waiting for me at the Y last night. He didn't send me the flowers ..."

"You got flowers?"

"Yeah, but I don't know who sent them. Anyway, Sandy lied to Cabot for me and I feel just awful about it. And then he smiled at me and I didn't think about anything else all night. Not even these stupid Nazi baby sellers, and Glinda is Billy Burke, the nice witch who got Dorothy Gale home."

"Billy Burke's not a witch, she's married to Flo Ziegfeld."

"No. It's a movie. My favorite. Everybody's favorite. I'm babbling."

"The future seems very complicated to me. All this talk about witches and watching TV and radar, and wars and flowers from strangers. It must be terrible for you. I've never said much, but you're the Hot-shot, Piper. Sandy's going to love you back, and if this Glinda person is real, well, she'll let him go home with you."

"I just wish I knew why this has happened. If I had a reason …"

"I can't tell you why. But, I'm glad you're here."

Carole went to the table and brought back the last chocolate doughnut wrapped in waxed paper. She put it on Piper's plate and offered it to her. "We've all been terribly selfish. You had your life and now it's gone. Maybe you're here to save somebody's life, but if that's true, it's a cruel fate. Falling in love isn't exactly a fair reward considering how miserable it can make you feel. Out of control and everything."

Piper went to the bathroom and splashed cold water on her face. If Goldstein saw she'd been crying, he'd get nosy. "I'd better get going," she said when she came back to the living room. "We both have to get to work." She picked up the doughnut and drank the last of her coffee. "Sorry about the blubbering. I don't usually boo-hoo it in front of strangers."

"We're not strangers, Piper. Not anymore. Whatever you need me to do, you just ask."

"I really need you to sit down and write everything you can remember about everything that happened after you met Mitch. Names, dates, places —what you wore to the clinic. Whatever details come to mind. It helps, really. And I'll do my part. Sandy is taking me to dinner and he doesn't know it yet, but I've got things I need him to do."

***

Sandy didn't bring red roses, but he did bring daisies and four yellow carnations and an answer to her most pressing question: Who sent the flowers? Cabot Jersey. "He had Charlie Cleveland order them. Cleveland didn't know if he should sign Cabot's name on the card, so he didn't."

They drove to Tops Drive-in and got fried chicken baskets and shakes to go. "We'll have more time to talk if we eat in the car," he said as he rolled to a stop in front of the theater.

"Yeah, talk we need to do. First, I didn't lie to you about Yuma and Sorenson. He really did jump bail. But …that's not the reason I was tracking him down. You have to be at least twenty-one to be a bounty hunter and I'm not twenty-one."

"That's how I knew there was more to the story." Sandy was drowning fries in catsup, but navigating them like a pro. No red drops on the white shirt he had tucked into his jeans.

"I forget you're older and wiser than I am."

"Stop with the sarcasm, girlie. What's this all about?"

"I'm spying on the Nazis, Sandy, and Sorenson is a Nazi. I think."

"I knew it was something serious. Not that serious, I admit."

She could see Goldstein watching them from the ticket booth and wondered if he could read lips. "That's it? You believe me?"

"I didn't know what to think at first. You knew where to find him. There had to be a reason. There's a reason for everything. So, I got big-mouth Cleveland to stand in for me and drove out to Yuma last night. Guess what I saw."

"You did what? I … I can't imagine. I mean, why would you do that?"

"Private airport. Scheduled flights. Some of which land at daybreak. Got me curious. And I watched it all. Including the Sorensons going home with a new little bundle of joy. I've seen a lot of strange things in my day, but never a baby delivered by an airplane."

Piper stopped mid bite on a droopy fry. "Are you sure it was a baby they brought home?"

"You saw the Missus. Did she look pregnant to you? But when Mr. Sorenson left for work at ten in the morning, she had the little girl with her and carried an infant out to the car to say bye-bye."

"How old?"

"I don't know." He spaced his hands about twenty inches apart. "This big, maybe. About a month old? There's more. Mitch and Honnolore showed up at Sorenson's a while later and picked up a different baby from the Sorenson's. I know it was a different kid because Mrs. Sorenson was holding her baby as she waved them good-bye. I followed them to a house back in Dago. I'll take you there tomorrow morning."

Mr. Goldstein was waving and pointing at his watch. "Oops, gotta go," Piper said. "See you at nine tomorrow?"

Sandy nodded, and finished a bite of chicken. "One more thing." He leaned over and planted a kiss on her cheek. "Be careful."

What does be careful mean? Stop? Proceed slowly? The only remaining questions for Piper were whether the baby selling supported the Bund, or whether the Bund was a cover for a crime syndicate. Maybe Edwina Blackledge found the answer.

***

Sandy drove her past a tan stucco bungalow in La Mesa and drove down the alley to observe the backyard. A thirty-ish woman was hanging freshly washed diapers on the clothes line. On the patio was a bassinette with a blue and white striped skirt. "If babies go to families out of state, this one is probably imported from somewhere else. El Paso, maybe?" Piper said.

He took her arm to get her attention. "I have to report this, Piper. I'm sorry, but I have to."

"ONI already knows." She looked at him earnestly. "They're watching the airport, and my job is watching the Bund and making reports to Admiral Bailey. So now you know the whole truth."

He started the car and coasted on idle until he was past the backyard, then shifted into first gear. "Seen enough, then?" He drove down El Cajon Boulevard without a word.

"Are you angry with me? I couldn't tell you upfront, Sandy."

He pulled into the Denny's parking lot and stopped the car. "I'm not angry with you, just pissed off at the Navy because I'm scared for you. This is big time stuff. I've got one more week of leave left, and my parents want to me to visit, and I can't bear to leave you spying on people who'll want to kill you if you mess up their money-making machine." He smacked the steering wheel with an open palm. "Damn it! You think I can hole up in Hawaii knowing you might be in trouble?"

Piper drew into her thoughts for a minute. "Would you rather I hadn't told you?"

"It's not your fault I went back to Yuma. What a bunch of bastards these fascists are."

"Do you want to help me put them away?" she asked. "The Bund isn't illegal, but black-marketing babies is." The realization fell on her like a boulder from the blue. All those crime movies on the weekends based on true stories? Sometimes, ordinary people really do get involved with the ugly underbelly of society. Maybe Mrs. Sorenson loved Suzanne, but maybe she didn't. Or maybe it was a sick kind of love that made Suzanne expendable if life got too complicated. On the other hand, the little girl was growing up. Mrs. Sorenson was the only mother Suzanne knew and it would break the kid's heart to be torn away from people who love her.

Piper felt herself trembling. This wasn't the world of selfies and gossip about rap stars. It was the time of big decisions by people trying to avoid a war the rest of the world was already fighting. It was a time of intimate, personal decisions by people trying to be happy.

"I'd do anything for you, Piper. Can we bust them in a week?"

Who needs a week? Life can change in an instant. Piper looked into Sandy's green eyes and felt herself wanting —no, needing his help. "Let me think on it for a while. Twenty-four hours. If I haven't come up with anything by then, well, you do what you have to do."

***

Captain Mike made time for her after lunch. They met at the Admiral Kidd Club, where they wouldn't be bothered or overheard, Mike said. He escorted her to the patio and ordered iced tea for her and a martini for himself. "You sounded so serious on the phone, I got worried."

"You said we should tell you about any plans to rescue Suzanne from the Sorenson's, and I have one."

"Oh, yes. Of course."

Piper knew instantly his plans had changed by the way he directed his attention to the wayward olive swimming in his cocktail glass. There were developments since their last talk with Admiral Bailey, but he wasn't sharing them with her. With Carole and Mrs. McKnight occupied with the wedding, and Jim working overtime to pay for the honeymoon, the urgency of the evening cabal seemed to have evaporated. She brought out her cell phone. "You said they want this. Suppose I use it as bait and cut a deal with Mitch. A sort of exchange."

"And let him know somebody's onto him? Suppose you wind up dead. I've given this a lot of thought, Piper. I can't put you in danger any more than I can put Carole in danger. It's not right. And the truth is we just can't risk a big operation for one little child, no matter how precious. Word has gotten to us that Hitler has announced Germany must prepare for total war. It's probably true, but even if it's not we've got to keep the organization in tact if we're going to track it. We can't learn anything from chaos."

"But, if we called the FBI in on this, couldn't they prosecute a civilian case against just Mitch and Sorenson?"

"The closest FBI office is in Los Angeles. There's scuttlebutt Hoover's thinking about opening a San Diego office, who knows?"

"We don't know for certain the baby ring could be traced back to the Bund because of all the political agitation on the Mexican border. Knowin' Mitch, he's probably playing all sides of the street to make a buck."

"And knowing Mitch, he isn't going to go down alone. He'll take the Bund down with him and you know it." As soon as the words were spoken, she knew he was right. "Besides, what about … this." He held up her phone." We call in the feds and they'll start asking a lot of questions about you, and they won't believe your answers. Where were you born? San Diego? Where's your birth certificate. Who are your parents and where are they? You'll be put in protective custody in some juvenile detention center and maybe transferred to some nut house when you tell them the truth. Do you want that?"

She shuddered. "God no." This was a part of her new reality she'd never considered. Maybe the authorities would think she was an alien. The thought of being prodded, tested, examined, and observed like a biological mutant made her dizzy with terror.

McKnight continued. "With this depression thing, millions of young people are moving around the country. Some of them looking for work, and some of them running away from crimes they committed back home. It's easier to hide when everyone's from somewhere else and nobody knows your name. The best thing you can do for everybody involved is keep a low profile."

It was his way of saying keep out of the way. Disappear if necessary. There can't be any official record of their meetings either.

"Yes, Sir, I understand." She needed a new identity.

Chapter VIII

"Don't know why but it seems like everybody's in a hurry to get hitched," according to Joe Tucker, Justice of the Peace. Piper wanted to tell him that she and Sandy wanted to live a little before the dying started, and by the numbers of couples waiting in his office, a lot of young people shared the same premonition. JP Tucker filled out the marriage certificate and gave them a discount ticket for the Pioneer Motel in Winterhaven. "Never seen so many newlyweds or so much melancholy either."

Sandy seemed determined to be cheery. He came back from the office with a key to room 213 and a mischievous grin. "Twin beds," he said when he slid behind the wheel and drove to the motel's rear entrance. "The guy apologized, but under the circumstances, I suppose one of us should thank him."

"I won't be a bother. If you fall in love with somebody, I'll pay for the annulment. I promise. And I'll keep my job. Investigation or not I'll pull my own weight."

He stopped the car and put his arm around her shoulder. "My question is, can you keep house?"

In 2018, there was a bedroom littered with her clothes, photography books and school assignments. She felt enslaved when it was her turn to run the dishwasher. By her desk was a Star Wars trashcan overflowing with Diet Coke cans and crumpled copies of her English paper drafts. She kissed his cheek. "I'll try my best."

"Then I say, your plan is about perfect for the both of us. You get the protection of a wedding ring, and I get home-cooked meals until I leave. That and the peace of mind knowing you're taken care of in case something happens, Mrs. Sanders."

There seemed to be an understanding between them that they wouldn't talk about the possibility of war. They spent most of their wedding night listening to the radio, alternating between news casts and music shows, and drinking sodas. "I cabled my parents that I won't be coming home before I ship out. They're used to the Navy changing its mind when it comes to medical personnel. I thought lettuce fields and fruit orchards were the last thing I'd miss about home, but now, I'd like to show you our farm. It's a pretty place."

"You cable them right back and tell them you'll be there as planned. I mean it. I promise I won't do anything too stupid while you're gone, but this is my situation and I won't have you changing your life because of me."

He held up his left hand and pointed to a slim gold band on his fourth finger. "Pardon the pun, but that ship has sailed."

"Changing your life too much, anyway, because of it."

He got down on his knees and crawled to her bedside. "I want you to ask yourself one big question, person who took me from a peep show to a Bund meeting. Do you, in your heart of hearts, believe that I could sit there and listen to Nazi garbage and think that this situation, as you call it, is something you should fight alone? If some little girl from God knows where is willing to put her life on the line for people she doesn't know, I certainly can't do any less." He crawled back to his bed, climbed on top, and rolled over.

She'd heard the sailors say they learned how to fall asleep anywhere in less than thirty seconds and she believed it now. Before she could think of a comeback, snappy or otherwise, Sandy was off in dreamland. How could he snooze when she lay awake, staring at the ceiling? And at him. Little girl? Was that why he didn't try to kiss her?

When they got back to San Diego, they both got news they didn't expect.

***

"Sandy got new orders," Piper told Carole over the phone. She'd promised to keep her in the loop, and this loop was rapidly becoming a noose of her own making. "Advanced medical training to commence immediately. He'll be stationed at the San Diego Naval Hospital."

"That's good news, isn't it?"

Were her misgivings so obvious? "I don't know. The plan was for him to provide me a new identity, not a new lifestyle. I mean, won't the Bund expect us to move in together? It'll look suspicious if we don't. And why the sudden advanced training now? Has Jim heard anything about a military buildup?"

"He's pulling double shifts until further notice. Is this the way it's going to start, Piper? I'm so scared."

"Me too," she admitted. Scared to death, and she didn't expect to be. She'd accepted that she and Jim weren't there to prevent the war. No two people could do that. But she didn't think the war would affect them so personally. They were Star Trek people, observers not participants, so why was she so committed to neutralizing Mitch and disabling the Bund? Now, nothing could persuade her to back off. She 'd figured out a new plan, one she hadn't shared with anyone but Sandy.

That's why Piper Hampton became Mrs. Christopher Sanders, she wrote at the first page of the journal she vowed to keep. If she ever found the time.

***

Mr. and Mrs. Sanders attended Bund meetings religiously. The Bauers were as ecstatic as Mitch was subdued. "Cabot said you were going to Hickam Field," Anatole said to Sandy after they set up chairs for the meeting. "And now I hear you're staying in San Diego permanently."

"Got a bunch of corpsmen who need instruction on finding a good vein on the first stab, and I'm gonna show 'em how. I've been reclassified as teaching personnel."

"Uncle Sam getting ready for a war?"

"I don't know. I do what I'm told and go where they send me."

"Piper still at the Y?"

"Not even a teacher guy gets a housing allowance right away, Mr. Bauer. My CO says it may be another six months. Can you believe that?"

Just a few minutes later, he saw Anatole talking to Mitch. In fix-it man mode, Mitch walked over to him and said, "I'll see what I can do about the housing situation." For someone who sulked through the entire meeting and the buffet afterwards, Mitch was quick to let

Sandy know he was serious about the offer. "Call me at the paper tomorrow afternoon."

"We would have given you a proper wedding," Honnolore assured Piper. "But elopements can be so romantic." She looked wistfully into the distance, as though remembering younger, happier times.

Piper continued to dry dishes and stack them in the cupboard. "We thought Sandy was shipping out. Guess that's how things go with the Navy."

"Mitch says you're going to keep working. Are you, really?"

"My money's going into a house fund. We want a family, you know." It still seemed strange to her how people didn't think she was too young to be married. JP Tucker didn't even raise an eyebrow and he had to suspect her permission slip was forged.

"Of course, you do. It's a woman's job. As many children as she can have without being depleted. You'll make a good German wife."

Three days later, when they saw the one-bedroom bungalow Mitch found in an eight-unit court in Hillcrest —no pets, no playing the radio with the door open after ten o'clock —Honnolore pronounced the place "adorable!" and measured the windows for curtains she promised to sew over the weekend. She took Piper shopping for material. How could Nazis be so evil and nice at the same time?

Mrs. McKnight was just as effusive. "You two make such a nice couple."

And she and Sandy were treated to a dinner at the Admiral Kidd Club.

"I wish Carole and I could elope," Jim confided to Piper on the dance floor. Carole had taught him the waltz and the box step in preparation for their first dance as man and wife, and he was practicing all over her feet.

"No, you do this right, Jim. You'll never regret it and Carole will love you forever."

They inched their way to the patio for a breather and looked out at a ship-filled San Diego bay. No bridge. No high-rise hotels.

"Does a church wedding really mean that much to a woman? I thought it was all for show."

"For the Kardashians maybe. For Carole, it's a dream come true."

"Inside skinny?"

"The truth, so help me."

"What about you? Sandy has real feelings for you. In case you can't tell."

It took a lot of effort to lie, but she didn't want to say she'd fallen for Sandy like a cedar tree. "I know, I could do worse. But I want to go home, Jim. I keep thinking about how sad my parents must be. No good-byes. My Mom is probably still beating herself up about letting me stay alone, my Dad, staring at pictures of our last trip to Universal Studios."

Jim took her by the shoulders. "Don't dwell on it. I've told myself a thousand times, things happen for a reason. If this is death, it ain't so bad. We've got people who love us."

Oh, hell. A fool could tell she was gushy for him. "I do love Sandy, Jim. That's just the trouble. He may die in the war. I don't want to be a widow. Especially one with kids to support. *That* would be hell."

"There you two are!" Piper looked up and saw Carole and Sandy standing in the doorway. "We wanted to see the harbor lights," Jim said.

Sandy took Piper by the hand and led her towards the dance floor. "*Harbor Lights* is my favorite song."

"Is that what they're playing?" Piper said.

"Yep."

She felt his arms around her and it instantly became her favorite song too.

***

Mrs. Stevens opened the boutique again and brought down a box tied with white ribbon. Inside was a collection of dainty peignoirs and nightgowns. "For newlyweds only," she said.

Piper was sure she had widow's weeds in there somewhere. Probably on the floor behind the ski boots. She chose a white satin nightgown with spaghetti straps and tiny blue flowers around the neckline. "This is pretty."

Mrs. Stevens pulled out a short blue chiffon robe to cover it. "There were a pair of … here they are … for in the morning. Keep your feet soft with lotion and trim your toenails." She held up a pair of blue satin slippers.

Piper didn't remember hearing that in Human Sexuality class. She swallowed hard. "You've been so kind to me. I'm going to pay this forward, I promise. Someday, I'll have clothes for the boutique."

The woman gave her a hug. "You were a good tenant. If you ever need a place to stay, I'll make room for you."

Carole came to the door, and Mrs. Stevens nodded. "You too, Miss McKnight. You both have a nice Christmas."

"Let me put this in my suitcase," Piper said. She didn't want Carole to see her all weepy. She didn't want to feel weepy. But how could she not? Almost overnight she'd gone from a child to a grown-up, and now she was a married woman. Honnolore sewed morning glory patterned curtains for her kitchen, and Mrs. McKnight gave her a Fannie Farmer cookbook. Jim and Captain Mike helped Sandy move a second-hand bedroom suite, a rose patterned chintz sofa, a lamp, and a green wing-backed chair into the bungalow. His study chair, Sandy called it because his dad had one. And Mitch —scoundrel that he was —helped paint the bedroom a pale yellow and the living room off-white. "Because white goes with everything," she explained to the men. Carole helped empty her car of clothes and second-hand linens in boxes marked bathroom, kitchen, and bedroom.

After the final trip, Piper noticed an unfamiliar box on the kitchen counter. Attached was note that read: To My Dear Friend. Love Carole.

Inside was a silver tea kettle. She held it to her heart. "It's wonderful," she said, "but it's all pretend."

"Okay," Carole said, and took the kettle to the sink. "We'll pretend to have a cup of tea."

"No, you don't understand ..."

"Carole filled the kettle with water and lit the stove. "Oh yes I do. You've got cold feet."

"I've got loads and loads of plain, old fashioned guilt. Sandy and I are married, but we're not married. Not in the same way people are supposed to be married."

"Oh, come on." Carole took her by the hand and they went to the living room. "You're not the first bride to feel awkward sharing living space with a guy..."

"It's the sleeping space I'm worried about. Sandy was supposed to ship out. Not be here. Everybody's being so damn nice and happy for us. I wish to God it was for real."

"I see. At least I think I do. Sandy knows about Suzanne."

"Yeah, but he doesn't know she's yours. He knows about Mitch and Edwina Blackledge, though, and he went back to Yuma by himself and told me he saw Mitch and Honnolore bringing in another baby. He was going to turn them all in, but I couldn't let that happen. There could be other babies involved."

Carole's eyes grew big as baseballs. "Not *your* baby..."

Piper sobered. "No. No ... the one he saw is with a family in La Mesa. We don't know how many others they're going to sell or trade, and we don't know what really happened to Edwina,"

The kettle whistled, and they went back to the kitchen. Piper rummaged around the boxes from Hansen's Second Hand and found two cups, while Carole got a tin of tea from the gift box.

"All this has been going on and all I've been thinking about is my wedding," Carole said. "How selfish can I be?"

"Don't be silly."

"Does my Dad know you're determined to see this thing through?"

"He told me to forget about it. But I can't. It's why I'm here. At least that's what I want to believe so my heart doesn't break into a million, trillion pieces. Jim doesn't want to go back, but I do, I think."

"It says in the Bible that a man shall leave his mother and a woman her family and they shall become one. I guess the difference between us is that, when I say for better or worse, I'll mean it." Carole scanned the bungalow and smiled approvingly. "I hate to say Honnolore is right, but your place is adorable. Let yourself be happy once in a while, Piper. Come on, we have a kitchen to unpack."

***

Sandy came home an hour early bearing flowers, a box radio, and hamburgers he'd scrounged from the mess. Piper greeted him with a, "Oh Lord, I'm a mess," and wouldn't let him near her until she'd showered and changed out of her shorts and into a pair of slacks and one of his navy T-shirts. They ate sitting on the living room floor, listening to President Roosevelt's Fireside Chat about the unemployment census, and the news wasn't good. Unemployment was on the rise again creeping upwards from fourteen percent. Manufacturing had fallen back to 1934 levels.

"It's damn hard arguing with the Nazis' success in Germany. You'd think they won the last war," Sandy said.

"The Germans may be making war machines, but Carole said Jim was working double shifts welding boats, so everyone's gearing up now."

Sandy switched stations again. "How about we leave the economy to Congress. There we go." It was big band music —Benny Goodman. Piper remembered her Grandfather's collection of old 78 records. Her first instinct was to reach for her cell phone and text her mother to save them for her.

"Teach me to swing?" she said.

"You bet!"

It wasn't jogging through the park, it was better. With her new military I.D. and a gate pass for her car, she could go to the 32nd Street commissary, PX, and even the Tropic Gardens Enlisted Man's Club even though she'd just turned eighteen. A couple of more practice sessions like this and she'd be able to Carolina Shag and Balboa with the best of them.

But what was she going to do about laundry? "There's a laundry service on Broadway. The Seven Seas Locker Club," Sandy said. "Drop off on Monday, pick up on Thursday. Or you can do it by hand and use the clotheslines in the backyard."

"I'll pay. Gladly," she said. This housekeeping gig was going to be tough. Sleeping arrangements even tougher. "I should take the sofa."

Sandy was adamant. "No way in hell."

"We'll trade off then."

"Nope. Bake me an apple pie."

"I've never baked a thing in my life. Can't I just go to Ralph's and buy one?"

"Ralph Miami sells pies?"

"Yeah, he goes into the grocery chain business when leaves the Navy."

She unpacked and took the top and middle drawer of the bureau, then put all her things in the top drawer because Sandy had more clothes than she had. Hats, ties, underwear, sweaters —white gloves, of all things —and some awful canvass leggings called snake guards. Unlike many of the young sailors, Sandy spent his money on extra uniforms too. They hung in the closet next to her box-office uniforms. His four to her two. When she hangered her green Stevens' Boutique taffeta that was her wedding dress, she thought about the last shopping trip she'd had with her mom, hunting for a prom dress that had to be sexy but not hoe-ish. Now, she'd settle for something that wasn't frump-ish. She'd try to be an old-timey woman.

She took a bubble bath with Sandy's razor and shave cream, swathed her legs and feet with lotion to get rid of the Barbisol smell, and clipped her toenails. The satin nightgown was the only one she had, so she slipped it on. With her hair loose about her shoulders, she looked like a goddess. A goddess who could use a tranquilizer. Mentally, she thanked Mrs. Stevens for the blue robe and slippers.

"Would you like a cup of tea, Sandy?" she said crossing from bedroom to kitchen through the living room. No answer. She went to the sofa and removed his reading glasses. What was he thinking of before he fell asleep? She lifted the book and read the cover: Field Wounds.

Task at hand. She went to the kitchen, pulled the cookbook from the top of the refrigerator and looked under PIES, Apple.

Chapter IX

Mitch was the last person she wanted to see, but like a bad penny, he showed up at the screen door as she was taking her first pie out of the oven. She'd made a list of ingredients and was at the grocers when it opened. "I need this stuff," she'd told the swarthy man at the counter.

"You never baked a pie before?" She shook her head no. "I give you some advice. Put the pie pan on a cookie sheet. It's easier to clean a cookie sheet than an oven."

He was right. She put the cookie sheet on the counter. "Can't talk to you right now, Mitch. Got to get to work."

"How about I pick you up for dinner?"

"Can't. Goldstein wants me to change the one sheets for tonight's movies."

"What's new?"

"*Snow White and Seven Dwarfs. The Awful Truth* is still running."

"They any good?"

"Why not buy a ticket and see for yourself?"

"You've been avoiding me since you moved in."

"I'm married, Mitch." She held up her left hand and wiggled her ring finger. "Remember?"

"No pie for me, I take it. You ladies and your romances." He eyed her suspiciously. "You look annoyingly happy."

"It's none of your business, Mitch Roberts." She forced a

friendly smile and rested against the counter. "You know, I think you're jealous of Jim 'cause he beat you to the altar. If you cared about Carole, you should've made your move."

He shrugged. "Old news, Piper. I'm pissed because I didn't make my move with you. Got to hand it to Sandy. Moved right in on Cabot's territory. We all thought you'd set your cap for him, even though I knew he wasn't your type."

She gave him a sisterly punch. "You never know about people."

"I know you and Sandy went somewhere east. Cabot told me. Are you a fan of hot dusty places?"

Maybe she could throw him off track. "If you must know, Sandy and I went to a motel in El Centro. The Y has a strict policy about gentlemen callers."

His scowl transformed to a sneering smile. "Well, well. You don't say. A country tryst."

"Just doing my part for the Fatherland. Sandy's a wealth of information." Her mind searched her Captain Mike file —the Nazis thought she'd been sent for a reason and Mitch wasn't buying the Sandy explanation. "You might want to tell the Bauers the Navy knows that Hitler and Japan are ready to leave the U.N. I overheard a phone conversation." It was time to flex a little muscle. "Besides, somebody has to find out what happened to Edwina and that missing hundred thousand."

Sweat beads appeared on Mitch's upper lip. "I didn't have anything to do with that" were the next words out of his mouth.

"And what is that, exactly? Murder and robbery?"

"Was that body they found in El Paso really Edwina?"

"Do you really care, Mitch?"

"Sure, I care. Organizing is hard work and murder spoils resolve." His voice was brittle.

"But they didn't find the cash, Mitch. Theft will inflame the resolve of the most dedicated Party official." He must believe she'd been sent by the higher ups by now. She decided to press on. "Blackledge got off a plane that landed at Sorenson's airport, and no one knows what happened to her between then and turning up dead in El Paso. Except you, of course."

"Sorenson said there was a man waiting at the airport. He didn't know who he was, but he's probably the guy who drove her to the Desert Palm Hotel in Yuma. I've got no reason to doubt him."

"I suppose not, with the insurance policy you took out on Sorenson. They've got a pretty child."

"I can explain …"

"No need. You make a few dollars on the side. No big deal." Piper recognized a sigh of relief when she heard it. "I may be in the market myself someday."

He took the bait. "Oh? Trouble in paradise?"

"If there is, it's my fault. I should have the doctor's report in few days."

"Your awful truth?"

"Big problems call for big solutions. A hundred-thousand dollars' worth. It doesn't matter. Not all commercial transactions require money."

Mitch leaned over and gave her a peck on the cheek. "I knew you were in charge of this poker game. Pie or no pie. See you later, sweetie-pie."

She locked the door behind him and changed into her uniform. She'd call Sandy as soon as she got to work and let him know the plan was ahead of schedule. She'd need that doctor's report sooner than either of them expected. And, yes, he could dig into the pie before she got home. "See you later, Honey," she said, then held the receiver away from her ear and grimaced. She'd never called anyone honey in her life. Maybe he didn't hear.

"Looks like we may have him right where we want him, Sweetheart."

She heard a click and hung up. He called her Sweetheart. It wasn't so bad. It was better than Josh calling her Peeper.

***

When she got home, Sandy smelled of Old Spice aftershave and had dinner waiting. Soup, ham sandwiches, and Nehi Orange soda. It wasn't fancy, but she was grateful. "How was the pie?" Half of it was gone.

"I was impressed with the crust. So, tell me what happened with Mitch."

"Did you really eat half the pie?"

"I brought home a friend. Ran into him at Largo Factotum…it's the Italian market near Sears …"

"I know it. Went there this morning." She cut a sliver of pie and gave it a taste. "Dang, that's good. What friend?"

"A guy who mustered out about a year ago. I warned him finding a job on the outside wouldn't be easy, but he said his parents wanted him home. They used to live up Sacramento way. Not too far from our farm."

"What's he doing back in San Diego?"

"His parents lost their farm. The only reason my Dad's still in business is because he can repair his own equipment and hasn't had to borrow money from the bank. Oh, here." He handed her an envelope that contained a check for twenty-five dollars. "It's a wedding present from my folks."

"Sandy, we can't keep this."

"We can't send it back. My parents will have a fit and send us fifty. You don't know how they are. And we are married …"

"I don't care. We're both working, we can't take money from people who need it."

"No, but we can accept a gift from people who'd be shamed if they couldn't send their only son a wedding gift. Mom says buy a table and chairs. They want us to come up as soon as I get leave again or send them a picture."

She stuffed the check back in the envelope and handed back to him. "Maybe we can give it to your friend. Where's he staying?"

"The YMCA on Broadway."

"That big hulking brown building? Wonder why they built it so far away from the YW. What's his name?"

"The YM was there first. WWI. And his name is Chester, but he goes by Cecil."

"His last name wouldn't be Beatty, would it?"

"You know him?"

She felt like someone slapped her. "No…yes. I mean I don't know him. Does he paint?"

"Mitch told you about him, right?"

"He's going to paint murals at the Trib," she said.

"What'd he tell you?" Sandy's sounded giddy. If he was a puppy his butt would be wiggling. So, it was true men loved gossip as much as women.

"Did who tell me what?"

"Mitch. Did Cecil get the WPA grant?" Sandy eyes were sparkling. "He submitted gorgeous designs. You ought to see them, Piper! He won't be able to buy the farm back for his parents, but he'll be able to send some money to help out now that his sister's moved out …"

"I want to meet him, Sandy. Jim will want to meet him too. Believe me."

"Jim's into art?"

"We're both fans of murals." It was miraculous. "I'll call Carole and Jim tomorrow and you call Cecil and have him come to dinner Thursday. I'll take the check to the bank too, and we'll give him the money to tide him over until he gets his grant."

Sandy gathered up the plates and took them to the sink. "Okay," he said from the kitchen, "but only half. I'm buying us a table and chairs this week-end and a few pictures. These walls could stand a mural or two." When he came back, he had another envelope in hand. "It's from Doctor Isaacson on a hospital letterhead. Your fallopian tubes are officially blocked and if they try to unblock 'em, they'll crumble. Sounds grisly enough to be true, huh?"

She read over the three-paragraph letter that delivered the bad news. "Geez, I'm glad it's not true. How'd you manage to get him to sign a fake medical report?" Isaacson didn't seem like a pushover when she'd seen him two weeks ago. His first words to her were, "What do you need?" and she almost slipped and said a pap smear.

"He didn't sign it. I did."

"Where'd you get the stationery? It looks authentic."

"It is. I made an appointment with him to ask him about …things …he's the ladies' doctor and does the newlywed counseling, and the 'stay away from the whores so you don't get gonorrhea' counseling, and how do I keep from getting my wife pregnant counseling. Which sounds a lot like how to not get gonorrhea counseling, by the way."

"He just gave you stationery?"

"I stole it while he was getting me … ah … other stuff …"

"What other stuff?"

Sandy was turning red. She'd never seen a grown-up guy blush before. He went into the bedroom and returned with a white sack. "It's a diaphragm and a spermicide. He said you'd need a medium. I wouldn't know. You know?"

"Don't worry," she said softly. "I know. Thanks. I mean, thanks for getting the letter taken care of. I'm impressed now." She brightened, and said, "Are you going to study?"

"Probably." He shifted his eyes to the sofa.

"Well, I think I'll take a quick bath. You gonna be awake?

"Yeah, probably."

"Good!" She took the sack and letter and headed to the bedroom. "Thanks for cleaning up. See you in a few…Honey," she said over her shoulder. Carole had advised her to let herself be happy, and she had decided it was good advice. She was sure she could make Sandy happy too. Until she faced reality. She had never told him about Manuel and his Senior Prom night and the champagne. Jim didn't expect Carole to be a virgin, but he was a 21st Century guy.

She sat down on the toilet set and felt the tiny flowers on her nightgown with her fingertips. Would it matter to Sandy that she was second-hand goods? The term turned her stomach. Women here only had the vote for seventeen years. Four elections. Yet, it didn't seem to bother him that she worked. Part of him must be non-traditional. Or …he didn't really care about her. That way, at least. She'd have to find out. He couldn't sleep on the sofa indefinitely.

She opened the bathroom door slowly. She could see the sofa, but not Sandy. She walked into the hall. "Sandy? Sandy, I have to talk to you. It's important. I think I ought to tell you …"

"That's a mighty pretty nightgown you're wearing, Mrs. Sanders," she heard him say from the bedroom. "Turn off the light and come tell me in here."

***

He looked at her in the moonlight, and she at him, wondering whether she'd made the biggest mistake of her life. He said, I love you and she believed him because, for the first time in her life, she wanted someone to hear someone say it and mean it. Everywhere she went people talked about war. The one in Spain. The one in China. The one in Africa. Everywhere she went people talked about the depression. How jobs were so hard to find. How millions of people lost their farms, their homes, and their families.

She said, I love you too. Maybe he believed her because he needed to hear someone say it. How could she now tell him the truth about where she came from and that she was going to leave? Yet, somehow, she got the words out.

"The world seems so mixed up," he said when she'd confessed. "It almost seems like we're all coming and going. There's nothing to keep a man in his grave anymore. Or his time slot."

"You believe me, then?"

"It sure explains why you've never baked a pie, and why you're dead set on fighting a war we haven't declared yet. It explains how someone like Amelia Earhart could just disappear ... three weeks before you got here, she just vanished into thin air. And Cecil once told me ... well, I'll let him tell you the story."

His voice trailed off in that sleepy way voices do when speakers are spent, and a kind of peaceful relief settled over her, her eyes eager to block out the night light. People and time may come and go, but sex was still the same language, she thought. There was a lot of comfort in that.

***

She awoke to a steady knocking at the front door. Sandy was

gone to a Saturday shift at the hospital —a note on his pillow read hugs and kisses, Sweetheart —and all she wanted to do was relive the romance of last night with a home-made latte. She glanced at the clock. Eight-thirty. Shivering, she slid into her shorts and a t-shirt and dragged herself to the living room. "Oh, god, what do you want?" she said to a flush-faced Jim. She staggered to the kitchen, lit the stove and put on the coffee pot.

"I need your cell phone charger."

"What for?" She unzipped the side pouch in her purse and handed him the cord. "I told you, I tried my car lighter. It doesn't charge."

He went to the kitchen table, and within minutes had changed the charger's cigarette lighter end to a wall socket plug. "Not enough oomph. I don't know why I never I thought of this before. Yes, I do. I keep thinking everything works the same here …or doesn't as the case may be."

She handed him the phone. "You think this will work?"

"Yep. If nothing else, you'll be able to take pictures again."

The screen lit up, and the familiar colored bars appeared, showing the battery was sucking up the electricity. So was she. They watched the screen like they were watching TV. "We got a phone yesterday. I was going to call Carole last night, but it was too late. I didn't want to disturb her at an inconvenient time …like some people," Piper said.

"So, what's up?"

"We're having a guest for dinner Thursday night. Cecil Beatty.

Can you believe that?" She heard him take an audible breath.

"No!"

"What do you mean no? Yes, for real. He's a friend of Sandy's. What do they say here? You could've bought me for a nickel."

Jim became all business. He got cups and saucers from the cupboard and a spoon from the drawer. "Damn, things are getting weird."

"Oh, yeah, they've been completely normal until now." Piper got cream from the refrigerator as Jim poured the coffee. "What's wrong now? You ought to take a lesson from your girlfriend and try to be happy."

"I won't be able to make it to dinner, that's all."

"Pardon the expression. Bullshit."

Jim reached over and took her hand in his icy fingers. "We'll be meeting a dead man. Remember you told me I knew a lot about the Trib building? You were right. Beatty died in the war. He was aboard the *Arizona* at Pearl Harbor."

"He's not in the Navy now. Sandy said he got out when his enlistment was over. To help his parents."

"That's not what his biography says."

"Maybe … maybe us coming back will change his biography. You ever think of the changes we might cause just by being where we're not supposed to be? Sandy calls it time slots. And we've been mis-scheduled. We're Amtraks." Her words were spoken to the unchanging, unflinching gaze of her partner in the paranormal who waited for her staccato plaint to stop.

"Maybe he re-enlisted when he couldn't find work after he painted the Trib murals. Or on December 7th. That's not complicated."

"And that's not necessarily the way it happened." She unplugged the phone and skimmed through her photos. "They're all there. Gees, you're brilliant, guy."

"That's what Carole says. But I got the info from one of the electricians at the shipyard. It's funny, Beatty's an electrician. Sort of. He was a radioman in the Navy."

"Is. He's not dead yet," Piper said.

"I hear determination in that. Are you going to warn him?"

"And spoil Christmas? Would you want some stranger predicting you're gonna die? Hi! My name's Piper, and *auf wiedersehen*? I've got three more years to decide. Meantime, I want to meet the guy who gave the world pretty pictures to look at. Here, take my picture." She handed him the phone, and posed by the refrigerator, then stuffed the phone in her pants pocket, and offered him the last sliver of apple pie. "You're coming to dinner, aren't you? You want to meet Beatty."

He nodded yes and used to spoon to finish off the pie in three bites. "I surrender. It'll be tough, but I'll come."

"Speaking of Carole …"

"Were we speaking of Carole?"

"Does she ever ask you questions about 2018? You know, about what people do for fun? What kind of technology we have? Were you a rich kid?"

"Mostly, she's just relieved America wins the war. I didn't mention the atom bomb, though. If her Dad gets wind of that, it could be real sticky considering the Manhattan Project was so secret. I'd wind up in some Navy brig for the duration."

"I'm afraid of that myself." Nuclear power might have comforted the Greatest Generation by ending the war, but it scared the hell out of everyone who came later.

"Did McKnight tell you to back off?" Jim put the dishes in the sink and ran some water. "No Dawn dish soap. That always gets me."

"You got the lecture, too?"

He sat at the table again. "I was wondering why the hurry for you and Sandy to get married. I mean, you must have had a great plan to snag Mitch, and I was sure you didn't have to marry Sandy for real. But, now I get it. You're going to set up a baby buy. Brilliant. Did you tell Sandy where you're from?"

"Yeah. Last night. Maybe he thought I was drunk or something. He said he believed me, but he didn't ask me any questions. If it was reversed, I'd be all up in his business, you know? I'd want to know everything he could remember about his former life."

"Different time, different people. Haven't you noticed how polite and private everyone seems to be? No road rage. No flipping off stupid people. The guys at work don't even say hell around women. Not that women are allowed in a shipyard."

"Yeah, that's gonna change when the war starts. My great-grandmother was a riveter."

"They say the yards are too dangerous. They'd crap their pants if they knew women flew bombing raids in Iraq in real live jets. Carole owns a girdle."

"Sandy didn't ask me who wins the war, Jim, but he has to knows it's coming. When do regular guys get orders to get specialized training in field wounds? One day he's a corpsman taking vital signs and handing out aspirin, and the next he's studying how to do a field amputation."

"He doesn't want to believe there's going to be a war. I guarantee it. Captain McKnight doesn't want to believe it. Everybody wants to think Hitler's just another political leader. Nutty as hell, but harmless. That's what all the guys at the dry docks say. Some of them say Heil! Have you shown Sandy your cell phone like you showed Carole? She believes what we tell her. It scares the hell out of her, but she believes it." He checked his watch. "Jesus, I gotta go. Where's your phone? I gotta call my boss and tell him I'm running late. By the way, you're looking mighty happy this morning, Mrs. Sanders. If I had to guess, I'd say you were in love."

"Like looking in a mirror, huh?"

Chapter X

Thanks to Jim, she had her mo-jo back. If there was any question she was somebody special, she could whip out her cell phone, and intimidate the hell out of Mitch Roberts. But Sandy? She decided to wait. She was changing. Into what —or who she didn't know. More patient, yes. Less ambitious, yes. What good was becoming a famous photographer if she couldn't share that fame with her family? She missed Josh most of all. How nice it would be to have him and Shelly-the girlfriend over to the bungalow for pie and coffee on a Saturday morning. They'd be shocked to see her in her in an apron, her hair piled on her head with bobby pins. Or maybe not.

She got pencil and paper and sat at the table. She'd just turned eighteen, which means in 1960, she'd turn forty-one. The same age as her Great Grandmother was in the 1960's or thereabouts. She searched her memory. What was Grandma Gussie's maiden name? Hensley. No. Hershell. Damn, she couldn't remember. The information was always there, the family tree was written in the front of Gussie's Bible. Why didn't she pay more attention to these things? "Because of you," she said to her cell phone lying on the table, its black eye staring at her.

Like Scarlet O'Hara, she'd think about it another time. Now, it was time to set the stage for Act Two. Armed with the letter-head Doctor's statement, she put on her uniform and went to see Mitch before her shift. He'd have a tough time killing her in his office.

She suddenly found it hard to breathe, and her hands began to tremble at the thought of being alone with him on his turf. Captain McKnight's warnings had done their damage.

***

It wasn't difficult to produce tears to go with the bad news about crumbling fallopian tubes. She saw Mitch grimace as he read the letter. He probably didn't know what a fallopian tube was, but the conclusion was unambiguous: no kids.

"Does Sandy know?" was his first question. He handed her the letter back to her as though it had monkey snot on it.

"I haven't told him yet. Bad news is sometimes easier to take when there's good news, too. But Carole knows. If you can do something for me, I can pay." She opened her purse and activated the record function on her phone before hauling out her wallet. "I can give you three hundred dollars on account."

She handed him a stack of bills. Inside, she was screaming for him to take it. After all, down the line he'd have something on her and Sandy the way he had on the Sorensons. "I know we'll have to wait," she continued. "If I got pregnant last night, it would still take nine months, right?" She made sure her hand stayed steady.

After dawdling for a few minutes, Mitch unlocked one of his desk drawers, put the money inside, and produced a little black book. "What do you want, a boy or a girl?" he said as he took a pen from his desk set.

Maybe he'd interpret her stammering as gratitude instead of fear. He actually *was* in the baby business and she was now an accessory.

"Eventually two of each. But a boy first, if it's possible."

"No problem," he said flatly as he scribbled in his notebook. "Believe me, Mrs. Sanders, there are girls all over America who just want assurances of a good home for their mistake. Millions of men on the move are always on the make. Even married women are susceptible to good-looking strangers and have to hide their indiscretions in case hubby comes home."

It was time to re-visit the Blackledge issue. "Was Edwina one of those indiscrete women?"

His sardonic smile disappeared. "She didn't want to wait. Couldn't." The fear she was sensing wasn't hers. For all his bluster, Mitch was terrified whenever he heard the name Blackledge. She decided to play another hand.

"She was seen at Sister Rita's."

"Blackledge was going to stay there but changed her mind. She wanted to go back to Chartman, so I drove her there. That's the last I saw of her."

Piper sat down in one of the two captain's chairs in front of Mitch's desk. Abortion was legal and safe —okay, safer —in the twenty-first century. She'd heard speakers at school talk about women who died from botched abortions "back in the day." Maybe Blackledge was a statistic. "Did you ask Chartman about her?"

"Alright, I'm a bastard. I didn't ask until New York contacted the Bauers about the missing money. Anyway, Chartman swears she was alright when she left his office."

"Start from the beginning."

Mitch pulled the other chair close to hers, sat down, and lit up a Pall Mall. "Like I said, there was a guy hanging around the airport. I picked her up at the Desert Palms Hotel and drove her to the Knickerbocker, and then out to the Bauers. She picked up the money, and on the way back to the hotel, she tells me she has a problem and needs to see the Doc. The next day, I picked her up and drove her to Imperial Beach. The little rich bitch could pay, so what was I supposed to do? Tell her no?"

"That would have been the better idea. Do the Bauers know you're the one who took her to see Chartman?" Piper asked.

"If you mean, do they know Blackledge had a problem, I didn't tell them anything. I know Chartman didn't tell them. Hitler made abortions illegal for German women. Industrialists and shippers all want their daughters to marry bankers and politicians, and the merchandise has to be top-notch. Is that so hard to understand? Edwina had the hundred grand. Maybe she was going to relocate to Argentina or Timbuktu."

"Who picked her up from Chartman's?"

"Chartman didn't know the guy. All he told me was the guy was dark."

"How dark?"

"He wasn't Aryan. Does it matter? Chartman doesn't want any trouble. He could lose his medical license if there was a scandal. It's either fewer abortions or more suicides. Take your pick." He smashed the butt in the ashtray. "What happens now?"

"I'll make my report. Eventually."

"Does your report have to include information about Edwina's trip to Chartman? I mean, the Bauers sent the Bund another hundred thousand. They mortgaged their house, and with Chartman willing to do operations in addition to deliveries, we should double the money we make real soon. New York doesn't have to know exactly how, or how much, money is raised. Right?"

"Was Edwina supposed to deliver the money directly to Party headquarters or to Alfred Blackledge personally?"

"That I don't know. You'd have to ask Anatole. Can you cover Chartman's ass on this?"

"I'll let you know. I think maybe we can work a deal."

Why did she feel even a smidgen sorry for Mitch? She spent her entire shift wondering what the hell was happening to her. These were Nazis. Bad people with evil motives who sewed curtains for her and fed lonely sailors sausages and sauerkraut. Couldn't they see that Hitler and his henchmen were using them? But, the fact was they didn't see. And she and Jim couldn't make them see. Then there was the baby selling. Who knows what kind of people he was selling them to? Child molesters. Serial killers. She had everything she needed to send Mitch away to prison. Yet, it was more likely, as Captain Mike said, that she'd be sent away as a spy, or, worse, as a crazy person. The only good part of all this was that now she had proof.

***

Everyone did a bit of schedule juggling, because Piper insisted what she had to show them couldn't wait until Thursday. Carole and

Sandy considered ten o'clock the dead of night, which struck her and Jim as hilarious, so they set the meeting at six o'clock. "I'll bring brownies," Carole said, and Jim brought two quarts of milk. In bottles.

"Don't ask any questions," Piper ordered as thy sat on the floor in a circle, "just listen."

She turned on her cell phone and put it in the center. Mitch's voice was loud and clear. When the recording ended, Sandy picked up the cell phone and inspected every inch of it. "You say this is a camera too?"

Jim took it from him and motioned him to get closer to Piper. "Let me show you." Sandy put his arm around her shoulders, and she instinctively leaned into him. Jim snapped the button and showed Sandy the photo.

"No film? Well, I'll be damned," he said. "Look, Piper. Don't we look like the perfect couple? You're so pretty …"

"This is why they say technology is seductive," Piper said as she rolled her eyes. "It is. Now what about the confession?"

"Okay, I admit it. I'm in love with the gadget. You say millions of people have these?" Sandy handed the phone back to her.

"Yes, and they're very handy. Now, tell me what you think about what Mitch said."

"It's what he didn't say, that got me thinking the obvious," Sandy said. "According to Mitch, Chartman said Edwina was alright when she left the doctor's office, but Mitch couldn't have known that for sure if he didn't see her after wards. The cops must have checked all the flight manifests flying into El Paso." He looked at Piper. "Unless Mitch is lying his ass off, Chartman killed her, Mitch stuffed her in the trunk and drove to a flea-bag hotel in El Paso."

"That's not likely, is it?" Piper said. Sandy was grinning.

"Nope." Sandy said. "Unless she was showing, Chartman would have done a Friedman test to find out if she was really pregnant. That takes forty-eight to seventy-two hours."

"Trust me, she didn't have to be showing to know she was with child. A woman knows as soon as she vomits," Carole said.

"Ah, but Chartman would want to make sure before he cut her." Sandy said. "Women have been known to mistake pelvic diseases and tumor symptoms for pregnancy."

Piper and Jim exchanged wide-eyed glances. Once again, they'd forgotten that cell phones weren't the only invention that revolutionized the world. In the 1930's, there was no such thing as an EPT. "What's the Friedman test, Sandy," Piper said.

"Short answer. The woman's urine is injected into a rabbit, and the rabbit's ovaries are checked to see if they've changed."

"Bet that's not too pleasant for the rabbit." Piper winced. "Does that mean they kill it?" Carole patted her hand and nodded a yes.

"What it means is that Mitch isn't telling you the whole story. Edwina must have stashed the cash somewhere," Jim said, "especially if she was stealing the money to run off with her non-Aryan boyfriend."

"The point is," Sandy said, "the timeline is all wrong if you want to believe Mitch. Edwina must have been here a few days at least."

"Maybe the money is still in the hotel safe," Carole said.

"Carole's right," Piper said. "Edwina would have stashed it somewhere. She comes from a wealthy family, and probably brought her own money with her. She didn't need to steal, even for her boyfriend, and she damn sure wouldn't give up the good life in New York to live in Argentina or Timbuktu."

"Agreed," Jim said. "We're all poor and we need to think like rich people. She wouldn't have stayed at the Knickerbocker. It's below Broadway. She would have stayed at the El Cortez. The Grant. Or the Del Coronado."

"Yeah," Carole said, "that whole Sister Rita story must be crap."

"Who took her there? Honnolore? And when? Mitch said he took her to the Knickerbocker and then went straight to Bauer's where she picked up the cash, and then took her to Chartman's the next morning. Like it all happened in twenty-four hours. Why the BS about a side trip to Harbison Canyon?" Piper said and turned to Carole. "Your father told me the Bund thinks ONI had something to do with this. Mitch acted like he didn't believe Edwina was dead. Maybe the Blackledge thing *was* a sting. Could your father have found out the Navy did have something to do with all this, and that's why he told us to back off?"

"There's no way the Navy would fake a girl's death," Carole said.

"*NCIS* did once." Jim said.

"What's that?"

"It's a T.V. series. Naval Criminal Investigation Service."

"The Navy goes into the entertainment business? Sign me up!" Sandy said.

"*My* point, gentlemen," Carole said, "is that the Bund is a legal organization. They're watching it, and Captain Mike said they don't want to interfere with it."

"Hoover did crack down on the Communist organizations a few years back." Sandy said. "I remember my parents talking about how he tracked down a bunch of Commies that blew up a senator's and a judge's house after the war."

"What war?" Jim asked.

"The Great War. I was born the year America got into it," Sandy said.

Piper clapped her hands three times. "Guys. Guys! Can we stay on task? Mitch Roberts, remember?" They were just like Josh. "What do we do now?"

"What does your gut tell you?" Sandy said.

"That I have more questions than answers. Was Edwina's picture in the paper? Did her parents offer a reward for information?"

There was a long pause. "There was nothing in the San Diego paper about Edwina's death that I can remember," Carole said. "Maybe Mitch did a little creative editing."

"How about the slags?" Piper said to Jim.

"What are slags?" Sandy said.

"*National Enquirer. Globe. People Magazine.* Grocery store check-out crap. When rich people die or get killed, the media covers it twenty-four seven," Jim explained.

"Same as now." Sandy stretched wide and looked at his watch. "We've been at this for over an hour. Four intelligent people and we're stymied. It's a good thing none of us works for your *NCIS*."

Carole collected the glasses and plates and took them to the kitchen. Piper was at her heels with napkins for the trash. "You're wearing that 'let's talk' face," she said, "What's up?"

"You guys are overlooking the important part, but I'm not," Carole said. "We both know Mitch likes to step in and rescue desperate damsels. I thought I was in love with him. Well, maybe Edwina did too."

"Guilty as charged," Piper said as she considered the implications. "Maybe Mitch knew Edwina better than he lets on, as in baby-daddy? If the El Paso police suspected murder, there would have been autopsy, the coroner would know she'd had a recent abortion. Maybe Alfred decided to pull the plug on an investigation to protect himself and the Bund from a scandal. Hard as that is to believe, considering …"

"Considering what?"

"Considering thirty-six years from now abortion will be legal. Terrible or miraculous, depending on your point of view."

"You're not kidding, are you?" Carole said, incredulously.

"People still debate whether it was a good idea, if it's any consolation."

"We haven't considered suicide," Carole said after a long silence. "I was tempted when I realized I was pregnant. If Mitch hadn't helped me out, I might have tried. Maybe Mitch talked Edwina into an abortion the way he talked me into an adoption."

"Did Mitch ever say he could have gotten you an abortion?

"I was too far along."

"Does Mitch ever go out of town? Like on assignments for the paper?"

"Sometimes. He went to M.I.T. to interview Vannevar Bush?"

"Never heard of him."

"He built an analyzer that could solve equations with eighteen variables. Got lots of press. Can you imagine that? Mitch was fascinated by the whole thing."

Yes, Piper thought, I can imagine. "This Bush guy must be one heavy-weight scientist. On the other hand, Massachusetts isn't that far away from New York. He could have spent some fascinating time with Edwina. Maybe got down to the Jersey dry docks. Being a reporter is a lot like being a detective. You have scads of free time and people expect you to be nosy."

The women joined the men in the living room floor. Jim was explaining the finer points of a cell phone's internet capability and the necessity for relay towers for transmission. "Listen up, guys," Piper said. "More speculation from a woman's point of view."

"Let's hear it," Sandy said, tossing the phone to Jim like it was on fire.

"Maybe Mitch was the father, and the mystery man is BS. Mitch flies to El Paso with poor, sad girlfriend," Piper said.

"Who maybe under sedation anyway," Sandy added.

"Yep, and he takes her to the hotel where they commiserate with each other about bad timing and how no one will know Edwina got rid of an Aryan baby. Something goes wrong. Mitch panics, and flies back to a desert airport with the cash," Carole said.

"But it still doesn't explain why the parents of a rich girl aren't paying private detectives, offering rewards, and being really pissed off about their daughter's death whether it's from an abortion or murder at the hands of some unknown boyfriend," Sandy said. "If it was me, I wouldn't sleep until I'd killed the bastard that killed my kid. I'd hunt him down and squeeze the life out of him with my bare hands."

Everyone got quiet. There didn't seem to be an explanation for the Blackledge's disinterest. "In 2018, parents who lose their kids to murder go on T.V. and talk about how necessary it is for people to grieve and go on together. They light candles and have vigils. The preachers call for forgiveness, and understanding, and beg people not to hate," Jim said. "It doesn't work."

"Then I'm damn glad I'm living now," Sandy said.

"We're thinking like Americans and they're thinking like Nazis," Jim said.

"Mitch could be lying about everything including the Bauers mortgaging their house to pay the Party the missing money," Piper said. "Did he see the loan papers? Just because they said they were in financial straits doesn't mean it's true. People lie all the time."

"Occam's razor," Jim said. "The most obvious answer to the question is the answer to the question."

"The obvious answer is that Mitch stole the money," Piper said. "He took my three hundred dollars, didn't he?"

***

Nobody was up to a Bund meeting. Even if Mitch had given her every detail and signed his confession in blood, there was still the problem of what to do with the information, and once again that two-ton elephant blocked their road. If they told the cops what they knew about Mitch, they'd have to tell what they knew about each other, too. And they knew what ONI would do no matter how much evidence they had: nothing.

We're still at square one," Piper said. "and it drives me nuts not being able to *do* something."

"You can do push-ups with me," Sandy suggested. He'd shed his having-company clothes and was on the floor working off the brownies in shorts and a sleeveless tee-shirt.

"You do push-ups, I'll count. Then I expect you to give me some options," she said. His body tensed and relaxed, tensed and relaxed, as his steely arms raised him up and down, making it hard for her to concentrate. How many has he done? Two or two hundred? He had a lot going for him, she decided. Looks, stamina, and he kept his toenails clipped too.

Sandy rolled over on his back and stared at the ceiling fan creaking overhead. "Twenty-five! You know what the options are." He was breathing deep. "We bypass Naval Intel and go straight to Shore Patrol headquarters. We have to treat this situation as exactly what it is. We're talking crime syndicate. It doesn't matter if Mitch is a member of the Bund or a Boy Scout leader, he probably killed Edwina and stole a hundred grand."

Piper slid to the floor. "Damn it! Now I know how my mom felt when my dad was right."

"You want me to be wrong?"

She laid next to him. "Guys make it sound simple."

"You're confusing simple with easy. This a simple problem with a tough solution. People are going to get hurt." He took her hand, laid it on his heart, and rested his head against her shoulder.

"What if they investigate me? That's what Captain Mike is afraid of."

"That's why we're going to do the hardest thing in the world to do right now —wait until we have evidence that doesn't involve you."

She nibbled his ear lobe. "Mitch was nice to me, you know."

"Yeah, he's a great guy. You want a baby? I'll buy one for you. You want to get rid of a baby? Sure, I'll arrange it."

"I'm just saying for a son-of-a-bitch, he's not all bad. You sound jealous, Chris Sanders."

"So why isn't he here now instead of me?"

She couldn't stop the words. "Because I *love* you."

Sandy jumped up. "Aha! I knew it!" He danced in place, gyrating his hips and wiggling his hands. "I knew it. I knew it. I knew it. I'm crazy 'bout you, Baby, and la-di-da for me! You luuuuv me."

She sat up and extended her arms to him. He lifted her to her feet, and they broke into the Shag. He danced her into the bedroom, and Piper knew there was more fun ahead —fun that excluded all thoughts of Mitch Roberts.

Chapter XI

Cecil Beatty looked like a true artist. Unkempt hair, a bushy mountain of a moustache, and clothes that needed pressing. He and Sandy laughed about tossing cow-patties and a guy named Jonas Miller winning a bake-off at the Sacramento County fair even before they downed two quarts of beer, so she knew they were true friends.

"You got yourself a darlin' little mare there, Sandy, my man," he said of Piper. "Yes, sir." Cecil gobbled down a second plate of macaroni and cheese and she added another dish to her expanding list of can-do recipes.

Carole and Jim added their own fair stories. Carole said she and her mother could quilt anything, including a canvass tent, and Jim related how he rode in a mutton-busting competition when he was six.

"Did you win?" Cecil asked him.

"Yeah, a sore butt from falling. If I'd had done that at six-teen on a bull, I'd never have made to seventeen. Them dang young rodeo guys will ride anything."

At least they weren't staring at their phone screens or playing video games. Piper caught Jim's eye and motioned him to come to the kitchen. "For heaven's sake, stop staring at Cecil, Jim. He's going to think you're hitting on him."

"I guess you haven't noticed how he's been staring at you, Miss Space Oddity. Anyway, it's no longer a hypothetical. A man's life is at stake here, for real." He haphazardly rinsed the dinner plates. "Do we tell him what we know, or not?"

It was one of those questions philosophy majors ask when it's past midnight and they've had a few hits off the bong. Josh had told her all about how serious everyone got all of a sudden, and she'd teased him unmercifully, ending with a Shelly-the-girlfriend *coups d'gras*: What would Jesus do? "We don't have to do it tonight. Let him paint the mural first. Just relax and don't screw up his good time, alright?"

They returned to the living room where the three children of the Depression were playing spades, their cheer having turned unexpectedly somber.

"What's going on?" Jim asked as he sat on the floor next to Carole. "Bad hand?"

"The radio just reported the Japanese have taken the city of Hangchow," Sandy said.

"Hitler supports Japanese expansion," Carole added. "My Dad told me."

Piper expected Cecil to make a concluding remark, but he sat quietly, as though wrapped up in the game, until the hand was over. "Here Jim, take my place. I'll wash, you dry, Piper" he said.

Before Jim could tell him mission accomplished, Cecil was on his way to the kitchen. Piper followed. Rinsing wasn't washing her Mom told her once. Germs are evil.

"I'm a pro at dish washing. I got paid for it in Sacramento. For a few days, at least." Cecil tied on her apron, and mixed washing powder into a bowl of water. "Sandy tells me you're into photography like Carole."

"I'm still learning. She's a real pro."

He used the copper wire scrubber instead of the dishcloth from the first fork to the last roasting pan Sandy had used for Navy meatloaf. He made cherry cobbler too. Cecil made the mashed potatoes and biscuits from scratch. She'd never seen guys cook so fast and confidently. Josh could boil weenies and her dad could grill, but these guys knew how much salt and pepper and onions to use without measuring or consulting her Fanny Farmer's.

"Did Sandy tell you my sister has disappeared?" Cecil asked when he'd finished using the last of the soapy water to clean the sink. He sat at the new-used kitchen table, brought out papers and a pouch of tobacco, and rolled a cigarette.

"He said she moved out."

"We ain't heard from her in over a year." He took a straw from the broom, lit it from the pilot light of the gas stove, and used it as a match.

"I'm sorry. Carole says a lot of young people are leaving home, especially if there are younger kids at home. I guess it's easier for them to travel to find work than it is for their parents."

"They wait for a miracle to save their farms. Did he tell you Beth disappeared once before?"

"No, but he said you had something to tell me."

Cecil was staring at her when she looked up. He got a bowl from the cupboard to use as an ashtray and sat at the table. "She was just a little kid. Almost two years old. I told Sandy at the time, she wasn't the same kid when I found her. He said separation can make a kid crazy. Circumstances change people all the time."

"I suppose that's true, and circumstances can get pretty weird. I know, believe me."

"I do believe you. Would you be upset if I told you I think I know about your weird circumstances?"

She eyed him warily. "I don't know. Maybe."

"It's plain to me that you and Jim aren't like any Americans I ever met. I'm an artist, so I study faces and peoples' posture; the way they look. You guys are a lot healthier than most people. Jim eats enough food for two guys his size. If I had to guess, I'd say you're foreigners of a sort. I think you guys were in the San Diego Trib building somewhere, somewhere in the future, and something weird happened and you wound up here, am I right?"

"Did Sandy tell you that?"

"All he said was you once worked at the newspaper, and you found out I was going to get the WPA grant from Mitch Roberts. I knew instantly that wasn't true. Mitch hates my designs. The Committee seemed to like them, but him? Guys like him never spread good news."

She nodded a yes. "You're right. Mitch didn't tell me. Crazy as it sounds, you're right on the money about me and Jim. We're not from around here."

He slapped his knee. "I knew it! Let me tell you how I think it was, and you tell me if I'm right about this too." He smashed what was left of his cigarette in the bowl and got root beer from the icebox. He poured them each a glass and lifted his in a toast. "Skoal! My guess is, your family never seemed like your family and your baby pictures look nothing like you. Am I right?"

Piper sat on one of her new-used dinette chairs. "That's right," she said weakly, and took a swig of root beer, praying inside he wouldn't ask her about the future because she didn't want to lie and she didn't want to tell him the truth either.

"Tell me about the murals. You must have seen my name on them if you know I get the grant."

"They're very much admired, I can tell you that. Jim and I were overwhelmed."

"They stayed true to color?"

"Not bright, but true to color."

"Son-of-a-bitch. That's my biggest concern, that the materials won't hold up." He leaned forward, his eyes hungry for information. "Did they put them under glass? I've been thinking that if they were covered by glass plates, sort of like the one-sheets at the movie houses, they'd keep better."

"Actually, I don't know if they did that. I know I never saw evidence that there was glass. You could ask Jim, though, he's studied the building."

"Did he work at the paper, too?"

"In a way."

"Oh, Bethy, I thank God you've come back to us! Your replacement was a nice girl but she wasn't you." His face bore such a loving expression, a mix between gratitude and remembering, and

Piper felt his embrace even though he never touched her.

"You really believe I'm your little sister?"

"I know it in my heart." He sank back in the chair, melting into it with one big sigh of contented relief.

"But how did it happen?" Could he really have the explanation she'd been seeking? Maybe she could learn from an artist what she could not think out.

"My mom left my dad, temporarily. We went to live with her family in San Diego. Her and my grandma took me and Beth to the newspaper to take out an employment wanted ad. While they were in the ad office, I was supposed to be looking after you. When I couldn't find you, mom got hysterical. Everybody was rushing around, looking for you, afraid you might have gotten caught in one of the presses. I went back upstairs to the offices, and when I turned the corner, there you were. No one seemed to notice you were wearing different clothes except me. Everybody said it was a miracle, and nobody questioned miracles back then. But it wasn't you. It was a different Beth."

Piper questioned it a million times over. "I can't understand how a two-year-old in 1919 can change places with a toddler in 2000. It doesn't make any sense, Cecil."

He took a pen from his pocket and grabbed a napkin from the holder. "That's what I thought, too, at the time. Then I heard about this German scientist who's been talking about a theory of space. I was in the Navy, when I heard some officers talking about it. According to this guy Einstein, space isn't a straight line. It's curved. So is time."

He drew a horseshoe on the napkin, and marked an "X" at each end, then drew a circle around one of them "This is you. And at the same time, there's this other little girl living in 2000. Think of it as you living in Sacramento, and her living in Alaska. Only instead of shared space, you're sharing time."

He drew another circle around the other "X," a straight line between them, and a door frame on the line. "You walked through the door and went forwards, and she went backwards. Fifteen years later, you both went through the door again. It makes sense if you see it Einstein's way." He removed a photo from his wallet and handed it to her. "This was Beth when she was nine months old. Look at it, Piper. It's you."

Piper remembered what she was told at the zoo. Humans are the only animals that recognize themselves. She'd never seen a baby picture who she recognized as herself. She'd only seen an infant people said was her —and heard Josh tell her about the day she was lost, the day his parents had taken him and little Patricia to the Trib to do an interview about the recent earthquakes in the Imperial Valley. She'd wandered off down a long, dark hallway. Everyone thought she'd been kidnapped. She could have been wearing different clothes. No one would have noticed in the confusion. Part of the plot of a diabolical universe, it seemed, as she saw herself in the baby's eyes.

If what Cecil said was true, her parents now had their real daughter back, grateful she'd been pulled from the collapsed building alive. Or mourning her death along with that of that of a security guard named Jim Crenshaw.

"Is it possible the door stayed open long enough for two people to step into the past?" she asked. For the third time, she folded the dishtowel. It must not have been square because when she tried to match the corners, the rest of the towel wouldn't lay flat. It was a metaphor for her life.

"Who knows where the doors are, or how long they stay open? Maybe Jim walked through the door alone and didn't exchange places with anyone else. Maybe he hitched a ride with you and is just back where he belongs."

Piper remembered what Jim said about Occam's Razor. The obvious answer to Cecil's question was that she did know when the door had opened and, if it opened once on May 7th, it might open again on that day next year.

"The Hampton family was good to me," she said. She loved them even though she never felt like one of them.

Cecil reached for her hand. "Einstein may be a fool. But, I want you to know, I'm sorry for not taking better care of you. It's nice you married my best friend. Guess there are things fated to be no matter what we do."

***

"So many questions, Jim," she said as they sat on the stoop. In two weeks it would be 1938.

"One problem at a time," he said. Sandy had taken Cecil to the YMCA, and said he'd drop Carole at her place on the way, but he was due on a night shift.

"Would you go back to 2018, if you could?"

"Only if I could take Carole with me. There's no way I can let her to go through the war alone. I guess my answer lies in a question I asked yourself and one you'll have to answer: Have you gained more than you've lost? In 2018, I ain't got a fiancé and no important job. Today, I got a message from Captain Mike that I'm going to meet the Maritime mole tonight. That's damn sure important."

***

Sandy agreed with Cecil about horse-shoe time. In a way. Only Sandy said the Head Honcho made a correction when he realized people were out of place, and he put them back in the right places. "The Lord works in mysterious ways," he concluded in his sleepy voice.

They were lying in bed, watching the neighborhood tom cat play in the moon shadows with a ball and string Sandy had attached to the outside. Piper named him Batcat because of his big ears.

"Assuming Cecil's right about this, how can you believe the Head Honcho knows what he's doing after a screw-up this big? Cecil's carried a ton of guilt for almost twenty years for something that wasn't his fault."

"I believe eventually things get sorted out. At least he knows now it wasn't his fault. He can die happy."

She bit her tongue. "Would you miss me if the Head Honcho decides to correct his correction?" It seemed like a fair question.

He kissed her forehead. "I'd be brokenhearted. I like you."

In romance movies, the guy was supposed to smother the girl with passionate kisses right about now, but Sandy's admission meant more to her than any 'I love you'. Still, were her choices a senile god who misplaced people or random science?

She'd never imagined a question like that, but she never imagined she'd have a Christmas where the best presents were from the German-American Bund: a 6X9 foot Persian rug from Engle's Carpets and an RCA Victor radio/phonograph player in a walnut cabinet.

"Mitch must have told them about our fertility problem by now," Sandy said when the delivery van had left, and he'd checked the gifts thoroughly for bugs. "Wonder if Mitch told them we're in the market for a baby. Maybe they'll give us one next Christmas."

"The Bauers can give me the moon for all I care. I love my red wool coat." Carole must have told him she'd tried it on at the Y Boutique. "People say Southern California as no winter. The hell it don't!" It reminded her of a picture she'd seen of Nancy Reagan. "But we said no presents, Sandy."

"A coat isn't a present. It's a necessity." They sent his parents twenty dollars. Cecil sent his parents ten.

Chapter XII

Hitler's order of March 1, 1938 instructing German nationals to abandon the Bund and its leaders to return to the Fatherland, signaled dark days ahead for his loyalists in America. Anatole read it aloud to a full house as soon as he called the meeting to order and ended it with a prediction. "The Communist Jewish lawyers in Washington have the politicians in their pockets. They'll be issuing a ban on all support of our *Fuhrer* before the year is up."

"Let 'em try!" Mitch shouted. "They can pass a thousand laws and it won't stop the love and loyalty in our hearts and our programs."

The response to his declaration was cheering and clapping, and salute, and throughout the night defiance highlighted every conversation as the men socialized and strategized over bratwurst and beer. As loud as they were, the women were as subdued as they served sauerkraut and potatoes with stoic determination.

"You ladies can go home. I'll finish cleaning up," Honnolore announced in the kitchen when the meeting was finally over. The two other women left, but Piper ignored her and returned to the hall with an aluminum tub to bus the tables. Anatole was trying to convince Sandy and Mitch that he could fold the tables and chairs without their help and got the same result.

"Give it up, Bauer," she heard Sandy tease, "you don't want to dislocate something important."

"I want to feel useful, gentlemen," Bauer said.

"Then lead us in a song." Sandy and Mitch broke into a chorus of *Deutschland uber Alles*, and she saw them smile as they sang to a resigned Anatole who had emptied a pitcher of beer into his glass. The consensus was Hitler's order was only for German citizens, not them. It was okay to disobey their leader; he was trying to appease the American government, not dismiss their work.

"There's simply too much to do," Honnolore said as they dried pots and put them in the store-room. Piper had never seen her so busy. Why did stress bring out industriousness in women?

***

From her ticket sales booth on the corner, Piper could see everything happening in the intersection of fourth and 'E" street, including the opening of the soup kitchen kitty-corner from the theater. Every day the line got longer earlier in the morning, and the soup ran out sooner. Unemployment, Captain Mike said, was inching towards 19%. "I've stood in lines like that," Cecil admitted when she told him and Sandy how terrible she felt for the men.

"That's why, no matter what they tell me to do in the Navy, I do it in a hurry," Sandy said. "There ain't nothing worse than being out of a job."

"And that's why I'm gonna re-enlist as soon as I've finished the murals," Cecil said.

The quandary was back. She left them sipping their Cokes on the stoop while she made sandwiches, wiping tears from her cheeks with a napkin she used as a tissue. A gun shot sent her to the floor. This time she didn't faint. "Sandy!" she yelled and crawled toward the living room where both men were crouching near the window.

"Stay down, Piper!" Sandy screamed back.

"I'm down! I'm down!" She reached him, and he grabbed her close. "What's going on?" she demanded.

They heard angry voices, and a siren. Then two.

Cecil stood and peeked through the curtain. "It's the Sheriff serving an eviction. The people across the way. Do you know them?"

"No," Piper said. "I've seen them a couple of times, but never talked to them."

Sandy stood at the other side of the window. "They got the guy's gun and got the cuffs on him."

Piper stood and watched the Sheriff and his deputies carry out the belongings of a man, his wife and three kids. "All of them live there? I never heard the kids. Never saw them. Didn't they ever go to school?"

"Squatters more than likely," Sandy said.

"Reminds me of when they evicted us from the farm. God, what a nightmare," Cecil said.

Piper saw the woman clutch her three kids, not any of them over ten years old, around her skirt, as they put her husband in a squad car. The kids didn't cry. They just watched the men dump their clothes and toys on the sidewalk. "Where will they go, Sandy?"

"Bonita. If they can get there. There's squatters in the hills that'll take care of them. He probably came lookin' for work, but so many of these squatters are farmers with no formal schooling."

The children collected their toys when the men left, and Piper saw the real tragedy as the mother stood alone. "She's pregnant, Sandy."

Sandy dug into his pockets, and Cecil pulled a handful of bills out of his. "I made sandwiches," Piper said and went to the kitchen. She brought back a sack full of baloney sandwiches and two dollars from her money jar. Among them they had eleven dollars.

"We can't let them in, Sweetheart. They probably have lice. Cecil and I'll drive them to the jail and try to get her husband out. The best we can do is take them to the camp in Descanso."

She hated herself for crying. "I'll be alright," she promised, "Do what you can for them, Honey."

Sandy and Cecil helped the woman load their clothes into the car and piled everyone into the backseat. Are lice difficult to get rid of? She didn't know. Maybe she could have bathed the kids and given the mom a sweater. She called Carole.

"Sandy was right. If you'd let them in, your landlord would have evicted you. Squatters are thieves and drug addicts. God only knows what the inside of their place is like now. Landlords have a devil of time. They have to fumigate for lice and roaches and pay a crew to clean up carpets. Worse yet, replace them."

"She's got three kids and another on the way, Carole."

"Life is hard. Most likely the State will take the kids. They'll be better off. Terrible things happen to kids in those camps. I get off in an hour. We'll come by."

She wanted to call Mitch. Maybe he could have Chartman

deliver the woman's baby and see that it got a good home. He said he helped married women take care of their indiscretions. Why not this one?

A call from Honnolore interrupted her consternation. "Why, Dear, you sound upset. Is there anything I can do?"

"We had an eviction that turned ugly in the court. They had three kids."

"Oh, that's always ghastly. Our *Fuhrer* has put a stop to that. The depression in Germany was so terrible. So many people hungry and on the streets. Women selling their bodies. Men selling their daughters. If only America had a leader who would care for his people the way the *Fuhrer* cares for his!"

By the time Jim and Carole knocked on the door, Piper was resigned to the fact that her new world was one of extreme inaction on one hand, and extreme action on the other. Mitch was a scoundrel, but she understood now why Carole felt she owed him a little gratitude. She did too. He didn't turn her away because she might have had lice.

"Are you all right?" Jim put his arm around her shoulder. "You should've called me."

"And woke you up when you're working graveyard? Never. Jobs mean everything."

"You got that right," Carole said. "I'll make us some tea." It was her way of leaving the two outsiders alone.

Piper searched his face. Had he learned the lesson she learned today, or had he begun to believe the fiction that they could lead a normal life in the midst of the oncoming onslaught? "I just have to toughen up, is all. Once and for all, I have to accept that we're just here."

"We have to do our part. That's all. Only a part. Not fight the whole damn war. Carole and Sandy are just the way we're going to get through it without going crazy, I think."

"I know you can't tell me who the mole at Maritime is, but can you tell me if it's the same person in the Bund?"

"It's not. I still don't know who the Bund mole is, but I do know, when the time is right, the mole will contact you. Captain Mike said so."

"Jim, I want to go to the meeting tonight, and Sandy's got the car. Will you take me?"

"We'll all go," Carole said as she came out of the kitchen. "We can have tea anytime."

***

The hall was overflowing. The unemployed were drawn to any port in the storm, and Anatole Bauer knew how to please an audience. "National Socialism is the only solution," he told them. "Every able-bodied man is needed and welcome to labor to feed his family with dignity. Everywhere in America, families are suffering. Tell us what happened today, Mrs. Sanders."

She should have been terrified, but Piper had asked to be recognized, and she was ready to tell everyone what she saw, ending with, "Do you know where Mr. Sanders is tonight? My husband is getting a man out of jail, taking children to a safe place where people will take care of them and sharing his time and money because he's a good man." She thought she might cry, then, but the tears had been replaced by simmering anger. She didn't want people to believe the Nazi propaganda, but she knew why they were listening to its preachers. "That poor husband and father wasn't threatening to kill a lawman. He was threatening to kill himself for the shame of not being able to take care of his family!" Was it true? She didn't know. It could have been, and it should have been.

The standing ovation she got was echoed by Carole as they cleaned up the church kitchen. They'd served two hundred tonight. "You were wonderful, Piper. They loved you. I can't believe you just got up there are gave them a good dose of the truth. Jim said young women in your time don't think anything of speaking out, but here it's still surprising."

"I meant every word. Somebody's got to help feed these people. If it's the Nazis, well, good for them. When the war comes, many of these men will be dead and many of the women widows. None of them will remember what they heard tonight, but they'll forget on a full belly," Piper said.

"Look what the cat drug in," Jim said as he, Sandy and Cecil came into the kitchen.

"You gave one hell of a speech, Sweetheart, "Sandy said and gave her a kiss. "I hope I can live up to it."

"Did they let the dad out?" She rinsed and dried her soapy hands and helped herself to Honnolore's hand lotion.

"Yeah, we drove 'em all to a motel on Highway 8 so they could get cleaned up and pack their stuff. They had a car at the squatter's camp, and Cecil fixed the fan belt. He cannibalized an old Ford they had out there."

"I told him to join the Navy," Cecil said.

"Will the Navy take him?" Carole asked. She'd finished drying the plates and saucers and was starting on the cups.

Piper looked at Sandy. "Will it?"

"I sure hope so. It'll keep him away from his wife for a few months. Maybe she can get some rest. We're going to help with the tables and chairs." He planted another kiss on her cheek. "Ain't she somethin', guys?"

Cecil gave her a soft elbowing to the ribs. "I told the guy to use my name," he said with a wink, and followed the guys back into the hall.

Had Jim heard? She had a big 'I told you we shouldn't tell' waiting for him if that's the way it happened. She rested against the sink, letting the possibility sink in. A married man with four kids might die in Cecil's stead. Was that preferable? Where had she read that sometimes it was better to do nothing?

Carole leaned over and whispered. "Check out Mr. Jealous in the left corner. If looks could kill, Sandy, would be dead."

Piper glanced through the window that opened to the hall and saw Mitch staring at the *tres amigos* stacking the chairs. He wasn't the only guy who could get things done on a moment's notice, and the Bauers knew it now. "You and Jim go on home. I can finish up here."

"You're sure?"

"You gotta work tomorrow. I don't."

She gathered the paper napkins and a handful of silverware and headed to the storeroom. They might have to rent a bigger hall, she was thinking, if membership kept growing. She heard a voice behind her. "Equipment coming through."

She turned around and saw a large man carrying two coffee urns. She recognized him as Fred Gunderson, the man who delivered her car. He put the urns on the second shelf. "That's got it." He slipped her a business card: Gunderson's Garage and Towing. "Holy-moly, your car needs a tune-up and an oil change. Call me tomorrow and we'll set up an appointment."

***

It might have been a coincidence, but Mitch showed up the evening after Sandy left for special training at the University of California San Francisco medical school three days later. "I'll be 800 miles straight north. If you need anything, Cecil said to call him. Keep the front door locked," he'd told her.

"How long will you be gone?" She was used to falling asleep on his shoulder. Was this separation anxiety swimming around in oceanic uncertainty?

"Eight weeks, but when I come back, I'll know how to cure your jungle rot and treat your gas gangrene. Ain't that great?"

Once again, prayer seemed like a good idea. "You bet, Honey. A jungle is definitely my honeymoon destination of choice."

Only she hadn't listened carefully to Sandy's reminder about locking up. Mitch gave a quick rap and opened the front door before she got to it. "How's married life?" he said as he sat in Sandy's study chair near the radio. She turned it on immediately upon rising. It seemed every minute there was news about the deepening crisis over seas, Japanese expansion in the South Pacific, Mussolini in Ethiopia. The bad news just kept coming.

"You've made a real cozy love nest for your sailor boy. I hope he appreciates it."

"He does, and shows it in ways you'll never know. What do you want, Mitch? I hope you have good news for me."

He was feeling the carpet with his fingertips. "Nice. Honnolore said you'd like the rug."

"She saw me admiring it when we were shopping for material. It was kind of her to remember. The Bauers have been very good to us."

"They'd better be, considering all you do for them."

She crossed her arms and leaned against the door. "Such as?"

"That speech you gave at last week's meeting? Hugh and Betty Krasner were there. You may not recognize the name. They're west region money. He owns a string of auto parts stores. He wrote the Bauers a check as big as their Packard 12 cylinder and said if all young couples were like you and Sandy, he'd have to start teaching his kids German. And guess who his wife is friends with … Magda Goebbels. She pumps out babies like Standard pumps oil."

Piper decided to let him stay. "Do you want some iced tea?"

"Got any vodka to go with that?"

"We don't keep hard liquor on the premises." Regretfully, she thought. People get chatty when they're a little mellow. She brought two glasses and a pitcher of fresh-brewed tea to the coffee table and sat at one end of the sofa.

"Are you missing your hubby," Mitch said.

"Of course. What a silly question."

"I just meant, he's not the only Prince Charming in town. Speaking of lovelorn swains, guess who in Hawaii is helping the Bund recruit."

"Cabot Swan? Really? It doesn't surprise me. He believes in the cause. Does he write to you?"

"Not to me. Honnolore. Figure that one out. He's almost as good an organizer as you are. I guess that's why Honnolore was hoping you'd marry him instead of Sandy. Although… he's heard a rumor the Navy is recruiting corpsmen for medical school. Any truth to it?"

She sipped her tea and made a quick wince. "This needs more sugar." She headed to the kitchen to buy time. Scuttlebutt was verbal Twitter; people would say anything for attention or out of envy if it had any ring of truth to it. "I'll have to ask Sandy when he gets back. I certainly wouldn't mind being married to a doctor." She brought in a box of sugar cubes Sandy brought home from the chow hall. "There, that's better. Well, neater at least. One of cooks said the box was out of date and told Sandy to give these to his horse. Why does everyone think Sacramento is the sticks?"

"Because it's all farming country with a big ol' capitol building stuck in the middle?" Mitch plunked two cubes into his glass. "I like sweet things.'"

"The truth is, Mitch, I don't know what goes on at the hospital. I just think of it as Sandy's job."

"Have you ever been to Berlin, Piper?"

Was it a trick question, or was he changing the subject for a purpose? "Only in my dreams. I hear Hitler is turning it into an urban Garden of Eden. *Look Magazine* says it's about time the center of the Fatherland got a facelift. What about you?" Vague memories of an article she had to read for her Social Studies class swirled about her brain. At the time, the words urban renewal and gentrification were meaningless, but stories of what Hitler was doing all over Germany were in every magazine. He was all about cultural preservation of the villages, but big on making Berlin the new Rome. Like her father, he loved architecture.

"Nope. I've got no desire to see the Fatherland. Not enough beachfront for my tastes. I like sand and palm trees and making money." He moved from the chair to the other end of the sofa. "I heard Honnolore talking about starting a group for *Die jungen Housfraus*. The Germans are big on clubs. She wants you to organize it, perfect little role model that you are. And Carole can take over when her and Jim get hitched and you go back to …New York? You'll have to leave eventually."

"You're so right. Just as soon as I get my merchandise. I certainly don't have time to start an organization now, though, between working and taking care of a household. I don't think I'll ever get used to not having a maid."

She was joking, but Mitch dug out his pen and scribbled on the note pad she kept by the phone. "I know what you mean. Everybody should have help. Call Sister Rita," he said as he handed her the paper. "She knows plenty of women who work cheap."

"That *will* be a blessing," Piper folded the paper and put it in her apron pocket. Whenever she assumed a top-dog attitude with Mitch, he got obliging. She'd remember that. "I thought about calling you after those squatters were evicted. If Sandy hadn't gotten the guy out of jail, I thought you could find a home for the baby. I'd say she was about six months along. A good candidate for a Chartman delivery, hospital wards being as crowded as they are now."

He helped himself to more tea, but only so he could move closer to her. "I'm always as near as your phone for anything you need, Piper." He toyed with the ends of an auburn lock. "I mean that, and don't think I'm not working on your problem. I've got the word out."

"There is one thing," she said without flinching. "If Sandy isn't back before Carole's wedding, I may need an escort." It was an empty gesture. As best man, Sandy wouldn't miss the wedding for anything.

"I'll rent a tux. But where's he off to, anyway?"

"A training conference. We don't talk medicine. It's all over my head."

"Somehow I don't believe anything is over your head."

"I'm glad we had this little talk. I'll have more free time now."

She patted her pocket. "And now, I have to get ready for work."

This time she locked the front door, then called Sister Rita and got directions. "I'll be out next Thursday, I'm getting my car tuned up on Wednesday."

***

Gunderson's Garage and Towing served the needs of the Pacific Beach's middle class. The first thing Piper noticed was how clean the floors were. No grease. No oil in the service bay, and the office tiles positively gleamed. The second was Gunderson speaking Spanish to his mechanics who doubled as detailers for cars with names like La Salle and Plymouth. When a car pulled in, a bell rang in the office, and whoever was closest to the pumps immediately stepped up with a greeting while another guy began cleaning the windshield. Amazing, she thought as she sat in the office looking through window glass so clean it was invisible.

"We don't give green stamps, just damn good service," Gunderson said. He lumbered into the office like a bear in a white uniform. "How're you doing this fine Southern California day?"

"Glad I ran into somebody who knows more about cars than I ever will. It never occurred to me my car would need something called a tune-up." She handed him her keys.

He reached down and patted her shoulder. "Tending to machinery is men's work." He went to the door to the bay. "Ramon! Give her the works, *por favor*." He threw her keys to a guy who couldn't have been more than fifteen. "Let me show you around the place. I keep a couple of used cars out back. Pick up good deals, get 'em in tip-top shape and sell them as second cars to people that can afford second cars."

They walked behind the building to a row of five automobiles that looked like the vintage cars Piper saw at Jack-in-the-Box car-club rallies. "Nice rides," she said, and inspected the leather upholstery as Carole had done. "No cracking. No tears."

"Fit for a king or a Captain, and I know a slew of them. Take Captain Mike, for instance. I sold him new tires just last week." He opened the driver's side door of a sea green Plymouth and rolled down the window. "Go ahead. Get behind the wheel."

She slid into the seat and Gunderson closed the door and leaned down. "I just found out this morning. Hitler's making his move in Austria in March. He's going to demand Schuschnigg's resignation and will appoint Seyss-Inquart as head of the Austrian government. Got it?"

"Austria. March. Schuschnigg out. Inquart in."

"That's it. The press may ask Admiral Bailey for a comment and he can't be caught off-guard. Tell Captain Mike. Sorry the introduction couldn't have been more polite. My office is probably bugged so watch what you say indoors."

Piper felt her hands griping the steering wheel so tight she felt she could tear it off the column. How could she know if this was a test, a trap, or for real? "I don't know you, Mr. Gunderson. Why would you tell me something like this, assuming it's true? Where's your evidence."

"Captain Mike told me to tell you —cell-phone tower." He

opened the door. "What do you think? Worth three-hundred dollars? Tell your friends, Gunderson's got the goods. I don't give out toasters, just sell cars that run."

She was officially in the spy business.

***

Where were the phone booths she saw all over the place except here, when she needed to call Captain Mike? She drove to the Admiral Kidd Club instead and used the restaurant's phone.

"If the password isn't cell-phone tower, I'm in trouble, Mr. McKnight. I just got a message from Gunderson: Austria. Schuschnigg out, Inquart in. Sometime in March. He said you'd understand, and to tell Bailey. Please tell me Gunderson is the mole."

"Where are you?' Captain Mike said, finally.

"At the Admiral Kidd."

"Wait there. I'm on my way."

"Would you like something, Miss?" the waitress said when Piper found a table on the patio.

"Yeah, a lemonade with vodka."

"Coming right up." Piper noticed her pockets were bulging with change. Her uniform was nothing like a ticket-taker's. She wore white shorts and a navy jumper-like blouse with short sleeves and a black necktie, and black open-toed pumps.

"Wait! Aren't you going to ask for I.D?"

"You're Miss Carole's friend, aren't you?"

Piper forced a smile. Had she stopped being invisible? "Yes, and

I'm waiting for Captain McKnight. Will you tell him I'm here? Forget the vodka. Just bring the lemonade, please."

That important job thing Jim talked about was beginning to make sense. What would she be doing on a February afternoon in 2018? Starting her second semester of college. Taking 101 classes and doing what she'd done for the past four years of her life. Reading textbooks, writing papers, waiting for the weekends so she could devote herself to studying for tests and posting her photographs on Facebook. Mostly, she'd be waiting to build a life. Now. in less than a year, she had more life than she'd had in the previous eighteen.

"You didn't waste any time, did you?" Captain Mike said. He sat facing the bay and told the waitress to bring him iced coffee. "And don't forget the cream, honey." She gave him a *faux* salute, and a gorgeous smile.

"I don't mean to be a pest." Maybe the message was a feint.

"If Gunderson didn't think you're ready, he never would have made contact."

"Then he's for real?"

Captain Mike glanced over his shoulder to make sure the waitress wasn't within earshot. "He's for real."

"It must be information worth getting to you, if he finally made contact. Why did he wait so long?"

"According to him, that speech you made last week convinced the Bauers you're for real. That makes all the difference in the world. You're part of their inner circle now. To earn their trust, you have to do something to convince them you've bought into the cause. Gunderson said even he was inspired."

The waitress was back. On a small tray were a glass of iced tea, a cup of coffee, and a martini with an olive skewered with a tooth pick, that she unloaded on the table while Captain Mike got out his wallet. "Thanks," he told her as he laid a ten on the table, "keep the change and keep them coming." He stirred cream into his coffee but devoured the olive and went to work on the martini. "She knows what I like before lunch," he said as the waitress walked away. "Are you ready to go to the next level?'

"What's the next level? I don't drink martinis."

"We have to set up a schedule and a place to meet so you can pass information without a spur of the moment luncheon date. I told my secretary we were meeting about Carole's wedding shower this time, but as soon as she's married, that cover goes away." He turned to her. "If I can't keep you out, I'll have to take you in. The information you gave us *was* important. We've been waiting for Hitler to make his move on Austria. It's his homeland. You've helped us with a time-line."

He picked up a fork, dragged it across a napkin, leaving four deep grooves, and passed it to Piper. He pointed to the bottom line. "Word to the wise. This is your track. Above you are people and armies and politicians. While you're operating from one set of facts, other people have different agendas and are working from another set of facts. Don't assume people are telling you everything or telling you the truth. Report what you see and hear and leave the interpretation to us." He put on his cap. "Good job, Piper. Order some lunch on me. I'll get with Bailey and get back to you." He stepped away from the table, then came back and patted her shoulder. "Oh, and by the way, congratulations to Sandy on passing his entrance exams."

***

With one remark, Captain Mike had proven the truth of his words. She'd been operating on the assumption that Sandy loved her for real, that they could trust each other if no one else. She had muttered a "Thanks, I'll tell him you said so," but sat bayside for a half an hour watching the clean water, wondering how it got so dirty in eighty years. Was she lucky to see how things had been, or was she condemned to live in a foreign hell hole until she died?

The worst part of the past was the waiting. Long distance calls, even to San Francisco, were budget busting for anything but a 'hi, I love you.' Maybe she hadn't lied to Mitch after all. Whatever was happening at the hospital was over her head. All those nights Sandy studied, God knows how many hours he dedicated to his books while she was at the work, and all for an entrance exam. He never said he wanted to be a doctor. Or … maybe he had, and she hadn't paid attention any more than she'd paid attention to his instruction about locked doors.

When she got home, the painter working on the squatter's place brought her a long box she recognized as a flower box and took off his hat. "Guess the Mister thought you'd be home, Mrs. Sanders. Your phone's been ringing off the hook."

Congratulations, you're now the wife of an official medical student, the card read. Be home soon. Love Sandy."

"Good news, Mrs. Sanders?"

"Old news, but good news," she said. The painter put on his hat and returned to his work. If her dad had kept something like this from her mother, Piper thought, there would have been hell to pay and flowers wouldn't have qualified as a tip.

Chapter XIII

Piper passed the Outpost Country Store and took the next right turn as Sister Rita directed and drove another two miles to a circular drive way that led to a big white house. "You can park under the delivery port to the right of the house. It'll keep your car cool," Sister Rita said. "Just ring the bell."

Piper got out of the car and walked to the back yard where she saw patio furniture arranged on a cedar wood deck. Further back was what looked like a small stable with a fenced in area adjacent that looked like a dog kennel. The lawn and gardens were well-manicured. Pregnant women didn't do the maintenance that kept this place pristine, Piper was sure. Carole never mentioned how lovely the Grove was outside. Maybe the residents weren't allowed in the pretty part.

She walked back to the delivery entrance and rang the bell. A woman in a white nurse's uniform answered the door. "Heil Hitler" she said and offered Piper her hand.

"Heil Hitler, Sister Rita?" Piper answered, and gently shook hands.

"You must be Mrs. Sanders. I've heard so much about you from Mr. Roberts."

"I'm glad, I think."

"Come in and yes, he speaks highly of you."

Carole hadn't mentioned Sister Rita spoke with a British accent; Sister was the English term for nurse. And she hadn't mentioned the living room looked like every English home she'd ever seen on BBC productions. The furniture was large, over-stuffed, with fading upholstery; lots of colors and patterns, but nothing bright. The carpets were worn and the lighting dim. The built-in book cases displayed bric-a-brac instead of volumes, and with magazines fanned out on each of the three end-tables and the wood-inlay coffee table, it looked like a doctor's waiting room. Above the fireplace hung portraits of King George VI and Adolph Hitler, side by side. Three-way loyalties made for interesting speculation as to the motives, not to mention the sanity, of the Grove's presence.

"We'll have our tea here," Sister Rita said and sat in one of the wing-back chairs opposite pink brocade sofa. She rang a ceramic bell that sat on the coffee table, and almost immediately a pregnant girl who looked about sixteen rolled in a cart of tea paraphernalia, sups, saucers, cream and sugar bowls, spoons and a teapot covered with knitted cozy.

"Thank-you, Margaret," Sister Rita said. "This is Mrs. Sanders."

"Nice to meet you, Ma'am."

The girl seemed healthy, but too thin, Piper thought. Like the squatter's wife. "It's nice to meet you. Have you been here long?"

"A month."

"That'll be all, Margaret," Sister Rita said.

When she'd gone, Sister Rita gave Piper a doleful smile. "Hers is a sad but familiar story. I try to make the girls understand that one mistake doesn't mean the end of their lives, that it's a temporary delay. Mine is a re-education mission, really The Bund camps do much the same thing for the boys, but you know that better than most, of course."

"You keep the Grove immaculately clean, Sister, I'm impressed."

"I hoped you would be. Like most organizations, we depend on Party disbursements. We're a comprehensive facility. Many of the girls come from poor circumstances. Many barely read or write. They attend school during the day. Those from the better classes, we counsel about going back to their families. If they'll have them. And what they might do if that's not possible. Older, married women, we send home with a good scolding."

As she spoke, Piper realized she was once again being schooled in desperation, gratitude and loyalty. With no State aid, where else would these women go? There was no welfare office. If they couldn't work, they couldn't eat, and if they couldn't read, they couldn't work even if jobs were available.

"Some of the girls took to the rails with their young men rather than lose them. Few of the men return once they've started lives elsewhere. As soon as the girl gets pregnant, the romance is over, and she's burned her bridges. Some throw away their lives in prostitution, demon run, opium …some of the infants must be saved from suffering. Beyond the stable is a row of trees, and beyond that there's a cemetery."

Piper felt her stomach tighten at her wistful words. Videos of addicted newborns were available on u-tube. Was Sister Rita's solution kinder in the long run? Eighty years in the future, even with

State aid, the problems of illiteracy risky behavior, and dissolution would still savage the lives of young women. They didn't ride the rails, but they wore tracks on their bodies. "You see a lot of sadness, Sister. I admire your efforts."

Sister Rita turned in her chair and gazed at the portraits above the fireplace. "My efforts are nothing compared to the heroic struggles of the *Fuhrer*. He bears the burden of us all."

The man with the funny mustache didn't return the adoration of his believers. He stared forward into eternity with the confidence of the regal blood line that hung beside him. Piper looked down at her white hands resting against the green taffeta that way she had at her grandmother's funeral. As then, she didn't share Sister Rita's communion with the divine, she only observed it, and wondered why people allowed themselves to be consumed by it. Strangely too, as then, her respectful silence was perceived to be exemplary humility. She counted off five seconds. He social communications teachers called it an "appropriate pause" before speaking.

"Mitch tells me you keep excellent records, a spotless kitchen, and have envious success with adoptions."

She may not have paid attention to history, but she was grateful to Mrs. Spurlock for insisting the class role pay to learn how to open lines of dialogue. Compliments pay big dividends.

"He's very kind. Let me show you."

Sister Rita led her to the foyer and then down a long hall to the rear of the house. Margaret and two other girls were washing clothes on the back porch that doubled as a utility room. A fourth woman, in a nurse's uniform also, sat a long table snapping green beans. "Sister Ann, this is Mrs. Sanders.

She stood and gave a modified salute with the same Heil Hitler greeting, as the girls gawked through the screen that separated the kitchen from the porch.

"Heil Hitler," Piper said. It reminded her of Shelly-the-girlfriend's story of her sorority's pledge week. "If you don't take the ceremonies seriously, they kick you out," she'd warned Piper.

"Is that why you quit?" Piper had asked and got a cold stare and a sharp 'no' in reply.

"Sister Rita's showing me around. I'm overwhelmed by the attention to detail. Even the floors shine," she said to Sister Ann

"We have a man who comes once a week. We have an electric polisher, "Sister Ann explained. "If only we had a machine to do the dishes."

There was agreement all around as one of the girls on the porch said, "Amen!"

"Someday," Piper said.

"Well, you might as well meet everyone," Sister Rita said. "C'mon ducks, meet the new inspector."

That's it, Piper thought, that's why Edwina was here. Mitch didn't mention that. "It's informal, believe me.," she said.

"You've met Margaret. The brunette is Carla, and the freckled one is Susan. Carla won't be with us much longer."

Indeed, Carla's very pregnant belly stuck out two feet from her frame. Piper caught herself before asking if it was a boy or a girl. No sonograms. "You definitely look like you're ready."

"Yes, Ma'am," Carla replied sullenly.

"It's nice meeting you. I can only echo what Sister Rita has said. There's a future waiting for you." It sounded vacuous even to her, but what else could she say to girls who didn't have the luxury of knowing a Navy corpsman who could get birth control without money or questions?

"Can Carla read and write?" she asked in the privacy of Sister Rita's office. "I know someone at the Y.W.C.A. if she needs a place to stay and I need someone to help with the housework two or three days a week."

"Mitch said you needed someone if you're going to organize for the Bund, but Carla isn't suitable." She had stacked two green ledgers on her desk that she'd taken from a file cabinet behind it. She patted them affectionately and sat down. "Five years of hard work boiled down to numbers and names written on pages of record books. Maybe that's why I keep them dusted and stored in a cabinet instead of on a shelf."

"What's the problem with Carla?" Piper went to the window and peered through the lace curtains at the girls who were hanging the wash on clothes lines hidden by tall hedges from the patio area.

"She wants to keep her child. She thinks her fella will come back to her eventually and they'll live happily ever after."

"Is there hope that he will come back? Maybe Mitch could investigate."

"Paul Jones wasn't hard to find. He's doing five years in the federal penitentiary for violation of the Mann Act. Carla was only fifteen and he was twenty-one. They were turned in by a drunk after a fight in one of the cantinas over in El Centro."

"Was Jones taking care of her? Did he have a job?"

"They both worked in the fields picking onions and carrots."

"Does he know about the baby?"

Jones swears he didn't know she was a minor, that he met her at a bar in El Paso. He's from Michigan. Mitch went to see him. Told him about the baby, and all he did was call her … unflattering names. How do you tell a child that her Romeo is a bastard when she doesn't want to believe it?"

For all her heil Hitler-ing, Sister Rita was a kind person. Sort of like Mrs. Stevens. Stern of the outside and jelly on the inside. "Maybe she could visit the prison and Jones could tell her to get lost in person. No, it's too late for that, I suppose. What are you going to do?" The memory of Carole's confession of suicidal thoughts made her choke. She'd seen many young women on the streets and wondered how they survived.

Sister Rita suddenly showed her age as her face hardened even as her wrinkled brow and staring eyes pleaded for understanding. "Carla will deliver a still born, according to Dr. Chartman."

"I see." Did Sister Ann deliver babies by plane, perhaps? Where would Carla's baby end up?

"But I do know a Mexican woman who's looking for work. Constance Garza. Clean, honest and speaks fairly good English. She won't flirt with the Mister either, and that's a serious consideration.

The girls here are too used to male attention." She handed Piper the ledgers. "While you inspect these, I'll take Maria to get her daughter. Constance works part-time at the Outpost. They're all from Puebla. Maria's our cook and her husband Enrique our maintenance man."

The patient record only went back a year, so Piper didn't find any record of Carole McKnight or Edwina Blackledge. She snapped a picture of page one, a random middle page and the last page that did record Margaret, Carla and Susan, including last names, due dates, visits to Dr. Chartman, and his fees for services. She photographed random pages of the bank account ledger, before stashing her camera back in her purse. She had evidence of the organization, but not of illegality. She scanned the walls for a State license of some kind but wasn't sure the Bund needed one for its philanthropic work. Didn't the IRS have a special designation for non-profits? Yes, but probably not for reproductive entrepreneurships in 1938.

She spied the file cabinet and wondered if there was a third ledger, one that recorded adoptive parents or those buried in the Grove cemetery. With her and Carole's testimony, perhaps she had enough evidence for the police to get a search warrant to find it, if it was there. She didn't have time to check. She heard the door open and turned to see Margaret's suspicious face.

"Sister Ann wanted me to ask if you wanted something to eat. They gobble down these things called scones."

"Only if you'll have some with me. Maybe we could talk."

"I'm not supposed to chat to visitors."

"There's no law against chatting. They don't beat you here, do they?" Maybe Margaret was suitable.

"I'll bring the cart."

"Never mind, I'll come to the kitchen." Margaret really did roll her eyes. When she met the girls she so much wanted to scream, "I'm one of you, still," but knew it wasn't true. She was regarded as an adult, and it hurt.

"How did you wind up here," she asked as they sat at the long oaken table. In the middle was a cobalt blue bowl full of lemons and cream and sugar bowls sitting on a white doily.

Margaret poured coffee and brought a basket of lightly browned and buttered wedges to the table. "I'm from Arkansas," she said as she got the cups and saucers from the cupboard. "Everybody told me I was pretty enough to be in pictures. You look just like Jean Harlow, they said." She sat down and tilted her head so Piper could admire her profile, and ran her fingers through her light brown hair. Piper was sure Mitch saw the resemblance, but it was wasted on her. She'd never seen Jean Harlow. "I had to change my name. Margaret Olson ain't a star's name. I called myself Lauren Michaels. Nice, ain't it?"

"You're certainly as pretty as any Hollywood starlet and that's a great name," Piper said. Margaret needed compliments, and she needed information.

"I was working over to Miss Sunday's Hair Salon. You know, sweeping up hair and making sure the combs were clean. Doing shampoos and making appointments. I saved up all my money for a whole year. Lied to my mama. Said Miss Sunday paid me a quarter when she'd pay me fifty cents. I saved thirty dollars!" Margaret's eyes glowed with pride. "Came out to Hollywood. Got me an agent right away. Went to few parties and met Ray Milland. Can you believe it? He was so handsome and so nice."

She climbed back into her shell then, taking her dreams and memories with her. From Glamour queen to discarded teen in less than ninety seconds. "Then I met this producer. So he said. When I told him I was in the family way, he said he already had a family. Gave me ten dollars and put me on the train to San Diego. I sure liked being on my own, while it lasted."

"How'd you meet Mitch?"

"I hung out near the nickel-snatcher."

"Nickel-snatcher?"

"The boats near the ferry landing that bring the sailors across the bay from North Island. The sailors pick up girls and pay for a night at a hotel sometimes. When I started to show, that was over. Mitch was there some nights. I'd seen him talking to other girls. Helping them out if they got in trouble. He bailed Selma out of jail once when she tried to hustle a cop. Anyway, he brought me here." She looked around the kitchen disgustedly.

"At least it's clean and safe. And you eat." Was Mitch into pimping, too?

"I hate it. It's no damn fun. That's why they don't want me talking to anybody, especially to anybody like you. I hate them all.

Carla all moony-eyed over Paul. And Susan talking about how she's going to become a nurse like Sister Rita. Ha! That's not going to happen. She's pregnant by her cousin. Sister Rita don't know that."

"She probably wouldn't tell anyone Susan knew if she did."

"Why not? She's such a bitch." Margaret shifted in the chair and let out a groan. "Oh, God. Let me go to sleep for the next three months and wake up when this nightmare's over!"

"I'd be happy if we had doughnuts instead of these blobs of flour," Piper said with a less passionate groan. Margaret looked at her, and Piper grinned. "They're pretty bad, Margaret. More coffee, please. I beg of you."

Margaret started to laugh and struggled to stand. "Coming right up." She brought a pot to the table, filled Piper's mug, and put the pot on a trivet. "You're okay for one of them Nazi sourpusses. Okay, Hitler's a great guy. I've heard it a thousand times."

Piper feigned a furtive mien and looked around. "We better be careful. Sister Ann might hear us."

"Naw. She left to take Carla to see Chartman. They don't figure we're alone because you're here, but what's the big deal? Where the hell would we go?" Instead of coffee, Margaret got a glass of milk for herself, twisting up her face as she stared at it before she sipped it. "Dang sure ain't champagne." She broke off a piece of her scone and dunked it into the glass like a cookie. "You know what I'm going to do after I drop this kid? I'm going back to Hollywood and make Mr. Producer's life a living hell. Maybe I'll blackmail his butt." She fished a pack of Pall Malls out of her apron pocket and lit up a cigarette.

"Are you going to name the baby after him?"

"No way in hell. Mitch says he got a family who'll take it. They'll name it. They're gonna give me a hundred dollars to get settled somewheres. Might as well be Hollywood, right? Course, my body's shot now." She leaned across the table and lowered her voice. "Mitch says Chartman can fix me. You know, so I won't get pregnant again. Ever."

She went to the sink, and opened the window, blowing the smoke towards it as she spoke. "I got a plan. I'm going to learn how to do hair styles. I used to do bobs. And I know a lot about make-up. I can get on with a studio. Get discovered that way. You know how Ray Milland got his start? He learned to shoot while he was in the Army and did some sharpshooting for a picture. True story."

She's a survivor, Piper thought. The Sisters wouldn't approve, but at least she had a plan she formulated on her own. It wasn't all that far-fetched either. Piper thought about the reality show Face-off and how determined the make-up artists were to win. "Miss Sunday can teach you. I'll bet she would, too. You wouldn't have to pay a beauty school, and you could save some more money." Margaret didn't say anything. Maybe she hadn't heard, or maybe she was hoping she could sleep through that too. Going home didn't mean failure, but it would feel that way, Piper thought. She recognized the fear as her own. "Sister Rita's been gone a while. Wonder what's keeping her?"

"It's noon. Constance has to watch the store while ol' man Figgs goes to fix lunch for his mother. She's in a wheel-chair. Can't last much longer, he always says, but she just keeps breathing."

"How do you know that?" Piper said. Margaret was realistic in her own way. She liked her.

"Sometimes I ride down to the store with Maria's husband. He tells me shit. Oh, damn, Sister Rita's back." Margaret ran water over the lit end of her cigarette and put the butt into the pack. "You won't rat me out, will you?"

"Nope. Your lungs, your choice." Maria's husband probably bought her the cigarettes.

Sister Rita, Marie and Constance came in the back door, past a rack of drying sweaters and the wringer washer. The moment they got to the kitchen, Margaret and her milk glass had melted away.

Constance was suitable. She'd stay with her Aunt and Uncle in Old Town, and her Uncle would drive her to work three days a week, picking up and dropping off the laundry on Wednesday and picking it up on Friday. For a dollar a day, she'd clean the kitchen and bath, dust and vacuum, and make dinner. Light housekeeping, Sister Rita called it. Tuesday's and Thursdays, she'd attend English classes until she was ready for secretarial school. Eventually, she'd fulfill every girl's dream: becoming part of the steno pool of a company. She wouldn't have to work in the fields. "And no boyfriends for a long time," Sister Rita confided. "Devout Catholics."

From what Piper knew about the Grove's girls, it was a strong selling point. "I'll have to talk it over with Mr. Sanders, of course."

The last thing he'd want was a Nazi spy in his house, even if she did clean toilets. Piper smiled, and nodded, and wanted to run.

"Of course, you just give me a call."

On the other hand, she'd made headway in her investigation. Edwina's non-Aryan chauffeurs were most probably the Mexicans Sister Rita employed. Whether Mitch knew that, or arranged it, she didn't know yet. Sister Rita had certainly made it clear she needed the Bund money, and that kind of need could just as certainly be a motive for robbery and murder.

As for the black-market baby ring, some of the girls involved cooperated. Maybe Mitch intended for her to learn that through a visit to the Grove specifically contrived to force her to ponder reality seriously. Was it possible that it was sometimes necessary to do bad things to accomplish good ends? Maybe Edwina's answer to that question is what got her killed.

Chapter XIV

Piper sat on the stoop watching the painter collect his brushes, trap, and paint cans from the bungalow across the walk and load them in his truck. He was at east sixty, she thought. Sinewy and hirsute. A leathery tan. He should be paying golf.

"I'll be shovin' off now, Mrs. Sanders. You enjoy this fine afternoon, now."

"I'll do that. But, before you go, there's something I want to ask you."

He put down his last two cans. Empty, Piper guessed by the way he carried both with one hand. "What's that, Mrs. Sanders?"

"You talked to the landlord before you started painting, I suppose."

"Well, sure. I like to paint before he strips the floors."

"Did he say anything about there being lice in the place?"

"Nope. He didn't say nothin' about no bugs. I sure didn't see any. He just said use the tarp, 'cause he had the floors done. It takes me longer when I have to be super careful. There weren't no stains on them or anything."

She hugged her knees close to her chest. "Thank-you."

"For what, Ma'am?"

"I just wanted to know."

He tipped his cap. "Yes, Ma'am. I'll tell ya. There weren't nothin' bad 'bout them squatters. They was just poor."

He stepped on his cigarette, picked up the butt and felt the end before putting it in one of his empty cans, and headed for his truck.

She wanted to call Sandy and tell him what the painter said, more than she wanted to tell him what she'd learned at the Grove. Cecil, too, ought to know how wrong they were about the evicted people, although she didn't know why it mattered. Maybe because she knew their world better than they knew hers, and it didn't seem fair. Margaret was so right. Nothing was fun anymore. She hated this San Diego. She hated everyone in it, except for Jim.

"You just got the blues, Piper," Carole told her. As usual, she was her bite-the-bullet self. Terminal grin-and-bear-it, Piper called it. "After seeing that awful place last week, you've a right to be blue, though." She'd brought a casserole to reheat before they went to the Bund meeting, and was rummaging around the kitchen for something to serve with it "Don't you ever buy groceries?"

"I'm used to calling Domino's and having pizza delivered when I have stuff to do."

"People deliver food to your door?"

Piper sighed. "Yeah, and I miss it. All I had to do is make a phone call … Did Sister Ann work at the Grove when you were there?"

"I don't remember a Sister Ann but there was another nurse there who would take the girls to Chartman's clinic when they were due and Enrique was busy. Oh, look some lettuce and a tomato. At least I think it's a tomato. And a can of peas." She got a saucepan from a bottom cabinet. "I forgot about that other nurse. I think her name was … Mrs. Palmer. I only saw here twice because only two girls delivered when I was there. After they left, three more came and I delivered right after that. Maria was there. And Enrique, her husband. I never met anyone named Constance."

Piper set the table for them. Jim was working overtime again. Carole's impending marriage to a good Nazi supporter seemed redemptive because Honnolore was cordial to her. Piper was convinced it was because a woman with potentially divided loyalties was no longer tempting Mitch, Honnolore's prized stud. "Constance is allegedly Maria's daughter but I'm not buying the story. She looked too old be Maria's kid," Piper said.

"It's a good bet she's not. When the whole world's in a depression, people do and say whatever they have to, to get work."

As she spoke, Piper reviewed the pictures she took of the ledger pages. "From the names and dates, I'd say the Grove handles its clientele in batches of threes. Did you all have your own room? I didn't go upstairs."

"The second floor is just bedrooms and bathrooms except there's a parlor. A second living room sort of, that's used as a classroom."

"Can you see the cemetery from the upstairs windows?"

Carole shivered. "Don't remind me. I had nightmares about how close it was to the house and how unsanitary that must be." She got the casserole from the oven and put in on a thick cotton pad on the table. "I … I heard a baby crying, once. The next morning, the girl in the room next to me said she was crying and hoped she didn't disturb me. Helen was her name."

Piper tried to sound nonchalant. "You didn't write any of this in your notes."

Carole eased herself into her chair. "I tried to remember, honest I did. But to tell you the truth, I didn't want to remember. I know it sounds terrible, but now that Jim and I are starting anew life, it almost makes what Sister Rita says the truth." She reached across the table and took Piper's hand. "I hope you understand. I'm not a monster but it's okay if I don't get Suzanne back."

Piper heard her stomach do a flip-flop. Or was it a gasp of relief?

"When you think you have nothing, you hang on to anything, even air. A shadow. A ghost. Whatever you imagine will take away the hurt and solve your problem. But Suzanne isn't my problem anymore. You said she had a home, and that's what Mitch said she'd have. Please don't hate me, Piper."

Piper stole a napkin from the holder and went to the back door. She blew her nose and stashed the napkin in the trash. She'd known since her meeting with Captain Mike about her plan that it was time to let the Suzanne situation go. Something told her Carole and Captain Mike had reached a tacit agreement. She'd give him another "first grandchild" with Jim, and he'd give her privacy.

She returned to the table. "I don't hate you. I hate that I'm here and wondering if my parents have forgotten me. It's not the same thing, I know, but I wonder." Carole had dished her out a mound of macaroni, cheese and chicken, peas and wilted lettuce with half a slice of wrinkly tomato sitting on top, and it reminded her of high school cafeteria lunches.

"I don't think you understand how ashamed I was," Carole

continued. "I was so stupid, and I hated that feeling like nobody wanted me because I'd been so foolish. Every time I tried to write notes, the feeling came back. It made me sick."

Piper wasn't hungry. Carole too was doing nothing but moving her food around on her plate. "I hate that I'm a grown-up, Carole. I saw myself in Margaret, losing all my plans and happiness, and being humiliatingly grateful I'm not off in some looney bin. And my loving husband doesn't even have the courtesy to tell me he's studying for med school."

"That's what's got your goat, isn't it? I mean, really what your upset about. Yeah, you still are a kid at heart. Men never want to fail, Piper. Oh, it's ok for them, but if their women find out, it's devastating. Failure is the same as saying, I can't take care of you. I call it good news only disease."

"Well, I hate that. So, we're even in the hate department." She expected sisterly commiseration. Instead, she got to watch Carole's face morph into amusement.

"We're quite the cry-babies, aren't we? People all over the world are suffering, and we're complaining about crap we can't do one single thing about. You know what we ought to so?" She took their plates to the kitchen and scraped the food into the trash can. "I vote we go to Bernie's and get chili dogs and limeades. Hell, we can afford it. Maybe we can find some old guys to flirt with. Don't looked so shocked. They love it, and it's safe."

They pinned up their hair, threw jackets over their slacks and silk blouses, and piled into Piper's coupe. "After we eat, we can joyride through the park," Piper said. She longed to smell the pepper trees at night and see the moon over the bay. She wanted to go by Josh's place too. She'd pretend he and Shelly-the-girlfriend were watching re-runs of *I love Lucy* that hadn't been produced yet.

"What about the Bund meeting?" Carole said.

"We're sick. Remember that."

Her words were prophetic. Chili over French fries, and chocolate shakes put the kybosh on the joy-riding. They ended up at Piper's, Carole stretched out on the sofa and Piper on the floor after trips to the bathroom, listening to Artie Shaw play *Begin the Beguine* on the radio.

It sounded familiar. She took out her phone. If her pictures were there, maybe her music was too. "Listen, Carole. I downloaded this for my Grandmother. It's Johnny Mathis' version in 1997. Guess that makes Cole Porter immortal."

***

Gunderson called at eight. Piper instinctively reached for her cell phone, then slid out of bed and stumbled to the living room to get the landline.

"This is Piper," she said. Her mouth felt like it was filled with oatmeal.

"Honnolore made an official announcement last night that you were ailing.

"Junk food overload. Me and Carole threw caution to the wind, and then hurled for real. What did I miss —anything important?"

"Some of the Navy guys brought their girlfriends to meet you.

Guess they wanted to see what their competition is like. You missed the fear in Sister Rita's eyes. She's scared you're going to recommend cutting off Party funding to the Grove. We had a meeting with her after the meeting."

"Oh, hell." She filled the coffee pot with water and lit the stove. "The place was efficient, and you could eat off the floors. Captain Mike might not want to hear that, but it's the truth."

"I'm supposed to come over and snoop. Allegedly, I put the wrong spark plugs in your car. You don't know the silliness of that. You couldn't drive with the wrong plugs. With the mister gone, I'm supposed to see if you've had a visitor. Mitch didn't come to the meeting, either, and he didn't call in."

Suddenly, she was wide awake. "Do tell!"

"What time did Carole leave last night?"

"Jim picked her up around midnight."

"Did he say anything about Maritimer?" Gunderson asked.

"Nope. What happened?"

"I'll tell you when I get there. Do you need anything?"

Just milk if you want it for coffee. I'm out." She turned on her kitchen box radio hoping to hear some news. Damn it! Why hadn't 24/7 news channels been invented yet? She took a quick shower and dressed. Why hadn't anyone thought of sweat-pants yet, either?

Gunderson must have called her from the market, because he was there, milk and cream in hand, before she could run a comb through her hair. "You forgot to put the percolator inside the pot," he said when she sat at the table to put on socks and shoes.

"Thanks. Have me tell you about a planet called Starbucks someday." When would she stop living in the future?

"There was a fire in dry dock number four. Around one o'clock. The cops will want to check Jim's alibi, so don't be surprised when they come knocking at your door."

"I haven't heard any news…"

"It's all hush-hush. Sabotage usually is."

"Jim didn't do it, Mr. Gunderson."

He was looking for sugar. There was nothing but Sandy's cubes. "Of course, he didn't."

"Was anyone hurt?"

"Two men were killed." He sat at the table. "Have you seen Mitch?"

"No. Did he have something to do with the fire?" The scent of fresh-brewed coffee filled the chilly kitchen and reminded Piper of Sunday mornings.

"He might have known about it, though. He haunts the pier."

"I know why, too. Waterfronts and damsels in distress have a lot in common. He definitely needs psychological counseling."

The look on Gunderson's face told her she wasn't making much sense. "I'll be right back." She went to the bathroom and checked her phone photo of the ledger. Carla Watson —if that was her real name. She might have gone into labor a month early. Science wasn't so precise here. Mitch was probably closing a baby deal. Did she still care? The danger seemed worth it when she was sleuthing for Carole and Suzanne, but now?

On her way back to the kitchen she got a call. "Carole says the cops are on their way here. Is that your cue to leave?"

"I'd better."

"Anything I need to tell Captain Mike?"

Gunderson gulped down his coffee and grabbed his keys. "Cabot Swan is on his way back to the states. Says he's got mono, and the Navy wants him quarantined in a hospital. It's more likely he's got syphilis and they want to cure him before he comes down for Captain's Mast here. I'll call you later."

"What'd he do?"

"Guys get in trouble for having VD." He gave her a half salute before speeding out the door.

Honnolore must be having a breakdown, Piper thought, admittedly amused. Two of her favorite guys were MIA, and two of her *deutsche madchen* had been out on the town without their men folk. All this wondering and driving and consternation, what a waste of time when they could be texting. On the other hand, it was nice not being tech-available 24/7. She could get used to having visitors.

This one missed Gunderson by two minutes. She opened the door to a guy in a blue uniform who looked about twenty-five. "I'm officer Conway. I'd like to ask you a few questions, if you don't mind."

"Sure. Okay. Come in."

He wasn't tall or particularly handsome, but he had bright green eyes and freckles on his nose, and Piper was glad she was wearing her wedding ring. "Carole McKnight said she was with you yesterday evening. Mind telling me what you did?"

We had fun, she wanted to say, and I no longer care about why I'm here. It sucks, but I'm going to make the best of it because I'm not a cry-baby.

"Jim dropped her off at three. We went to Bernie's for dinner at five. Ate chili, and spent the evening listening to music on the radio. Jim picked her up at twelve-thirtyish, after work, and I went to bed. To sleep. Because I had a tummy ache and was feeling blah with the blues. Amen."

He looked up from his notebook. "Is that all?"

"We had chocolate shakes. I guess dairy and chili fries don't mix well."

He closed his notebook and put it and his pen in his breast pocket. "Sounds like you girls got your story straight."

"I hope it sounds like the truth, because it is."

He handed her a card. "If you think of anything else you'd like to tell me, give me a call."

Is it okay if I call and tell you I think you're cute because my husband's a douche? "I'll do that, Officer."

"Alright, because perjury is a crime. You know that, don't you?"

"I do know that."

She watched him walk down the walkway, feeling an unfamiliar pang in her belly, like she was missing something. Her face felt warm. She'd call Carole and ask if there was anything she'd left out, and could Carole come up with a valid excuse to call Officer Joe

Conway because it was great fun messing with him?

"I knew you'd like him. Me too. You're not one for pretty boys," Carole teased, "He's so serious, he's a riot."

"Is everything square with Jim? He's not in any trouble, is he?"

"I called my Dad. He'll put them straight. How're you feeling?"

"Like the last thing I want to do is go to work today. Maybe I'll go grocery shopping." Piper spotted her recipe box on the kitchen and remembered the cards that came with it. One card had a recipe for scones. Maybe she could improve upon a classic. "Have you seen Mitch lately?"

"I'll have him call you when I get to work."

She got more than fresh tomatoes and cheese at Largo Factotum. The headline of the morning paper read: Maritime Fire Kills Two. She couldn't chance there wouldn't be a copy on her way out, so she fished around in her purse for a nickel and paid for a copy to carry. "Tragedy," Larry said when he added up her basket on the register. "More bad news for the workin' stiff."

In the car, she read the article about the fire which said nothing more than 'that's all we know now.' Next to it was an update on the brutal murders of San Franciscans Hazel and Nancy Frome, wife and daughter of an executive with Atlas Powder Company, in El Paso. Below that was an article that rivetted her attention: Body of Jane Doe in San Diego Bay. She turned to page A-8 and saw the face of Carla Watson —as dead as Edwina Blackledge.

***

Where was Sandy when she needed him? Living his life.

Celebrating getting into med school. Planning a Jim and Carole future for them. All she had to do was forget she ever met Carla Watson. She drove home and locked the door behind her. She checked the bathroom and the closets, too. The coffee made her jittery, she told herself, not the fear clawing up her spine. No one knew she'd seen the paper. She threw it in the trash, then retrieved it. What did Sister Rita say her boyfriend's name was? Paul Jones. Federal penitentiary. Maybe Officer Conway could get her in to see him. Not without an explanation.

She sat in the living room, blinds drawn, shaking and cold, seeing Captain Mike's fork-tines imprinting on her brain the way they dug into the napkin. Other agendas. Other facts. A nice way to say people lie. She and Sandy were supposedly married to give her cover to solve a crime. When did that change to hearts, flowers, and cures for jungle rot? When she put on a gold band and screwed her brains out. When Carole told her Suzanne wasn't important anymore. When she decided the Grove was doing a job no one else was willing to do. All of the above.

She grabbed her uniform, her work shoes, and emptied her change tin. The phone was ringing when she left. Probably Carole. It didn't matter. She had to run, but where? Why the hell did she give Mitch three hundred dollars?

Chapter XV

The truth was, if she'd let Sandy report Mitch and his black-market babies to the police, Carla would still be alive whether she was a suicide or a murder victim. And she and Sandy wouldn't be married or spying for Captain Mike.

"Call McKnight and have him meet me at church," she told Gunderson.

"I'll call him."

Twenty minutes later, she was at St. Joseph's Cathedral sitting in the pew under the protective gaze St. Tereasa, and watching the votive candles flickering at her holy feet. The dark, stone, Romanesque church was their new meeting place. Captain McKnight was devout, his staff learned. He went to confession once a week, usually on Friday mornings, but sometimes he met with the Bishop to discuss a fund drive or to serve as a sponsor for some poor kid who needed a Confirmation outfit. Occasionally, he and the Bishop would have lunch at the Admiral Kidd. It provided excellent cover.

"Gunderson said the cops had been 'round to see you. Did they spook you?"

"Officer Conway? Of course not. This did." She handed him the Jane Doe article she'd clipped from the paper.

"I don't understand."

"Really? Understand this, I'm out. Done. Through."

"Do you know her?"

"She's one of Mitch's girls. I met her at the Grove Wednesday, ready to deliver. Now, Mitch is gone and she's dead. If he didn't kill her, he damn sure took the kid. I not going to be a part of illegal activity and I'm not going to end up floating in the bay."

"You're too valuable …"

"You've got Gunderson in the Bund. You don't need me."

"Not true. Gunderson has a business to run. They know him as loyal, but he can't raise money or recruit. Especially young people. Most of all, he can't snoop. You're a rising star, and Mitch Roberts is in love with you, according to my daughter."

"Flattery won't save my life."

"Mitch was observed at Brown Field saying good-bye to a nurse carrying an infant on board."

"You're tailing him?"

"Trying to. Thanks to you. Now we know where the baby came from, and who the mother is … was. Thanks to you. Your information about Cabot Swan was invaluable. We can isolate him. You're an intelligence asset we couldn't have created even if we knew how."

He leaned forward on the kneeler for a minute. Was he praying, or trying to find the words to persuade her not to call the cops? "I thought you'd get over the spy stuff when you got married. I thought you'd be like Carole. She doesn't know just how deep Jim is in …"

"Jim helped you kill those two men last night, didn't he?" She felt that clawing in her gut again.

"They're the enemy within. They're sabotaging commercial

shipping vessels, and eventually they'll sabotage battleships too. Do you think war is a game?"

"No but ..." She couldn't finish her sentence because the 'but' part was 'I'm scared.'

"You say, we win this war, eventually. But how do you think that happened? People like you and Jim and Gunderson laid the groundwork for victory by getting our operation up and running before the war's declared." He sat back on the pew. "Get with Gunderson. He'll teach you how to protect yourself."

"I keep thinking about Carla's parents. They must miss her."

"I've seen families tell their sons to enlist in the military just to have one less mouth to feed. Providence works in strange ways. We're going to need every man we can get, and every spy we can get. Consider yourself drafted." He handed her a small box, patted her hand, picked up his hat, and left.

Inside was a silver .38 caliber pistole the size of a squirt gun and a box of bullets. Was this true equality? If Jim had to bear the oppression of war, why not her? She couldn't do anything for Carla now. She dropped two quarters into the donation box, and lit candles for Margaret and Susan. Was it alms or a bribe? She lit one for herself, put the box in her purse, and for the next three weeks, practiced everything Gunderson taught her about her new best friend —an Italian named Beretta.

"I've been there myself," Jim said when she invited him to the make-shift firing range Gunderson constructed near Descanso. She could hit tin cans from a whole seven yards. When she hit five out of eight, he gave her a thumbs-up. "You're no Annie Oakley, but you ain't bad for a millennial."

"Did you, in your wildest dreams ever think that …

"No. I never did," he said curtly and took her gun. He put on the safety, cocked the hammer, and fired. "FYI. Did your handler tell you that these pistols can fire even with the safety on? It's one of the reasons they're not very popular. It can come in handy, though. Be careful."

"We're not supposed to compare notes, are we? I mean, we never talk about our work …people-wise, that is."

"The fewer the people and the less you know, the less you can tell. Two things you gotta know to stay alive: who the big guns are, and how to keep big secrets."

***

"Carole called. I took a message. Mitch will see you at five." Goldstein was stocking fresh candy bars in the glass case under the counter. "And Mr. Conway called. Call him. And Jim, and Sister Rita, and Mrs. Bauer. What am I running here a secretarial service?" He stood up and wagged his finger at her. "You have too many friends for a married woman. They're going to get you in trouble, these friends."

His warning was a little late. "I'm sorry, Mr. Goldstein. I really am. I'll tell them not to call."

His finger was getting workout, but his eyes were glowing. "No, no. If I knew who everybody was … Miss Popular. You should tell a body who he's taking messages from. Your husband leaves and all of a sudden, your dance card is full. If you weren't such a good worker… Well, you're not, but you make the boys spend their money. It's the honey-brown hair and the brown eyes. If men didn't go where they're looking, movie stars could be ugly."

"Schmoozing the customers was part of my job description, as I remember." She tried to muster a happy face. "Popcorn?"

"You think I don't know Officer Conway? In my line of work, you got to know every cop on the force. These navy boys. I was young once. City boys meet country boys and trade bad habits." Goldstein rubbed his chin. "Unh … Are you happy with your husband? You know what I mean? In the bedroom."

Piper felt herself blush. "Oh, yes! He's a good man. The best." Did her boss really ask her such a personal question? If he hadn't seemed so serious, she would have laughed. "I'm very impressed."

"Okay. Good. How 'bout you call me Mr. Marvin?" He tore open a box and handed her a new roll of tickets. "I'm giving you a raise. Fifty cents an hour is nothing to sneeze at. You should put something aside. Build some assets. You think I don't know the New Testament, maybe? You got to grow your portion."

"Thank-you, Mr. Marvin." She remembered her mother's 'rainy-day fund,' the one her father knew nothing about, and made a mental note: start a cash stash.

"Alright, go to work. Tell your friends if they're going to leave messages, they better make sense, at least. I need details. And they should leave their phone numbers. What if you don't remember them?"

"Yes, Sir. And thank-you again …Mr. Marvin." Leave it to a former czarist to cut to the chase. He heard war scuttlebutt too. As the clock creeped towards five o'clock, she told herself she'd recovered from the shock of seeing Carla's picture, and was ready for Mitch.

***

"Can I take a pretty girl to dinner?" Mitch was his usual flirty self. He did have a way about him.

"You bet," she said as they walked to his Olds. "We have to talk."

His smile faded quickly. "Oh-oh, it sounds like I'm in the doghouse."

Piper opened the car door, got inside and reached for her seatbelt. Habit. Mitch got in and looked at her with puppy-dog eyes. "Am I in the doghouse?"

"You're lucky you're not in the jail house. And don't pretend you don't know Carla's dead. Drive."

He drove to Tops Drive-in and ordered burger baskets. "It happens."

"By it, you mean murder?"

She saw his shoulders jerk. "You think I killed Carla?"

She stared him down. "I think new mothers don't go for a swim in the bay. *Somebody* dumped her there."

Mitch turned his attention to drowning his fries in catsup. "Chartman said her blood pressure couldn't take the stress. She had a stroke on the delivery table."

"And you believe that bullshit?"

"He said he'd take care of it. I didn't know he'd put her in the water, I swear." His voice was cold. Matter of fact. She was almost done with her hamburger and he'd only taken two bites.

"Who drove her to Chartman's?" Piper demanded.

"Maria Garza."

"Where's the baby?"

"Las Vegas."

She got her change purse and handed him fifty cents for the food. "How much did you get for it?"

He took out his wallet, and counted out two hundred and fifty dollars, and then another two, and gave it to her. "Five hundred down, and another five hundred on delivery. Sister Anne keeps two-fifty for the Grove and gives the other two-fifty to the Bauers."

No wonder everybody was having shit-fits when Mitch didn't show at the Bund meeting. It was payday. "And Chartman? What's his cut?"

"The two-fifty I gave you. He won't get paid for Carla. He won't complain. We don't pay for mistakes and he knows it."

Piper put the money in her change purse. "From now on, I get a hundred and twenty-five. I leave it up to you who pays my share."

"Big deal. The price of a baby is now seven-fifty. Inflation's nothing new. Rich people will pay anything to get what they want."

"And another thing. We keep this arrangement between us. Sandy and the rest Bund don't have to know. I've got an image to maintain. You know all about that, right?"

Mitch's smile was back. "Got it, partner."

Let Mitch think he'd hooked her like he hooked the Sorensons. When and if she had to run, she'd have legs.

***

Mitch rolled to a stop a half a block from the theater. "Wonder what the Shore Patrol is talking to Goldstein about. He'll throw a fit if they bust him for underage patrons on porn night again. Take care, Pretty Lady. I have to see the Bauers."

Too bad he's such a cad, Piper thought, as he pulled away from the curb. If he minded her horning in his profit margin, he didn't show it. But then, he understood greed that fed on the desperate.

One look at Mr. Marvin's somber face as she neared the ticket booth, and she knew the SP was there on business. "What's wrong?" she asked her boss.

"Come with me," he said, and ushered them to the rear of the lobby. "You can use my office."

Piper steeled herself. She was ready to tell them everything, even about the gun and the one-hundred fifty dollars in her purse. Maybe they'd take pity on her. The older of two men looked her straight in the eyes. "I'm sorry, Mrs. Sanders, it's my sad duty to tell you Mr. Sanders is dead."

Chapter XVI

Carole, Jim, and Cecil were waiting for her at the house. She had little to tell them except there would be an investigation. There was nothing to do but bury him and break his parents' hearts. "They said I should tell them, but I can't do that. I barely know them. What would I say?"

Cecil shielded his face with his hands, but they heard his soft sobs. "I'll tell them. I know them well. I'll tell them you're in shock."

"It's the truth," she said, as she curled up in the study chair. She remembered the older sailor caught her on the way to the floor, but little else. She woke up on Mr. Marvin's red velvet sofa, and the younger sailor patting her hand.

"They didn't tell you how he died, or who discovered the body?" Carole's news chops had reappeared. She might as well have said do they know Mitch Roberts did it?

"He didn't show up for class Friday morning. When they went to the barracks, he'd missed bed check too. A Frisco cop found an abandoned car and called the base. He was inside. They said his pants were open. They suspect he picked up a hooker."

"Sandy wouldn't do that," Jim said. "No way in hell. I don't believe that crap for a minute. Right, Cecil?" He was sitting beside Cecil on the sofa and put a hand on his shoulders. "I don't believe it, Cecil. Our Sandy wouldn't do that."

"We're calling off the wedding," Carole blurted out.

"Oh, no, you're not." Piper said.

"Not the marriage, the wedding, Jim said. "We're eloping tomorrow. We've already called the Reverend. It wouldn't be right to have a celebration with all that's going on. Sandy's death has nothing to do with the decision. It's just … the world's gone nuts. The rumor is Japan has poison gas and might use it on the Chinese in the North. Does that remind you of anything?"

Piper shook her head no. "I know it should, but I don't remember."

"The gas attacks in Syria. 2018. Do you think the Isis bastards invented thc idca?"

"Are you sure, Jim?"

"Not a hundred percent, but the dominoes are starting to fall, Piper. The British are urging recognition of Italian rule in Ethiopia despite Haile Selassie's begging the UN to help."

"A showy wedding would be unseemly," Carole continued. "Not to mention expensive. We're going to need every cent we can save if we're going to weather the storm."

A knock at the door interrupted them. "Are you expecting someone?" Jim whispered.

"Absolutely not."

"I'll get it," Cecil said and opened the door to Captain Mike.

"Dad," Carole said, "Have you ..?

"Heard about Sandy? Yes, I came as soon as I could." He closed the door. "Piper, if you'll let me, I'll make the arrangements. Just tell me where you want him buried"

"I'll have to check with his family."

"Let me know. As soon as the autopsy is finished…"

"Autopsy? The SPs didn't say anything about an autopsy," Piper said.

"You've heard more than we have," Cecil said. "Spill it. All of it."

Captain Mike looked around at their angry faces. "I don't know if this is following protocol, but I might as well tell you while I have you all together." He found an empty spot at the end of the sofa and parked his cap. "First blush says a gunshot caused the death, but they want to do an autopsy. The San Francisco police want to have an official cause of death, and we want to see if Mitch Robert's bullet is a match. Sandy was naval personnel, but it's civilian turf so we're cooperating. It's a good thing, Piper. We want to find Sandy's killer as much as you do."

"Yeah. Right," Cecil said.

Captain Mike glared at him. "It's unlikely the bullet came from Mitch's gun, but it's the only lead we have. What we do know is one of the last people Sandy saw was Cabot Swan."

"He's supposed to be in quarantine at a civilian hospital," Piper said.

"Only twenty-four hours to make sure he hasn't got malaria, they told him. It was a cover story. Not a very good one, in retrospect. You don't get malaria from VD. Piper, I can't tell you how sorry we are. We know Swan found out about the medics' plan and we were hoping Sandy could find out how if they met. They were friends."

"You recruited Sandy for a mission and now you think Cabot killed him?" She turned to Cecil. "We'll need boots to get through this bullshit."

"We're not sure" Captain Mike said. "Cabot says he met Sandy at a nightclub, had two beers, and left him at 8:30 because Sandy said he had to get up early for class. He went to the head, and when he passed the bar, Sandy was talking to a woman. He must have been seriously talking to her because Sandy didn't notice him. Cabot didn't have any gun residue on his hands or clothes, but the body wasn't discovered for twenty-four hours, so he had plenty of time to wash up good."

"Cabot may be a fascist, Mr. McKnight, but he's not a killer," Piper said.

"I know, it makes no sense."

"Let me talk to him. He trusts me. I guarantee it. But no bugs. I want to talk to him with a Bund lawyer present."

"I don't know about that…"

"If he talks to me, he has no expectation of privacy."

"How do you know that?"

"*Law and Order*. People will learn a lot from television, if they pay attention."

"There was a History Channel, too," Jim said. "Remember?"

Piper waved him off. "Well, Mr. McKnight?"

"I'll set it up. I'll call you tomorrow and you can fly out of North Island. What's your job status?"

"Goldstein gave me ten days off, so I've got two weeks…"

Captain Mike turned to Carole and Jim, who were sharing the floor pillows. "I'll see you at home. I told your mother I might be late."

"Maybe we should all call it a night," Piper said. "I appreciate you all coming, but there's really nothing to do yet."

Carole and Jim gave her hugs and kisses, and followed Captain Mike, but Cecil took a seat at the dinette table, and stared at the rug as though he hadn't heard a word. Piper went to the kitchen and started a pot of coffee, then passed him on her way to the bedroom.

"Make yourself useful. He took most of his stuff with him, but I'd appreciate you taking the rest to his Seven Seas locker," she said.

Cecil came to the doorway and watched her stuff a duffle bag with clothes and shoes. "He was a good man, just not a perfect one. No man is, Piper."

"If you think he broke my heart, you're right. He had me believing he loved me. I'm sorry your friend is dead, but that's all he was to both of us. Obviously."

"I heard people get pissed off when people die, and they don't get to say good-bye."

"Oh, he said good-bye. With flowers and an enclosure card: I'm now in medical school." She threw the duffle bag at his feet. "We both know there's only one woman Sandy would have left that bar with. He was a too-convenient husband to me and a liar to you."

"You think he was with Beth?"

"Cabot Swan couldn't kill time, let alone a human being. Your

Einstein theory is interesting, but it's crap. Beth ran off with Sandy and left you and the rest of your family barely able to eat. That's not imperfection, it's cruelty. Don't tell me you didn't suspect it. Why else would you show up unannounced in San Diego with baby pictures of Beth? My brother doesn't carry around my baby pictures."

Cecil lifted the bag to his shoulder, took it to the living room, and set it upright. Piper followed and stacked Sandy's study guides and textbooks next to it. "I won't lie to you. I was suspicious when I heard he got married out of the blue like that. I thought it might be to Beth. They went together through high school" He opened the bag and started packing the well-used material. "His father bought our farm for five cents on the dollar plus back taxes. But it wasn't Sandy's idea or his money. We agreed we wouldn't let that ruin a friendship. My family left Sacramento, and Sandy re-enlisted." He folded over the duffle bag ends. "I wanted that job, Piper. To get paid to paint, I'd have done anything. Believed anything. I wanted Sandy to convince you to use whatever influence you had to get it. I don't blame you if you hate me for it."

Was not telling a man he was destined to die a form of lying? It was certainly a form of cowardice. She was afraid he'd hate her. "Let's just say you owe me, big time."

"Name it. Anytime. You got a lock for this?" he asked. She checked the kitchen catch-all drawer and brought him a padlock and two keys. "Beth couldn't stand being poor. That's the way mama explains her running off like she does."

"How do you explain it?"

"She likes men and she likes to drink. As soon as I met you, though, I knew why Chris married you, and I wish …I wish you were my kid sister. You're the kind of person I'd want my sister to be."

"Save it for my eulogy, if I'm the next on the list. What I need to know is, did Sandy tell Beth about me, about where I come from?"

He looked away. "He told me a little about you. I don't know what he told Beth."

"Different facts. Different agendas," she mumbled.

"I don't understand. Is it that important?"

"It means your sister might know what Sandy knew about me too. If so, she holds my life and my freedom in her hands. Do you have an older picture of Beth? I need it to show Swan."

"One thing, Piper. If Beth ran off with Sandy, why would she kill him?"

"She didn't." But Mitch Roberts knows who did. It was probably the same person who killed Edwina Blackledge.

***

Piper called Mr. Marvin and let him know she was taking a flight to San Francisco to identify Sandy's body. "It's the damn Nazis," he told her every other sentence as he explained how she and Sandy would be together in heaven. It was one of the better Christian beliefs, he adhered to. The Bauers, as usual, were solicitous and blamed the Godless Communists. Sandy was waiting for her in Valhalla. One look at the four-prop crate she was to fly in, and she was praying to everyone's God. If this was state-of-the-art flight equipment, the troops were in trouble.

"Rules are rules," she told them all when they asked why she had to go 'up there' when they could fly the body 'down here.' "What if it's not him? He might have family up there." She said and promised to call if got too hard alone.

"I can fly up there. Just say the word," Mitch declared Sunday morning over doughnuts and coffee. It was a newsman's idea of breakfast. "The good news is, the Bund in Frisco will give Swan the best lawyer they have." He also ran a story about thwarted young love, pointing out that there were no children from the marriage.

"All he needed was a proper headline: Piper Sanders is Single Again, Unencumbered and Employed. Line Up!" she'd told Gunderson on the ride to the airport. He'd been appointed chauffeur and chaperone of the young widow in her most vulnerable time.

"You're not fooling anyone with a brave front. You love Sandy. It doesn't matter if he turns out to be a man instead of a saint," he said, and she cried for the first and last time, she promised herself.

***

Cabot couldn't hug her when she and attorney William Alexander, Esquire, walked into the jail's interview room because he was shackled to the table, but his first words were, "Give me your hand."

She reached across the table, and he bent down and kissed it. The SP knocked on the window and scolded him with a wag of his finger.

"The Bund stands behind you, Mr. Swan, you have the German Consulate's word on it." Alexander stated. "Baron von Killinger is prepared to give you all the help you need."

"Thank God, because I'm being railroaded here. I didn't kill Sandy, Piper … you gotta believe that."

She patted his cold, clenched fists.

"Alright, let's take it from the top," Alexander said. "Tell me what you told the cops."

"It's like I said, Sandy called me in quarantine and said we should have couple of beers when I got out."

"How did he know you were in quarantine?" Piper asked.

"He was on rounds with the interns. It was just a coincidence. Anyway, he gave me his number and I called him when I got out, and we met up at the Underground …Something. Underground Hedgehog, maybe. Some bar. I can't remember."

"What did you wear to the club?" Alexander asked. "Your uniform?"

"Unh-unh. Sandy sent over a pair of his denims. I had to roll up the bottoms because he's two inches taller than me. And I wore a sport's shirt. The wear on the outside kind. It'd been warm all that day, so I didn't bring a jacket. I didn't know that at night it gets cold here. Not like in Hawaii where it's hot all the time."

"Back to the timeline," Alexander said.

"Yeah, okay. I met up with Sandy about six, after chow. I asked about you, Piper. I've heard so much about you from Mrs. Bauer. She bragged on you and Sandy, and I admit, I was jealous. It could have been us. I guarantee, you'd be popping out cygnets if you'd married me."

A man in despair talking about baby swans put a lump in her throat.

"The Bund appreciates such an enthusiastic approach to marriage and procreation, Mr. Swan," Alexander said. "What else did you talk about?"

"How he got into med school. I told him I'd heard about how hard the test was."

"From who?" Piper asked.

"The corpsmen at the dispensary at Pearl. As soon as I got there, I decided to do a little sight-seeing, and one of the sights gave me the clap that turned out to be thunderous applause."

Piper saw Alexander's shoulder shake with a silent chuckle.

"So, the next morning —when it hurt like hell to pee —begging your pardon, Piper —I went to the dispensary. I knew they'd give me a ration of shi ... grief … but I was in pain," Swan continued. "Anyway, as I'm waiting in hall line —which is always long after the week-end —I heard these guys talking in the office about how they flunked some test they'd taken. I remembered all the studying Sandy did, all the time reading textbooks. So, when one of the corpsmen came out and called my name —to shorten the line I guess they decided to do some work —I went inside and asked them what would have happened if they'd passed the test. One guy said, med school and jabbed me with a needle eight inches long. I'm not stupid, so I wrote Mrs. Bauer about it. The test part not the needle part. She probably heard me yell across the ocean."

"Go on about Sandy and the club," Alexander said.

"We drank two beers. We each bought a round. And then he said he'd have to make a short night of it because he had classes early in the morning. I got up to leave …and he said, wait take my coat because he didn't want me to relapse. I put on his pea coat and decided to take a whiz before walking back to the hospital housing. It's like a barracks only it's not. More like a brig if you ask me. It's a goodly hike. And when I came out of the head, he was still at the bar, talking to some gal. I walked past him, but he didn't notice, so I figure he was putting the make on her. I'm sorry Piper. It wasn't nothin' I'm sure." He sighed and sat back in his chair. "I don't think he was picking her up or anything. Honest, she was just a girl. If anything, she was probably coming onto Sandy. Maybe he knew her from the hospital …"

She patted his hand again. "It's okay, Cabot. That's what people do in bars, schmooze and booze. Right?"

"What time did you get back to your room?" Alexander said.

"Eight fifteen. I know because that's when I signed in."

"Was there anyone else in the house when you signed in?"

"Sure. The OD, a guy who was in quarantine with me, and two guys restricted to barracks for disorderly conduct. They were carping about how unfair it was because they were just resting, but it was bullshit. Sorry, Piper. But it was. The *Fuhrer* would never allow that kind of laziness. Orders are meant to be followed and if the order is you work, well, you work."

Alexander stopped taking notes and reached for Cabot's hand now. Piper saw a look come over his face that she hadn't seen since her Dad attended Josh's high school graduation. It wasn't love. It wasn't pride. It wasn't respect. It was, as Magda Goebbels put it, *Vaterehre*. "There's no English equivalent, but literally it means Father's Honor. As in Fatherland or ancestral honor," Gunderson explained. Magda's remarks had been published by the *Berliner Beobachter*, and they were the topic of Bund meeting to celebrate Hitler's birthday.

"You went straight back to the barracks after you left the bar? No detours, no side-trip to the hospital cafeteria for cigarettes, perhaps?" Alexander asked.

"Straight back. Check the sign-in sheet. I should be fourth on the list after chow."

"And you told this to the investigators?"

"At least five times."

"Then I'm filing for a *habeus corpus* hearing. They have to charge you or let your go." Alexander closed his notebook, stuffed it in his briefcase, and gave Piper a nod. "I've had enough of this nonsense. I'll give you a few minutes."

Before Alexander opened the door, Piper leaned over the table. "I'll make this fast, Cabot. They're censoring your mail. Stop writing Honnolore. I'll explain it to her. The government wants to know how you found out about the medics' program. Tell them names, dates, time. Just like you told me. Tell them everything you remember. That gets you off the hook with the Feds. You didn't know it was secret info. Got it?"

"I got it."

"The Bund is a different story." She took Beth's picture out of her purse. "Was this the woman with Sandy at the bar?"

"Yeah, that's her. You know her, right? Lizzy That's what the bartender called her. I heard him. That makes it okay, doesn't it?"

"For me, yes. But not for Sandy or the Bund. He was recruiting her without their permission and she's got to remain out of the case. If she gets involved, the San Diego Bund will be in big trouble. Don't tell anyone, not even the Bauers. Sandy took a big risk. It probably got him killed by the Communists because this Lizzie's related to a VIP. You never saw her before or after, can't identify her because it was too dark in the bar, and never heard her name. That's your story. No more blabbering. Got it?"

"I understand."

"That squares you with the Bund. I'm trying to help you Cabot. You tell the right things to the right people and you're out of here in forty-eight hours. Keep your mouth shut about Lizzy, and you'll be alive to tell your grandchildren about how you foiled the Commies. I'll keep in touch."

She stood, and looked at the window, then walked around the table and gave Cabot a kiss on the cheek. "I know you didn't kill Sandy. I never believed for a minute that you did," she said as she left. The SP had pulled open the door and was just about to say something but stopped when Piper gave him a grief-stricken smile. "He's innocent and I had to let him know I believe it."

"Yes, Ma'am, but the sign says no fraternization with the prisoners…"

"Thank-you for everything."

She called Captain Mike as soon as she got back to her hotel. The words *habeus corpus* were as magical as abracadabra, but it was the information about the medic's program that got Captain Mike to promise Cabot's release would take less than forty-eight hours. "Loose lips really do sink ships even unintentionally," he said.

"He's young and stupid when it comes to espionage, Mr. McKnight. I showed him a picture of Carla Watson and he identified her as the woman Sandy was sitting with. It's ridiculous. It was too dark for him to get a good look at anyone in the bar. But give me a week or two. I'm working on a theory about the man behind the trigger."

The bartender had called the woman Lizzie, but she was on the run, and everything she told him was probably a lie, Piper concluded. There was nothing to tie her Sacramento, and she probably disappeared the second she learned Sandy had been murdered. In any case, she'd leave it up to Alexander to worry about it. Like Jim said, the fewer the people and the less you know…people want to protect a young wife from the shame of a wayward husband. In this case, that agenda worked in her favor.

***

Morgues are kept cold for a reason, according to Sandy. "Cadavers don't thrive in hot, wet environments."

She'd laughed. "They're dead, Honey. They can't thrive

anymore anywhere."

"But the rest of us aren't going to like dealin' with them. I mean, there's dead and then there's ugly dead. The body gases expand until boom! The body explodes like an apple fritter. It's not a pretty sight and it smells like hell. Wonder what it must be like to be a morgue maître'd."

But Marin County didn't have a morgue. The coroner, J. Ray Keaton, did autopsies at the Keaton Funeral Home mostly. At least the building wasn't ugly. She wrapped her Christmas coat around her tightly, stupidly thinking Sandy might notice and know she still loved him. They had a commitment between them, even if the Winterhaven words meant little at the time.

"I'm Doctor Jordan. Mr. Keaton's assistant. This is routine for me, but this may be your first experience …"

"I saw my grandmother at her visitation."

He'd come out of a door to the left when the bell rang; he was a shortish guy with a bushy mustache Piper couldn't stop staring at. "Oh, this," he said as he twisted its handlebar ends, "I'm entering it in the County Fair moustache contest."

"Very distinguished."

"This won't be like a visitation. No mortician's make-up. He's not disfigured, if you don't look at his chest. A large caliber bullet leaves a big hole. By the looks of it, the shooter was close. Probably less than six inches away."

"How can you tell?"

"When the barrel is pressed next to the body, there no room for the gun residue to spatter; it goes into the clothing and into the body with the bullet. There's nothing but a star-shaped mark near the wound."

The hallway seemed endless when they passed through the double doors to the inner sanctum, but suddenly she was in a room empty except for a table with a sheet draped over a long, lumpy blob. Dr. Jordan took the end of the sheet and drew it up and away from the head, exposing Christopher Sanders' pasty flesh and blue lips.

All she could see was him smiling as he kissed her good-bye. "Hi, Sandy," she said. "It's me, Honey." Her fingertips found his cheek. "I just came to say good-bye again. For everybody. And to thank-you for all you did for me." She looked up at Jordan, the tear tracking down his face taking her by surprise. "Yes, it's my Sandy." She patted his once warm and comforting shoulder. "Bye, Honey. I love you, Dear."

She couldn't stop the tears no matter how hard she tried to keep them at bay. She slid an arm under Sandy's neck and bent over him to hold him close one last time. He was one of the first casualties of the war, she thought, and for the first time she truly understood why her parents went back for grandpa's funeral. She didn't remember signing on the for this part of the plan that afternoon in Winterhaven, but that 'till death do you part' clause had come to pass.

"Captain McKnight said to tell you Mr. Sanders' parents have requested burial in the family plot in Sacramento. It's your decision, of course. I have papers for you to sign," Dr. Jordan said softly.

They walked down the hallway and through the double doors again. I really should go back and ask Sandy what he wants, she almost said. "How long with the autopsy take?"

"I've a good head start. He should be ready by tomorrow morning."

She signed Mrs. Piper Sanders four times and took a cab back to the hotel. A Sacramento funeral meant another trip, but, to borrow Carole's term, it would be unseemly for her not to attend. How does a widow act? Wat does she say? She couldn't wear her green dress. Maybe Mrs. Stevens had something black at the closet boutique. Nonsense, she decided, she had a hundred and fifty dollars. She and Honnolore would go shopping, swollen, red-rimmed eyes and all.

"You can afford a widow's wardrobe now," Honnolore told her on the way to Dalton's Department Store. "Did you know the women of royal families always travel with one black ensemble just in case someone important dies while they're traveling?" It sounded dreadfully depressing, but practical.

She bought her first little black dress, another rite of passage to claim adult womanhood, for three dollars and forty-nine cents, including tax. The sales clerk escorted them into a private dressing room reserved for brides and widows, she explained, as soon as Honnolore disclosed the purpose of their shopping trip. A consultant entered the room soon after with a complimentary box of white thank-you notes embossed with black scroll work. "I'm Miss Lillian. These are for flowers —make sure you keep track of who sent what."

"Thank-you, send them out with our order," Honnolore instructed.

"We offer a selection of veils from netting to traditional lace, but today so few women wear full-length veils. May I suggest a three-quarter face veil? Something that covers the eyes, and a small black hat."

"We'll see that," Honnolore said. "That way, you won't have to fool with the veil when you kiss the casket," she said to Piper.

"Kiss the what?"

"In the church, you'll be the first to say good-bye. You go up to the casket and kiss it. It won't be an open casket, will it?"

"No."

"Good. You won't faint, but you'll be on display and the first to be led out of the church."

"I had no idea this would be so complicated." Piper whispered.

"You'll need black accessories too. You have black pumps, but gloves, purse and handkerchiefs?"

"Do I need all that stuff?"

Honnolore was direct. "Yes, you do. You don't want Sandy's parents to think he married beneath him. It was an elopement, after all. That black dress fits nicely. They can tell you're not pregnant. It will help if you tell his parents something like how sad you are that Sandy died before you could bear his child. Or something to that effect. Best to answer awkward questions before they're asked."

Honnolore was Old World old school. "When do I take off the

netting?"

"After graveside services, and you arrive at the reception. Tell his mother you need to freshen up."

Miss Lillian brought in a black linen suit and a white silk blouse, black slacks and a black and white polka-dot blouse. "Of course, you can wear a simple black arm-band with regular clothes, but you're going to want clothes for travel. Some things you can wear more than once. Will you be going by plane or train?"

"Plane. The Navy's arranging things for me. I don't think I need all these things, really."

Honnolore ignored her. "We'll take them all," she told the consultant. "That will see her through anything the Sanders have planned."

"Yes, Madame."

Piper expected the worst. The bill? "Twenty-three dollars' worth of fashion," Piper said as she showed her new wardrobe to Carole.

"You can donate whatever you don't want to the Y-boutique."

"After a year, maybe. I thought it was silly at first, but as usual, Honnolore is right. I need to be super-respectful around Sandy's parents. If it gives them comfort to see his wife traditionally grieving over him, then good. They'll never get over this. Never ever."

"Will you ever get over it?" Carole put hangars in the clothes and hung them in the closet. "I see Cecil brought back Sandy's duffle bag."

"This bag is Sandy's San Francisco's stuff. I can't open it. I miss him too much. I'm so screwed up. I never thought I'd feel like this in my life. Honnolore bought me a prayer book. I've never went to church back home. I feel like such a hypocrite every time I read from it. I keep thinking he'll call me and tell me it's another Navy SNAFU."

"Look at this way, Piper, his parents will believe he was happily married, however briefly. That will comfort them more than any prayer in the universe. You were a part of his future."

"You and Jim didn't elope Sunday." The first thing she checked was a ring on Carole's fourth finger.

"No. We're waiting until you get back from Sacramento. Jim insisted, so it's not all me. You're my maid of honor and that's that. Is Mitch going to Sacramento with you?"

One issue at a time, she reminded herself. "Cecil's flying up with me. He's buying a suit as we speak. He didn't want to go, but I said, okay, I'll get Mitch to escort me to your best-friend's funeral. That's all it took." Yes, that's all it took, and what she didn't tell Carole: Beth might be there.

***

Who can explain the purposes of God? How can we, imperfect beings, of His creation, understand the ineffable, know the unknowable? The answers are easy. No one, No, and no. What we can do is trust that His purposes are goodly. His design is perfection, and His ends are just as well as merciful. We lament the too-soon passing of Christopher Sanders, beloved son, honorable husband, promising medical student and proud serviceman, steadfast friend.

But, it wasn't too soon for God. His timetable is not ours. Only His comfort is promised to us, not the days and years of long life. Only His grace is delivered to us, not a miracle for each pain or trouble.

Christopher Sanders is in bliss. While we, properly so, mourn his absence, but never mourn his destination. He is conversing with the angels, recounting his love for us who remain here for only a fleeting time. We will meet him again, and there will be no more tears or partings, and no regrets.

They prayed. Our Father … and then it was time. Piper's wobbly legs couldn't carry her. Cecil held her arm, steadying her steps, whispering, "Lean on me," as they approached the cherry-stained pine box. She knew what was inside, remembered his cold, white skin, and an ache the size of the sea had taken up residence in that part of her reserved for the Hamptons and her yesterdays. She pressed her lips against the wood and embraced it as she would have embraced him. Her arms ached, and they could not be filled with memories of his kisses and his body pressed against hers.
In the future, women could bear the children of their deceased husbands, but not now. She was empty.
"My condolences, Mrs. Sanders, Reverend Alquist said softly, and Cecil guided her down the aisle to a waiting black limousine.

The driver opened the door for them; celebrities for the moment. She forced herself to breathe. Cecil wiped the sweat beads from his face. "We made it," he said.

"Was she there?"

"She's dyed her hair. Hiding from the cops, probably. I don't blame her."

"Are you okay, seeing her? You know she's alive at least." Piper took one of the three handkerchiefs Honnolore insisted she buy, out of her purse and patted her face. "This is the hardest thing I've ever done. I'll never forget it. My heart is like lead."

The driver opened the door and handed Cecil a white envelope. "One of the guests asked me to give this to Mrs. Sanders."

Piper couldn't force her hand to stop shaking. "Read it, Cecil. I can't."

He removed the lilac-colored paper, and read:

Chris loved me until there was you. You made him happy.

He told me so. You're all he talked about. Beth.

PS. Tell Cecil he looks swell in a suit. It's his first.

Chapter XVII

Everyone who sent flowers got a hand-written thank-you, including the Krasners and Mr. and Mrs. Alfred Blackledge who sent blood-red roses. As parents of a child murdered by 'the historic enemies of the Fatherland' they understood her pain, they said.

If the propaganda films coming out of Germany were any indication, it might be true. She couldn't believe what she was seeing. The violence on the streets were like America's inner cities on steroids … until Hitler came and saved them. Was it that chaotic before he came to power? Absolutely, Gunderson assured her. She was born after the Great War, but he had served in France. The Germans were utterly destroyed, he'd told her. No people could tolerate the dislocation and economic collapse of such a defeat for long, and there was no question the war continued for them within their borders. Only they were fighting the Bolsheviks for control of Germany's destiny. Fascism was Germany's answer to communism, misguided and oppressive as it was.

Even a good American like Gunderson could separate fact from fiction among the jumble of chaos.

She believed herself to be so smart, so capable of outwitting these yesterday folks with their funny fanaticism and fascination with their goofy *Fuhrer*. But she was wrong about so many things, about so many people. Alfred Blackledge didn't search for his daughter's killer among the Bund because he believed it was a political assassination by the other team. Telling him about Mitch, even presenting him with evidence, wouldn't persuade him a fellow believer would betray him or the cause. She was beginning to understand it the way she now understood that just because a guy has a conversation with a woman in a bar doesn't mean he doesn't love you.

"Mornings are hell," she said to herself as she made a pot of coffee for one and tried not to think about Sandy. As she waited to hear the gurgle-gurgle of the percolator, she caught herself swaying back and forth in her chair, and humming *Harbor Lights*. It would sound crazy to Josh and Shelly-the-girlfriend, but a guy who can dance and buys you a red coat really is a prize. She'd have to stop strolling down memory lane, however, if she was going to live out her Piper life and not the Mrs. Sanders-the-widow life.

She looked out the window before she answered the knock at the front door. If it was Mitch, she'd have him wait until she got dressed, but it was Jim. Her robe would do. "This is a surprise. But c'mon in and kick some sense into my stupid head. Somebody has to."

"Not what I expected from a grieving widow, but okay. Take a ride to the beach with me?"

"I'm picking up a 'Carole-doesn't-know-I'm-here' aura in that invitation."

"I just dropped her off at work, and no, she doesn't know I decided to check on you."

"A guy who works sixteen-hour shifts and overtime must have oodles of time to check up on a girl who threw away her memories in a duffle bag. Sounds right to me. Let me get dressed. There's coffee in the kitchen."

"Cecil called me. He stashed the duffle bag you gave him at the Y. If he'd put it at Seven Seas, it'd taken an act of Congress to get it back. People do nutty things when they're upset."

"Nutty things?"

"You reacted like any person would have who was slapped with a shock. He thought it better to wait until you were sure you wanted to get rid of the stuff, is all. Hell, you're Sandy's wife, you're entitled to be … okay, maybe nutty ain't the right word. Rash? How about passionate? He understands."

She hated being understood. It made her feel like a kid, the way understanding Margaret made her feel like an adult. How come she couldn't decide which she hated the least? The world was crazy.

Jim was strangely quiet as they sat in his car watching the morning mist hover over Ocean Beach. Piper thought at first it might be a guy thing, not knowing what to say to someone who just got back from a funeral. After all, it could have been him if it was discovered he had anything to do with the Maritime explosion. That realization might make a guy tongue-tied.

"How's Carole? Still single, I hear."

"I figured you'd think I was the biggest cad that ever walked the planet," he said without looking at her.

"Coward's more like it. On the other hand, if Sandy's death was political the way Alfred Blackledge believes it was, I'd be scared too. And I am."

"As long as Sandy's murder remains unsolved, all we can do is speculate," he said. "And wait."

"I know Carole wouldn't give into fear. Not when it comes to marriage."

They hadn't had a down to earth conversation in months. Piper hadn't seen the worry lines creasing his forehead, nor the changes physical labor had wrought on his body. The once-gawky security guard was now muscular, his face chiseled with manhood. He'd made foreman and his demeanor reflected the responsibility he carried. She should have realized that at the shooting range. Why didn't she pay attention?

"It ain't fear, it's reality knocking at the door. We love each other, Piper. So much, I can't believe how I feel. I can't make her a target, and that's what she is. You and me are the spies, but the people around us are sitting ducks. You ever consider that Sandy was killed because…never mind."

"Because of me?" The thought had crossed her mind a thousand times. During lonely hours, she'd retraced her steps with Sandy from the moment they said I do. She remembered how Carole told Jim everything without thinking of the consequences. Yes, some people weren't cut out to play dangerous games. What made her think she cold?

"Captain Mike tried to dissuade us," Jim reminded her. "Admiral Bailey tried to keep us out of it, but we were determined. Well, be careful of what you wish for. The game of life isn't a game."

It sounded like McKnight's bayside lunch speech. "I know the argument. You're too valuable now."

Jim fished a small tin box from his shirt pocket. "You know what's inside? Two cyanide capsules. I've had them since I made foreman because of what I've seen and heard. We're installing sonar equipment in ships destined for Russia, and somebody might want to know the schematic information for the Wolf Packs —German submarines. I can't let them make me give them top secret information."

"Holy shit, Jim, what happened to the less-I-know the less-I-can-tell speech! Tell them no and get out!" she demanded.

"Sure, and sell out the United States of America. Could you do that? What if helping to save America is why I'm here?"

"But … does Carole know?"

"She tried to stop us too. She gave up saving Suzanne. She planned a wedding. Planned a life. All the time knowing the Bund will end when America goes to war with Germany and the real spy game will begin. The Nazis will expect us to spy for them here or go to Berlin. They'll ask me to build boats for them or worse, blow ours up." He held the tin tightly. "My handler has instructed me to go, Piper, if and when the Party calls me to Berlin. I was contacted by the German mole. He's checking my racial purity and my commitment."

She threw her arms around his neck. "No, no. don't leave me. You can't. You can't leave Carole. It's too much for Captain Mike to ask. Doesn't he care about his own daughter's happiness?"

"Captain Mike isn't my handler." Jim patted her like a baby. "I work for the OSS. Who knew I'd become such a good welder, huh?"

"Damn them all!" She let go and opened the car door, sucking the sea air into her lungs. "I hate this life. It's sad and dirty and deadly … What if you and Carole got married and disappeared? You could wait out the war in Montana or Canada like the Vietnam resisters did."

"Would you do that?"

"You're damn right I *will* do that. Beth Beatty disappeared. Carla Watson disappeared. Why not Piper Hampton. I've done it once already. And not by choice."

Jim put away the tin box and started the car. "Okay, I'll take you home and help you. I don't know who Beth and Carla are, so they must have done bang-up disappearing jobs. Let's go."

"What?" She closed the car door, and Jim backed the car out slowly.

"I'm helping you get out of this mess even if I can't … or won't."

"No, wait." He stopped. "I can't leave Carole alone with you risking your life every day."

"She's gonna do her part. She's gonna keep working at the newspaper and feeding the likes of Mitch Robert's exactly what the navy wants her to. Maybe she can figure out who killed Edwina and Sandy. Mitch ain't going to Germany, that's for sure. He's too valuable here. Sort of like you."

Piper went into her thoughts, surmising that Jim was on a mission. He was playing her, but why? Because Captain Mike didn't want to tackle the mission himself. "Okay, out with it."

"Nothing."

"Like hell."

"Okay, Piper. What are you going to do when the Bund is declared illegal and goes underground? Will you spy for the Fatherland? Because that's what they're going to ask you to do. You married a Hospital Medic 2nd Class, why not a HM Chief? Better yet, engage in a little pillow talk with a Captain or an Admiral and pass along the information to the Bauers."

"No friggin' way. I'll do a lot to save my cover, but not trade sex for information for either side."

"Never? What if Captain Mike asks you to do for ONI what you did for Mr. Goldstein. Because that's what your country is going to ask you to do. Men trust you. Honnolore's already made you a regular Teutonic heroine." He started the car again. "But, I don't blame you. If you'd rather avoid a fate of wining and dining Nazi traitors and giving Uncle Sam the info, you'd better run."

They drove through the marshland that was San Diego pre-Mission Bay Park, and through Old Town when it was nothing more than an old town. It felt like a Disney Yesterland exhibit in winter to Piper. Lonely. House after house bore the stigma of hopelessness: signs reading foreclosure, bank auction, estate sale. Pennies on the dollar plus taxes, Cecil had said. She jotted down the phone numbers of agents. If she was to court the True Believers, she couldn't do it out of a one-bedroom bungalow. Maybe she couldn't get in on the ground floor of Mission Hills, but she might could raise enough money to buy into Hillcrest or Kensington.

"You've convinced the Bund you're a true follower, now be a true leader. Mitch is her prized fixer, but Cabot Swan has the key to Honnolore's heart, and you saved him. Captain Mike said Alexander didn't have to file any papers, you know."

"No, I didn't know."

"He didn't have time. You got all the glory for saving Swan from a bogus murder rap and saved the Bund a bunch of time, money and bad press in the process. You can't beat that for street cred if you have to impress a crowd."

He sounded like Josh's football coach when the Hoover High Cardinals lost their third game in a row. Half pep talk, half reminder they needed practice, and both messages delivered with a slight edge to let them know who was in charge. Maybe this was Captain Mike's new MO. When there were crummy orders to relate, pull out Big Gun Jim Crenshaw to handle the little lady. A lot they knew. All she had to do to impress the Bund was be herself.

***

She didn't wear her veil to the Bund reception on Thursday, but her little black dress was freshly dry-cleaned and unadorned except for the red, white and black swastika arm band on her right sleeve. On Gunderson's advice, she prepared a few remarks of thanks for everyone's support, and paid tribute to Sandy by recounting his loyalty to the *Fuhrer*. By way of closing, she plagiarized ideas from the best;

We are only promised comfort and grace, not miracles for every pain and problem, but you've all made it easier for me and I thank you from the bottom of my soul. Heil Hitler!

"Well, you wowed them again," Mitch said as he walked her to her car. "The Krasner's wrote two checks this time. One for you. Watch your mailbox. Oh, Honnolore told the Krasners you work at the theater downtown, and they're looking for another job for you. Can you type?"

"No steno pool for me. But they don't have to do that. The Navy picked up the tab for the funeral and I'll get my allotment next month." She took his arm.

"Never turn down opportunity."

"Okay. I could be a desk clerk. Or a bookkeeper. I keep track of money very well."

He slipped her a white envelope. "I was waiting for an opportune moment. Susan Beaman dropped her bundle of joy when you were in Sacramento. A boy. Healthy and living in Missouri. She's on her way home to Oregon."

"And Margaret?"

"Any day now. Sister Rita's had to double up. She's got five girls this go'round. It always gets busy in the Spring." He gave her a wink. "When the sap rises."

"I'll be able to start that women's group. Tell Honnolore I'd like to meet with her when she has time and strategize."

He took her hand. "She'll be pleased. She thinks of you as a daughter."

When they reached the car, Mitch opened the door for her. Her eyes lingered on his for a few seconds, then lowered them as she spoke. "Sandy was a good guy, Mitch. I didn't know what to do, and Honnolore helped me do things right. I'm grateful to you, too. Just when I though you couldn't be a better friend, you stepped up."

She gave him a gentle kiss on the cheek and got behind the wheel. He closed the door, mumbled something unintelligible, and waked slowly back to the house. Genuine as her gratitude was, she was happier by far to know Honnolore had seen a PDA directed at her golden boy. The biggest favor Honnolore did for her was teach her she was always on display.

***

Mr. Talbott reminded Piper of her high school math teacher. His big black-rimmed glass made him look like an owl, and he combed his thinning hair straight back. His lips were annoyingly odd, permanently pouty like a fish always ready to kiss.

"We like to settle death claims as soon as possible, Mrs. Sanders. We at We at Mutual All-risk know how anxious people are about their finances during times of grief." As he spoke, he was unsnapping a red leather attaché case and removing a file. "I'd rather be speaking to your lawyer or a male relative, of course, but I understand you have neither."

"I didn't even know my husband had life insurance, Mr. Talbott. How did you know he'd died?"

She examined his business card again, so she wouldn't have to watch his lips move. He'd called early, nine o'clock. Insisting on an appointment ASAP so he could get back to the home office in L.A. on the noon train.

"He registered the policy with the Navy." Talbott handed her a copy of the policy attached to her marriage certificate, and a death certificate signed by Dr. Jordan. "Most husbands conduct the financial aspects of marriage. Mr. Sanders wanted to make sure you were taken care of in case of … and that case is now. Now, you'll notice this policy has a double indemnity clause for deaths related to unforeseen circumstances. Murder certainly qualifies. Our capital sum payout is a hundred thousand dollars. Properly invested —and we can help you with that later —you should be able to live comfortably for the rest of your life."

Behind the death certificate was the coroner's report, and a letter attesting to the accidental nature of Sandy's demise. RE: Requested Autopsy: completed, Dr. Jordan wrote in the first paragraph.

"I don't understand. Your company requested an autopsy?"

"Yes, we received the inquest results. It's stapled to the report, but you understand, we had to rule out suicide before we pay out such a considerable sum. You'd be surprised how many people try to bilk the company in times like these. Men get desperate."

She put the papers on the coffee table, making sure they were in a neat pile. "Did you see the pictures, too? The hole in his chest?"

Talbott's lips transformed from fish mouth to bird beak. "He could have ingested poison and made it look like a murder by having someone shoot him after he was dead," he said coldly. "I've seen it before, and you only had the word of your friend that you were together on the night of Mr. Sanders' death. I understand you failed to show up at a meeting of some sort."

She rose from Sandy's study chair and stared at him. "Is Mutual All-risk satisfied now?"

"I have your check right here." He offered it to her, but she pointed to the table.

"Leave it and get out."

"Mrs. Sanders, I didn't mean to suggest that you … or be rude but …"

"Because of you, my Sandy was carved up like a Thanksgiving turkey. Maimed. Disrespected."

"They did a magnificent job of restoration. You could have had an open casket … I'll need you to sign for the check," he said meekly.

He put a release form and a pen on the table and stared at the case on his lap. She picked up the pen, bent over and scribbled her signature. He put everything in the file folder, stuffed it in his case, and snapped it shut. "The policy is probably among his papers, but I'll mail you a copy of everything we have. Good morning, Mrs. Sanders."

He'd only been in her house fifteen minutes at most, and suddenly, she was wealthy.

She dressed and went to Central Savings Bank. "Do you handle foreclosures?" was her first question after depositing the check in her savings account that paid zero interest but did include a free safe deposit box. Mitch's payment brought her 'cash stash' to four-fifty.

Blood money, she thought as she stacked three hundred of it in the tray. It was her down payment on a baby. More importantly, it was proof Mitch knew Sandy was dead before the Shore Patrol told her. It could have been a twinge of conscience, but it was a mistake. Did he suspect she caught it, or had he convinced himself she was too blinded by greed to notice?

Chapter XVIII

"Mrs. Sanders? This is Susan Beaman from the Grove. Do you remember me?"

Piper was fully awake now. She looked at the wall clock. Eight-thirty. "Of course, I remember. Are you alright?"

"Yes, Ma'am. I'm oaky. Margaret asked me to call you. She got your number from Sister Rita's desk. Please don't tell."

"Don't worry about that. What's going on? Are you calling from Oregon?"

"Unh-unh. I'm at the Santa Fe station. Mitch just left, but Margaret said I could change my ticket for a later train so … "

Mitch had lied again. "Go to the snack-bar and wait for me. I'll be right there. Do you understand?"

"Yes, Ma'am. I'll wait."

Her heart was racing. She knew Margaret would be the one to give her the break she was waiting for. She just wasn't sure when. In fifteen minutes, she'd showered, brushed her teeth, thrown on her black slacks, the polka-dot blouse, her black blazer, and her penny loafers, grabbed her keys and was headed downtown. Don't speed, she kept telling herself, you don't need a cop asking questions.

Susan was waiting at the snack-bar looking like a squatter in a faded blue cotton dress and pale as white ash. She caught sight of Piper and waved.

"C'mon, let's go to Bernie's. I need breakfast," Piper said.

"My train leaves at ten," Susan said. "It's nine already."

"Cash in that ticket. I'll buy your another."

At the counter, the clerk handed Susan fifteen dollars, and ten minutes later she and Piper were sitting at the back booth at San Diego's premier greasy spoon. Susan was chowing down a grilled cheese sandwich and Piper was gobbling eggs and bacon.

"What does Margaret need?"

"You're the home inspector, right?" Susan said.

"That's right. If there's anything wrong out there, I'm the person to tell. I'll set it right." It was almost true.

"Margaret said she's changed her mind about being fixed, and could you make sure it doesn't happen?"

"I'll see her first thing in the morning. I promise. Is there anything else you want to tell me?"

Susan took a sip of her soda. "We … me and Margaret, are sorry about your husband. Margaret saw the article in the paper. She's the only one who goes to the Outpost —you know, out in public. She overheard Sister Rita telling Maria that you probably won't need Constance to come clean for you, too. It's awful to lose someone you love. Especially that way."

Piper saw sorrow in her eyes. "It's downright hell, isn't it, Susan?"

"Yes, Ma'am, it is."

"Did Margaret say if she overheard anything else, or saw anything else in the paper?"

"Like what, Ma'am?" Susan said warily.

"Like about Carla Watson."

She saw Susan swallow hard and look over her shoulder. "Margaret said she's dead. That's why she changed her mind. She doesn't want to go under the gas. Especially after what Gina told her."

"Gina?"

"One of the new girls. See, Gina's speaks Spanish on account of she's from Texas too … like Carla. She's white, but anyways Gina never told Sister Rita that she understands everything Maria and Enrique talks about. Like how they told her Dr. Chartman was upset 'cause he had to do a C-section on Carla. Whatever that is."

"It's when the doctor has to remove the baby from the tummy. It's usually done in emergencies."

"Oh, yeah. I heard about that. Is that what it's called?"

"Yep."

"Huh. Well, anyways, Gina says that Chartman is what she called a native speaker. Even though he's Anglo, he's not an American. Anglos are what Mexicans call all white people." She hesitated. "But Chartman schedules all the births so there aren't any emergencies. Sister Rita told me he gives you a drug that makes you go into labor when it's time. As soon as I got to his office, he gave me a shot and I went right into labor. It was horrible! I'll never have another baby as long as I live."

"Would you girls like some dessert?" Candi, the waitress with the big name tag, asked them.

"Just pie and ice cream for me, please," Susan said. "Apple if you have it."

"I'll pass," Piper said, "but I'd like a coffee." With an appetite like a rescued castaway, Susan would soon recover, Piper decided. "What happened after you had the baby? Where did Maria take you?"

"She wasn't there. Maria dropped me off at Chartman's and Constance and Maria's brother, Federico, took over. Constance stayed with me, and then they took me to the Knickerbocker Hotel. I stayed two days. Constance brought me meals and then she said Federico would take me to the train station. Except, when he came, I was sick. Chartman came to the hotel and said I should stay another two days."

"But Mitch took you to the station this morning."

"Constance and Federico said they wouldn't take care of me no more. Mitch stepped in. He made sure I ate and took the pills Chartman left for me."

"Good ol' Mitch." Things started to fall into place. Abandoned and without proper care, Carla probably died of infection. Probably in the hotel room. The thought of what Carla must have endured alone made Piper ill. Hopefully, she was dead before they tossed her into the bay. Constance and Federico could have told Mitch she died of a stroke, and didn't want an instant replay with Susan, no doubt. But, surely, the coroner would have known Carla had delivered a baby. Did he not wonder what happened to it? Then again, the police would hold back pertinent details.

"Will you write to me when you get home? I want to know you made it back safe. Promise me you'll go straight to a hospital if you feel the slightest bit sick. Did Mitch give you any money?"

"He bought my ticket and gave me five dollars to eat on the trip."

Twenty dollars for a baby. His profit margin was phenomenal. She gave Susan twenty dollars. "Use this for cab fare if you need care, and have the hospital call me. You have my number at home, and here's my work number. She wrote BE-4-7154 on a napkin.

Susan folded the money into the napkin. "You're giving me all this money. Why?"

"It's a gift from the Stevens-Goldstein-Sanders Foundation. Now, tell me your plans when you get home."

They weren't big plans, like Margaret's. Susan wanted to finish high school and work with the local veterinary to take care of farm animals because she wasn't smart enough to be real nurse. She wanted to perm her hair. Someday have a car like Piper's.

"We don't have time to shop now, but you can't travel in that rag. You have a lay-over in L.A.? Use part of the twenty to buy yourself a few clothes."

In the ladies' room, Piper put just a hint of blush on Susan's pale cheeks and combed her hair the way she knew Honnolore would have done. "You're such a pretty girl. Take care of yourself." She was Honnolore, now, giving Susan a crash course in life survival. How to get respect from the people around you? Look like a traveler, not a victim of a mistake only you are paying for. Don't talk to strangers. Don't let a man sweet-talk you into going anywhere. Use a condom.

"What's that?"

"A man's disease protection. A poor woman's birth control. Get a diaphragm, Sue."

"Only married women can get those things."

"Bullshit. Send me your address, and I'll mail you one."

"I'm going to save some of this money for a stamp!" Susan said with a smile. The first Piper had ever seen her wear.

Yes, it all came down to money and connections. Rich people paid for babies and had Navy friends with airplanes to fly you to Sacramento. She bought Susan a private compartment, so she could sleep in a bed, and order as much apple pie as she wanted from a steward who would bring coffee to her with a silver pot, and say, "Yes, Miss."

At noon Susan was on the train to Salem, Oregon, and waved Piper a good-bye. She might even enjoy the trip with forty-five dollars in her purse. In Piper's heart was her thank-you and a promise she'd take care of herself.

***

Piper noticed the guy in the beige linen suit because he was one of ten people who walked to the Coastal when the "all Aboard" sounded over the PA system. She thought he was a passenger, but he returned to the station as she did. Was he expecting someone who didn't show? Yet, he was watching her as she walked down the center aisle and turned left to the side exit to "A" Street. By the time she reached the door, he was at her side. She stopped, and turned to go back to the waiting room, and heard a thickly accented voice say,

"Just keep moving, *Senorita*. Outside," as something prodded her ribs.

He wouldn't kill her in public She could use her purse as a weapon. Her hand went to her left arm and gripped the strap. "Don't try it," he whispered. She felt his arm embrace her shoulder and steer her toward the door. "Where's your car?"

"Half a block up the street." She smelled strong cologne. Was he after her cell phone?

"Walk," he commanded.

The lunch hour was over, and the sidewalks were deserted. Make up your mind, she told herself. He's going to kill you. She wanted to scream, but her throat was dry. Was this the way Sandy was killed? Adrenalin was flooding her heart; she could hear it galloping in her chest. Make up your mind. It's him or you. The words echoed loudly in her ears.

For an instant, she was at Ocean Beach with Jim crouching next to the car, dizzy, and seeing white sparklers. If she fainted, maybe he'd run away. No, he'd put her in the car and put a hole in her chest. The cops would find her like they found Sandy. Unarmed, there was little he could do to defend himself.

Make up your mind. It's him or you and the car is three feet away. Make up your mind to live instead of him. You have to live. For Sandy, for Jim, for Uncle Sam. Every ounce of courage she could muster went straight to her hand.

"Get in," he ordered as he opened the passenger-side door. "Slide over. You drive. We're gonna to take ride."

She put her purse in her lap and opened it. Beside her keys was her Baretta. She wrapped her hand around the grip, and as the man sat down and brought his feet inside, pulling the door closed, she pointed the gun at his chest and fired two shots. His body convulsed twice. He turned his head and looked at her, his eyes wide with surprise. She fired again, this time with the barrel pressed against his suit. He fell against the door, then slumped forward. She heard his gun hit the floorboard with a thud. She grabbed a handkerchief from her purse, snatched up the gun by the barrel before he could recover it … if he was still able … and threw it on the backseat floor.

She was panting, her brain in overdrive. The police station was three blocks away. The Trib and Carole, five blocks. But, reporting the attack meant questions about who and why? She didn't want to involve Susan or Margaret, but the cops would demand explanations. If she was arrested, they'd search her purse and find her phone. A stranger had tried to kill her. Because she was a spy? They'd never believe it. And they wouldn't believe she didn't know him. If she called Captain Mike or Gunderson, one way or another, the cops would get involved. Only she would pay a price for the son-of-a-bitch's mistake, either in jail or a mental ward. Her cover with the Bund would be blown. Like the girls at the Grove, she'd be a prisoner of circumstance.

She put her gun back in her purse, started the car, and drove East into San Diego's back country. She couldn't look at him, but she wasn't afraid either. She'd seen Sandy. Touched his skin. Understood, he was no longer in the shell we know as the body. So, why were tears wetting her cheeks? She was afraid —but only because she realized how alone she was. She'd have to cope all on her own.

DESCANSO TEN MILES. She took the off ramp to the right, but instead or turning right, she turned left and then left again, doubling back to an on-ramp and the access road that went under the highway, hidden from view by trees and foliage. She rolled to a stop. Purse in hand, she went to the passenger side and opened the car door. Gingerly at first, and then determinedly, she searched his right-side pockets. Car keys, three extra bullets, some change, a folded note she'd read later, and wallet and a train ticket from his inside breast pocket. She put them in her purse. She went to the driver's side, got in the car and closed the door. After searching the left -side pockets, which yielded a money clip —she'd count the money later —a pack of Juicy Fruit gum, and a condom. She stashed them in her purse too, braced herself against the door, and used both feet to push him out of the car.

He fell to the ground, but his legs were still inside. She started the car, and let it move in idle. His body weight pulled them free. She stopped the car again and got her camera from the back seat. She'd need photographs when and if the time came to present evidence. She took five pictures, one from each viewpoint like Dr. Jordan had taken of Sandy and displayed on the wall board in the morgue.

Much as she wanted to drive home and shower, she knew she couldn't drive around in a crime scene for long. The three slugs she plugged into her would-be killer had gone through his body and lodged in the right door panel. It was like being surveilled by a three-eyed Cheshire Cat. Luckily, there was no blood splatter, but there was still a pool of blood on the front and backseat floorboards that would have to be removed. But what would absorb it? Kitty litter. Shredded newspaper. Sand. She'd have to go home and change clothes for a cleaning job.

She put on a pair of Sandy's old bellbottoms she cut for shorts, pulled on one of his old tee-shirts, and found her sandals. She found a half a can of motor oil under the sink, and blanket, hat, and saucepan in hand, she headed to the beach. There'd be a small crowd at the beaches on a Saturday afternoon, but even if someone noticed her bringing a few pot-fulls of sand to her car, she'd tell them the truth, "I spilled motor oil on the floorboards."

No one would offer to help clean up a spill, but they wouldn't be suspicious when she dumped pails of dirty sand into the trashcans, either … all three of them as she stopped at different beaches up the coast. By sunset, the goo was gone. There was a stain, and there were three holes in the door where she'd dug out the cartridges with a screw driver, but a good scrub with lye soap and a lot of elbow grease had all but erased the blood evidence.

By eight o-clock, she was showered, drinking tea, and staring at Hector Garza's personal effects spread out on her dinette table, exhausted but unconcerned when she heard the news of an unidentified male body discovered under a bridge off Highway 8 East. "Give me time, I'll tell you who he is," she said over her shoulder to the radio.

Think of keys. Puzzle pieces. Diaries. An unwritten memoir, not booty from a dead man. If it was her laying in a sheltered ravine, she'd have her belongings and nothing else. Carla Watson had floated up from the bottom of the bay, the newspaper reported, despite snow chains wrapped around her ankles. No one mourned her at a graveside service. Yet, her ascension may have been her spirit's way of reminding the world she had lived, and deserved justice. These objects before her had never lived. There was no reason to fear them.

Garza's gun was first. She'd retrieved it from the floorboard the way she'd see it done on TV, lifting it by the barrel with a pen, grasping it with her black handkerchief, and laying it on a newspaper page, before carefully folding the paper and carrying it into the house the moment she'd gotten home. She'd wrapped it in a cotton kitchen towel and stashed it under her sink for safe keeping, but where to hide it now? She got Sandy's leather shaving kit from his San Francisco suitcase, emptied it and placed the gun inside, then put it in the bottom drawer of her dresser under her bed linens.

What was the last story she read in English Lit? *The Portrait of Dorian Grey*. He never would have gone crazy if he'd never looked at the picture hidden in the attic. She'd store all of Garza's property in her safe deposit box.

She inspected his keys next. He had a car key, a house key, and what looked like a locker key that bore an imprint of the number twenty-eight. She took that key off the ring, and added it to hers —

if anyone asked, it was the key she'd used at summer camp in fifth grade —and put the others in the kit. She put the fifty-two cents in change in her coin purse, and the condom and the gum in the trash. The bullets went into the kit.

The money clip was next. She removed the thirty-six dollars and the clip went into the kit.

The note read 8:30 AM, confirming that Susan was his target, and she added it to the kit. That left the wallet —one of those long slim ones men carried. This time she removed the driver's licenses she'd glanced at before. One was issued in Sonora, Mexico, and the other in California. Neither bore a photo. The address on the California license showed a L.A. address —El Segundo Boulevard. No surprise there. Mitch didn't include Hector in his list of who got a cut from the baby-selling business. Was he someone Mitch didn't know? Maybe it was supposed to be a one-time shot at the Bund's hundred grand and Edwina was a casualty of a heist gone wrong.

Still, Susan was his real target. He must have been really pissed off when his plan to dispose of her in had been derailed. He must have seen her and Susan talking, overheard Susan utter the words Carla and murder to a woman in black, and realized she was no longer a Miss Nobody that no one knew or cared about. I just got in the way, Piper thought. Mr. Garza probably didn't even know who I am. All he knew was that she could identify Susan, and would be suspicious if she didn't keep her promise to contact her when she got home. One thing for sure, Hector wasn't much of a pro if a girl like her could take him out.

She felt paper in in the opposite flap and pulled out two twenties and two tickets with receipts stapled to them. For reimbursement maybe. The first was a round-trip ticket from L.A. to San Diego, dated for the twenty-second, six am. The second made her dizzy: a round-trip airline ticket from L.A. to San Francisco dated for April thirteenth, the day Sandy was killed, returning April fourteenth. She returned the tickets and licenses to the wallet and put it into the kit.

The ticket wasn't a confession, but it was as close as circumstantial evidence gets to being a confession. Even if she hadn't given Sandy and Carla justice, she'd at least saved Susan's life. Maybe Margaret's too. She called the YMCA and left a message for Cecil to call her.

"You owe me a favor," she told him. "Here's what I need you to do."

***

As far as anyone at the Grove knew, Piper was making a courtesy call. Now that her husband had passed, she wouldn't be needing a housekeeper, and she wanted to thank Sister Rita for her trouble in person, and she'd like to see Margaret too. "I thought I'd take her to the Outpost and get her a few things for her trip home. I'm meeting with Honnolore in a few days, and I think giving the girls a hand in returning to society would be a wonderful project for my new women's group. Your work is too valuable to continue without more assistance."

"Then you're going ahead with it? Under the circumstances we thought … But we should have known you're not one to wither on the vine. What a generous idea!" Sister Rita said, and rang her little bell. "Gina, this is Mrs. Sanders. Get Margaret, will you?"

Gina gave Piper a polite curtsy and hurried off. Margaret was in the parlor before Sister Rita could finish another sentence.

"I'll have her back in time for lunch," Piper said as she waved from the car window and drove out the circular driveway.

"You talked to Susan?" Margaret said as soon as she turned onto the road.

"She called me yesterday morning. She'll call me as soon as she gets home."

"I saw Carla's picture in the newspaper. She's dead."

Piper nodded. "I saw it too. Where did you get the paper, from the Outpost?"

"Yeah. They killed her. I know it."

"They who?" Piper stopped the car by the side of the road halfway to the store.

"Dr. Chartman, and whoever he's working with."

"I don't think Carla's death was intentional. She had problems and they didn't take her to a hospital. But, that doesn't mean they didn't commit a crime. If what Gina says is true, Chartman is probably in the country illegally. But there's no doubt someone deliberately dumped her body, and they believe you and Susan might identify her. The cops would investigate the Grove."

Margaret gripped her arm. "I don't want to wind up like Carla! Can you help me, Mrs. Sanders?"

Piper patted her hand. Margaret let go of her arm but left a red patch of skin behind. "Keep calm. One issue at a time. Try and remember. Did Sister Rita say anything about Carla's picture being in the paper?"

"Not to any of us girls, as far as I know. But, she's not real big on reading English newspapers. All she reads are translations of the German papers. But Mitch may have told her. Somebody called her, and she got really upset. She called Maria into her office and closed the door. I couldn't hear what they said, but I could hear voices."

"Tell me about the day you saw the paper. Who took you to the Outpost?"

"Enrique."

"Did he see you reading the newspaper?"

"I don't know. I saw it in the bathroom when I went to take a pee. Ol' man Figgs saw me go into the restroom. He had a paper, too, at the counter and was talking to Enrique about the article, I'm sure…"

"Okay. Let me tell you how this is going to go down." She drove to the Outpost and parked across the road. "You see that guy sitting in the blue Chevy? That's my friend Cecil. He's going to buy a soda, and when he leaves, we're going inside and shop. You get whatever you need for your trip. A little overnight case, soap, shampoo … toothpaste. Whatever you'll need on the train and pack the bag on the way back. When we get to the Grove Cecil is going to pretend he's the baby's father, come to marry you. His mother's thrilled and waiting in Fresno. You pick up your bag and leave with him. He'll take you to the "YW" where a lady, Mrs. Stevens, is waiting for you. She'll take you to the Salvation Army in the morning. Got it?"

"Yeah. I guess, but what about the adoption? What about the money Mitch promised me? I can't go home broke …"

"Don't worry, the baby will still be adopted." She handed Margaret Hector's thirty-six dollars. "Keep this in your purse. When it's time for you to leave, you'll have your money. You just play the scene with Cecil, Lauren Michaels. It's the role of your life."

***

Sister Rita reeled into the parlor and plopped into her chair. "Is it possible Margaret has been communicating with the baby's father all this time?" she asked Piper.

Piper let out an audible 'phew!' and eased no to the sofa. "I had no idea romance and joy could be so boisterous! Margaret acted like she was being rescued from a fate worse than death. She must have been writing to him … did she ever make a long-distance phone call?"

"Not that I know. But if a man is willing to make an honest woman out a fallen maiden, who are we to interfere?"

Piper lowered her eyes and counted five. "God be praised."

Gina stood in the hallway, peeking around the doorway at the two seemingly overwhelmed women. "Would you like some tea?"

"Oh yes and a spot of sherry, I think, Mrs. Sanders. What do you say?"

"I say, amen."

Sister Rita unlocked a cabinet next to the fireplace and brought out a bottle of sherry and two small glasses. She sat on the sofa next to Piper and poured them each a glass. "Let's toast the happy couple. Margaret wanted to be a movie star, you know. She never would have made it. The girl couldn't act her way out of a paper bag. Too sullen. Too self-absorbed to notice anything going on around her. I think she'll be happier as a wife and mother."

"To Margaret and Tom," Piper said, as she lifted her glass. They gulped down their first glass and sipped at the second. "This is very good sherry," Piper said.

Gina rolled in the tea cart and gave Piper a smile. "I have scones in the kitchen."

"I'll get them, Sister. You sit here and relax," Piper followed Gina into the kitchen, and stacked three of the globs on a plate.

"You don't have to worry about Sister Rita. She always takes a nap after her afternoon sherries," Gina whispered with a giggle. Margaret never mentioned that.

"All I know for sure is that Margaret wanted to leave the Grove, and, if Carla was murdered, I want to find whoever did it. Our *Fuhrer* doesn't take kindly to killing German women."

"I hope Margaret will be happy with Tom, but she won't. I think she made a big deal out of nothing. She's into drama. Me? I've never had it so good."

One girl's prison is another's refuge.

***

The Salvation Army's Door of Hope had been around since 1931, and like the YWCA, could always find room for emergency cases like Margaret. Most girls don't come with sponsors, Piper was told when she handed over a hundred-dollar donation to cover costs when she signed her in.

"Do you know the name of the father?" Major Victoria Jones asked Margaret as she filled out the admission and consent forms. "For the birth certificate." Jones explained.

"I'm giving the baby up for adoption," Margaret answered.

"There still has to be a birth certificate. State law. And the adoptive parents will want to know the baby's origins, name, date and time of birth."

Margaret complied but told Piper as they sat in her new bedroom that it was weird.

"You never gave Sister Rita any information like that?" Piper asked.

"Nope. The new parents fill out the birth certificate, Mitch said."

"You have Maj. Jones call me when it's time, and I'll come, if you want me to. When it's time for you to leave, I'll have your money for you. I'll take you to the train station, too. What will you name the baby?"

"Sandy," came the quick reply. "It fits a boy or a girl. I hope you don't care."

"That's nice," Piper managed to say without a tremble. She was getting used to curve balls.

"Your friend, Cecil? He did a good acting job." Margaret said wistfully. "He almost had me believing he wanted us."

It was the first time Margaret referred to her baby as part of an us. "He's good guy. My husband's best friend. The good ones are out there." She could see Margaret selling tickets for Mr. Marvin. She loved movies the way Cecil loved art. "You're safe here. Think about your future."

It was as true for her as it was for Margaret, she thought as she drove to her bungalow. She had the time and the money to do whatever she wanted —except go home. That's when the tears started. If she could go back in time again, she'd save her Sandy.

Chapter XIX

Nothing more was printed in the morning paper about the Juan Doe found at the Descanso exit. Like Carla, his fifteen minutes of public notice —you couldn't call it fame —lasted about five, the length of time it took to read the story on page A-8. First thing Monday morning, Piper went to the bank and transferred the contents of the shaving kit into her safe deposit box, bought a tea cart at the used furniture store, and called Gunderson's garage.

"Call me stupid, but I thought the darn thing would fit in my front seat. I ripped the hell out of the front door panel. Do you know where I can get it fixed?"

"I know of a place where they'll reupholster the whole car for seventy-five dollars. What color?"

"White soft leather."

"You got it. You need a loaner?'

"I'll drive Sandy's Chevy. I can drop the car off if I can get me a ride home."

"Naw, I'll have Sandoval's pick it up. I'll call 'em now."

"How long will it take, do you think?"

"A week, maybe. You goin' back to work?"

"Friday, if I can stand the boredom until then. I'm meeting with Honnolore sometime this week. I hate sitting around all day. Too much time to think." Said no one ever. But she meant it. She wouldn't feel safe until those bullet holes in the door panel were covered up.

"Try to think positive," was Gunderson's advice.

Not that she could tell anyone now, but she believed she'd solved Edwina Blackledge's murder by committing one of her own. She had to dump all her assumptions about Mitch, and it was tough going, but once she did, it wasn't all that difficult to figure out.

As she pieced it together, Mitch did take Edwina to the Grove for her inspection after picking her up in Yuma. He took her to Knickerbocker Hotel, too, but for an inspection of the temporary lodging provided for the girls before they went home. They certainly couldn't stay at the "YW" and the Bund couldn't afford A-1 hotel rooms. He never said she registered there as a guest.

He also took her to the Bauers where she picked up the money, but what happened to it? That had her stymied until the day Honnolore took her to buy her widow's wardrobe. "You really shouldn't carry cash to San Francisco, Piper. Traveler's checks are safer," she said.

"What are those?"

"Pre-paid, like money orders. Only they're replaced if they're lost or stolen because the bank verifies your signature when you buy them."

She remembered how uneasy she felt until the Mutual All-Risk Insurance check was in the bank. If Edwina was a courier for undeclared money, she'd know how to carry money safely without a paper trail. Central Savings Bank sold Traveler's Checks, and, she discovered, the A-1 hotels did too. And, if she did buy them at the hotel here first night in San Diego, Hector, Mitch, Maria and

Enrique wouldn't have known. After she was dead, whoever killed her must have been sorely disappointed.

As for Edwina's trip to Chartman's, all Mitch said was she had a problem. They both believed that problem was a pregnancy, but maybe it wasn't. Maybe Edwina wanted to inspect Chartman's clinic. Perhaps word got out that Chartman wasn't legally an American doctor, and the Bund didn't want any problems.

Mitch said Chartman assured him she was fine when she left with some unknown dark man, but also said he didn't know how she left. How could Chartman know with whom, but not how? Because he wasn't there when she left. She remembered her first visit to the Grove when Sister Rita left her alone with the admission and financial records. He probably did the same for Edwina. It's likely he stepped out, maybe went to lunch, and when he returned Edwina was gone. Abducted by Hector.

Only two questions remained. How did her corpse get to El Paso and where is the money, whatever it's form? Sandy's suggestion that she was put in a trunk and driven there was plausible except that riding sixteen to twenty hours in a trunk would have made it impossible to sneak a smelly cadaver into a hotel room. No, Piper thought, Jim was right about Occam's Razor: the most obvious answer to the question is the answer. Edwina got to El Paso by plane and Hector flew her there.

This is 1938, she reminded herself. There is no civilian radar. Commercial passenger flight is still relatively new, and certainly not available to poor people. There are no security check-ins, no removing your shoes or traveling with a comfort animal. The aircraft she and Sandy saw at Sorenson's airfield were not jumbo jets, but twin-engine prop planes that could fly low.

She picked up her key ring and stared at the locker key. What if, she thought, this is not Hector's key, but Edwina's? If Edwina didn't have the money or the traveler's checks with her when she went to Chartman's, where is her cash stash?

She heard a knock and a man's voice. "Mrs. Sanders? I'm here for the car."

She'd removed her car key and tied it to a piece of cardboard with her name printed on it. She opened the door to a young man about Jim's age wearing dirty coveralls and a scraggly beard. "You're from Sandoval's?"

"Yes, Ma'am. Mr. Gunderson said you have a car that needs fixin'."

"The yellow Coupe at the curb," she said and handed him the key.

"Oh, she's a beaut. Don't worry, I won't be hot-roddin' her none. Mr. Gunderson said I should give you one of our business cards so you can check on the car. See, it has the phone number right here."

"Thank-you … Sam. Are you Sandoval?"

"No, Ma'am. I'm just the guy who does the work. We're real busy too, considerin' the way things are. You ever been to our shop? We're on India Street. Have a good day."

"You too," she said. And he probably would because she had

someplace to go, something to do. She got dressed and went to the theater. *You Can't Take It With* you was still playing and Mr. Marvin was struggling to add a one-sheet for *There's Always a Woman.* "Two comedies, Mr. Marvin?" she asked as she held the glass window open for him. It shouldn't have been a two-person job, but the window never stayed open all the way.

"Yeah. You want to know why? Because that numbskull of a distributor of mine has a new promotion idea. A night of laughs, he calls it. Ha! It ain't gonna work, and you want to know why Missy Where-you-been? Because people will compare one with the other. This one's funnier. No, this one's funnier. People will get divorced. When you coming back to work?" He climbed down from his step-stool and searched her face. "That copper, Conway, he's been around. I tell him, stay away from that girl. She just lost one man she don't need another so soon."

Piper counted five. "Thank-you, Mr. Marvin." He had no idea just how thankful she was. "Did he say what he wanted?"

"I know what he wanted. Unofficial business. Monkey business. How are you? Come inside. I got to get rid of the candy." They walked into the theater and stopped at the snack counter. Goldstein went behind and got a box from the floor. "Mostly chocolate but some other candy too. Give some chocolate to McKnight."

She perused the case and saw he'd added something new. "What are Black Crows?"

"Licorice drops. Five cents."

"Any good?"

"Buy some and find out, already. I give you a box of candy and you want I should let you have new merchandise for free?"

Piper took a dime from her change purse. "No. I expect to pay for them."

He took the coin to the register and rang up five cents. As quickly as he dropped the coin in the slot, he fished it out and held it up to his eyes. "Where did you get this dime?"

"Probably in Sacramento. I don't know. Why?"

He brought it to the counter. "It's a kopek. A Russian dime. How did it get to California, do you think?"

"May I see it?" He dropped it in her hand.

"I tell you how it got to California. It came by way of a Communist. They're all over South America. Mexico, too. Fighting the Fascists. Somebody in Sacramento is a Communist. Maybe a farm worker. And here you have it in San Diego?"

"I'll pay you in pennies." She counted out five on the counter.

"No, I take the kopek. Like a good luck charm. I save it for my grandchildren. If I ever have any. My daughter and her husband, they only think about swimming pools. A fancy house. No children."

Damn it! How could she have missed the Russian writing on a dime? The kopek was, like the airline tickets, just circumstantial evidence —Hector might have flown all over the world, for all she knew, and collected foreign coins —but she needed to keep every piece of evidence she could find. She tried not to clench her fingers. Possession was nine-tenths of the law. He'd let her see it and she wanted to put it with Hector's stuff. But, he wanted it. "Alright, but if I don't ever have any children, it will be your fault. Detective Conway may want a swimming pool instead."

He raised his hands to heaven. "May this woman never marry a policeman! They love swimming pools. I know. I hear things. Keep the kopek."

He put the pennies in the register, slammed it shut and got the candy box from the case. "You really want to come back to work?" he said as he handed it to her.

"Yes, I do. How about Friday?"

"Is happy you make me. An old man shouldn't be alone running a big business. Thank-you for the thank-you note for the flowers. A true lady you are. Maybe you can help me with these guys from the Defense Department, yes? They want to lease my building. The upstairs part they say they're going to make hotel rooms for the soldiers. What do you think?"

"I don't know how much help I can be, but …."

He grabbed some papers laying near the register, stuffed them in a yellow envelope she recognized as government issue, and handed them to her. "Can you read this by Friday? It's borsch to me."

"Okay, sure, but you really ought to see a lawyer."

"And ask him what? Look like a fool when I talk to him because I have no idea what's in these papers? You read them, and then we make an appointment with the lawyer. See you Friday."

He turned away from her to tend his corn-popper. Making money in the theater business is all about concessions, he said more than once. In other things, too, she was learning. She put the kopek in her change purse, put the box of outdated candy under her arm, and walked north to Horton Plaza, wondering why Mr. Marvin had never spoken of his family. Maybe for the same reason she never spoke of Sandy to anyone. It just reminded her he wasn't there anymore. Did Alfred Blackledge and his wife talk about Edwina? Would they be pleased to know Alfred was right, it was a Communist who killed Edwina? Not for any lofty political goals, but out of greed. She caught herself leaping to conclusions again. Idle speculation had to stop. Patience and attention to detail would pay off.

***

Margaret had a baby boy so there was no problem finding him a home, according to Maj. Jones. "You should have called me," Piper told Margaret on the phone. She'd called for her ride to the train station. "I told you I'd come."

"It just sort of happened. Yeah, it hurt a little, but not as bad as I thought. Sister Rita had me scared to death. The doctor said some women have a hard time, some don't. I'm one of the lucky ones."

"You're sure you're ready?" From Piper's point of view, she was more than lucky considering what happened to Carla and Susan, she was blessed.

"Yep! Can you come get me today?" She sounded like Josh asking for a favor with full expectation it would be granted.

"Do you have something decent to wear?"

"They gave me yellow dress. It's ugly."

"We'll go shopping."

Two hours and five dollars spent at the used clothing store, and Margaret had enough clothes to fill Sandy's suitcase. Piper bought her pale pink lipstick and a soft rose rouge at Woolworths. They ate burgers and drank coke at the counter. Margaret was encyclopedic about Hollywood. Piper recognized few the names of any of the stars she talked about except the ones she'd seen recently and the big ones like Jimmy Stewart and Clark Gable. Vivien Leigh was crazy, and Katie Hepburn swung the gate both ways. "You don't have to go home, you know. You can make it here, Margaret. Live on your own. I know some people."

But Margaret shook her head no. "Uh-uh. Miss. Sunday's expecting me. Maj. Jones let me call her all the way in Arkansas. Ain't that something? Imagine talking to people so far away. It's like magic almost. I'm going to start a whole new life and live on my own."

Funny how Margaret thought of her old life like it was a new life, Piper thought as they drove to the train station. Maybe it would be, now that she had experience more of the world than most of the people in Jacksonville. She could tell her customers all about Vivien Leigh and Jimmy Stewart, and they'd think she was the luckiest, prettiest girl in town.

For the second time in less than a week, she'd bought a first-class ticket out of town for a stranger and was waiting for the PA system to announce departure. This time, however, as they sat near the lockers, she was scanning the waiting room every two minutes for suspicious-looking men.

"Are you waiting for someone?" Margaret asked her once when she noticed her reconnoitering.

"Just want to make sure there's no one watching us before I hand over your money." She took out two-hundred-dollars in twenties and gave it to her. "You'll need to eat lots of meat."

Margaret took a quick look around too before stuffing the cash into her bra. "I can't believe you're doing this for me. I don't know what to say, except thank-you a thousand times. Tell Mr. Hitler thank-you too, when you see him."

"I'll do that. Can you think of anything else you can tell me about the Grove …"?

"I talked to Gina yesterday."

"You called her? Margaret, you're supposed to be with Tom!"

"Yeah, I told her we got married and we're with his mother in Memphis. I went there once. I wanted her to tell Sister Rita so they'd buy the wedding story and wouldn't suspect you of anything. I know they're mad about losing a sale."

"You know about that?" Piper said tentatively.

"Nobody takes in strays unless they're godly like Maj. Jones. I'm young but I ain't stupid, even if I did get knocked up. I figure you're a cop or something. When I heard about you husband, I started paying attention more to stuff that was going on. You came through for me. I know I can trust you."

"That you can," Piper said, and remembered something she heard Shelly-the-girlfriend say once: money talks, bullshit walks. "I never once thought you were stupid, Margaret."

"I don't know if this means anything to you, but when your friend came to get me, and I saw what kind of car he was driving, I thought about something Gina had told me."

"The Chevy belonged to my husband. What about it?"

"Maria and Enrique were talking about a guy in a blue Chevy being at an airport, and how they thought he might be a cop. At the time it didn't mean much to me. Anyway, Gina told me they forgot all about it until Cecil came to get me. Maria's scared that the guy they heard about might be connected to you. Enrique told her not to worry, that there's thousands of blue Chevys around."

"When you say 'they' thought he was a cop, who is they?"
"I don't know the names, but the guy who owns the airport and Maria's cousin. They had his license plate number checked. Something about the feds scouting around for possible places for landing fields. Like the one they're building at Treasure Island. I didn't know that was a real place. Is it important?"

What was it Captain Mike said? ONI didn't want Sorenson to know he was being watched. Well, he knew.

"Very Important. I'm no cop, but I am in the information business. I buy it. Like a reporter. If you talk to Gina again, maybe you could let me know what she has to say. Call collect. You have my number."

"That I do," Margaret said with a laugh.

***

She'd done it. She'd recruited her first source the same way

Mitch did it, with kindness to people who needed help. She'd also learned another valuable lesson; It's not just about what you see, or how you look. It's about who sees you.

***

From the train station, she drove to Central Savings Bank to visit her safe deposit box. If she missed a Russian coin, she probably missed a lot of other important information in Hector's stuff, and this time she'd make notes. "I'll be at least a half an hour, so if you have a customer who needs his box, give me a head's up."

"Do you need a chair?" the woman said dryly.

"Actually, that would be great."

The manager intervened. "Mrs. Sanders is a preferred customer, Miss Patterson. Please follow me, Mrs. Sanders, we have a private room available." He led her to a small but comfortable room that looked like a den and had a desk, a chair, and a reading lamp. "Can I get you a cup of coffee, perhaps?"

"No thank-you. I'm alright."

The first item she pulled from the box was the air-line ticket issued by Golden State Airlines. What airfields do they use? she wrote on her note pad. The attached receipt was for $12.00 from the Randall hotel. How far is the hotel from UCSF? Who paid for the room?

Next was the money clip. It was silver with a red circle insignia that had a black hammer and sickle on it. She drew a picture of it. She noted Hector's California address, 1492 El Segundo. Drive there next Wed, she wrote. Check for pilot's license and if he flies for Golden State, she added. Hector might have a locker at his workplace that would explain the little key.

She picked up his keys. The first was a car key with a logo she didn't recognize. She drew a picture of a large red and blue shield, a bird with spread wings, and a smaller shield on the bird that bore a picture of a fox. The second was a latch key —was it still considered breaking and entering if she used it? The locker key she already had on her key ring, so he got her keys from her purse and studied them. Car, house, Sandy's Chevy, Safe Deposit Box, and Hector's locker key. Why had she put it with hers? Just in case she could figure out where his locker was.

Maybe Hector had done the same, just in case … yes, it could be Edwina's key. Perhaps she carried it in her change purse.

She put everything back in the box except the keys, locked it, and returned it to the teller. "Tell your manager thanks for letting me use the office, Miss Patterson."

The woman smiled sheepishly. "I will. He told me about your loss, and I want to say … I didn't know. That is to say, I'm sorry you lost your husband. There must be many documents you'll need to store. Just seeing them can be painful. If there's anything I can do, let me know."

"Thank-you, I appreciate that." It was true. She hadn't received the copies Talbott had promised to send, but she'd have to store them and Sandy's personal effects somewhere safe. It was another one of those grow-up things that complicated her life.

***

She stopped at Largo Factotum and bought a big can of tomato soup. When she got home there was basket of fruit on her doorstep with a note from Honnolore: Call me. Bund Meeting tomorrow?

Absolutely. At least there she was appreciated. All the Navy ever did for her was get her husband killed. She called Honnolore. "Of course, I'll be there. I want to see everyone. And it's time we talked about the women's group."

"Sister Rita told me about your idea to help the girls return to society, Piper. It's wonderful. We can discuss it while we're cleaning up, and maybe announce it a week from tomorrow. I've got some wonderful news of my own, but you'll have to wait like the rest." She had that giddy schoolgirl lilt in her voice again, and Piper thought maybe Cabot was going to be the surprise.

"I'll see you tomorrow then. And thank-you for the fruit. I've been so busy. Did Gunderson tell you what I did to my car? What a dumb thing to do. Next time, I'm calling Mitch."

"You tell him that, too, Piper. He'll be thrilled, believe me."

For all her scheming, Honnolore was a good apple. She knew how to make people feel good about themselves. It was a gift Piper could borrow. She called Carole. "Can you come by after work? I have real fruit and soup."

***

Carole made grilled cheese sandwiches to go with fruit salad and hot soup. Piper called it a comfort dinner, and she liked it the term because, "We both can use a lot of comforting."

Piper held up her sandwich and stared at it. "I'm looking for a sign.”

“Of what, bread mold?”

“A sign that says, I am the perfect house for you, buy me.”

Carole took half of her sandwich and held it an inch from her eyes. “Will it tell me which bank you robbed?”

“It might tell you Sandy had life insurance.”

“Thank God!” Carole placed the sandwich back on her plate and let out a heavy sigh. “I understand. It must be awful staying here. Too many memories.”

“Sandy said he’d take care of me, and I know I need a reason not to go to Germany with the Bauers. If I get a house, let the Krasners get me a job, maybe pretend to marry Sandy’s best friend ...”

“Oh, Lordy, not Cecil! He’s already pretended married to Margaret. Who, by the way, sent him a thank-you card at the YMCA. Didn’t he tell you?”

Piper sank back in her chair. “Well, slap me and call me stupid, Honey Child. When’s he moving to Ar-kan-saw?”

“He can’t. No return address. I thought for sure he’d call you.”

“I’ve been out all day making sure his southern belle got on the train home.”

“Well, who knows. People find love in the strangest places.”

Piper detected sadness. “I don’t mean to be unseemly, but did Jim decide to run off and play secret agent before or after you met Joe Conway?”

“Who? You mean Detective Freckles?”

“He’s been doggin’ me and I figure it’s you he’s after. The last he knew, I was married until Goldstein set him straight."

Carole laughed. "Nope, it's not the man in the blue flannel suit. It's no one you know."

Piper scolded her with a wag of her finger. "You stay away from older married men, Carole. One got Margaret knocked up and kicked around."

"His name is Ensign Beauregard Donald Bailey."

"Impossible. Parents who give a kid a name like that, want him to stay single. Is he related to Admiral Bailey?"

"His son. Coast Guard. Flies fixed wing planes out of Lindbergh Field. The admiral brought him to dinner in February. Jim told me he'd been recruited by a German agent right after Christmas. I think we both knew what that meant when he signed on with the OSS. He tried hard not to want to do it, but he's like you, Piper, even if you don't realize it."

Piper felt a sudden chill as she recalled her last conversation with Jim. She cupped both hands around her mug. "We are from the same century."

"And you're both searching for a reason why you're in this one." She paused as though measuring her words. "Jim loves me, but not enough to stop looking, the way you can't stop looking for Edwina's killer and taking down a black-market baby ring. It's like, if you don't have a mission, you have nothing. But really, you just have nothing to lose."

"Does Jim know about Beauregard?"

"You mean, are Jim and I still sleeping together? Yeah, I want him for as long as I can have him." She cringed. "Don't look at me that way, Piper. What would you have done if you'd solved the mysteries and put Mitch in jail? Would you have stayed married to Sandy? Would he have stayed married to you?"

Piper went to the bedroom and came back with Beth's note. She gave it to Carole and put on the kettle while she read it.

"I prefer to believe that Cecil's sister is telling the truth," Piper said as she opened the tea tin. "I think Sandy and I would have made a go of it. If he got killed in the war, I'd be as sad as I am now. Only … only I might have had his kids to raise. As it is, the best way I can honor him is to kick the crap out of the Nazis. It's not a mission, and it's not about the 21st century. It's about Sandy's mission. I watched him study night after night for that exam because he wanted to save lives and cure my jungle rot on our honeymoon …"

The sobs were unexpected and came with tears, but they brought Carole to her side.

"I'm so sorry, Piper. I don't have your courage. If I did, I'd never have given up my baby because I didn't want to make my parents mad. I can't be a widow any more than I could have raised a bastard. The truth is, I'm deserting Jim the way I deserted Suzanne. Please, please, don't do anything I have to run away from."

It was the truth of people and circumstance that made life so sad. Long after they'd cleaned the kitchen and Carole had driven off with a pear for Jim, Piper sat in a living room lit only by moonlight. Funny, she thought, that Carole was so in love with Jim, only she wasn't. And she wasn't in love with Sandy, only she was. As for courage, she was afraid to turn on the radio in case they played *Harbor Lights*. Afraid to call Gunderson and tell him communists had infiltrated the Grove all because it meant complicated questions and explanations, and the threat of incarceration. "Don't go to the Bund meetings anymore," she'd told Carole before they said good-night. "I'm about to become the best Nazi in town."

***

Piper was at the public library at nine a.m., with drawings tucked under her arm as she searched for the reference librarian. She found Miss Ellen, a plump fifty-ish woman with a pink handkerchief pinned to her blouse, poring over a stack of cards and marking them OVERDUE with a black stamper.

"Excuse me, Ma'am," Piper whispered.

The woman looked up and smiled. She must be accustomed to interruption. "Well, good morning to you, and what would you be needing on this fine day?" she said.

"I was wondering how to go about finding what these symbols mean. If there's a reference book or something."

Miss Ellen reached for the papers in Piper's hand. "May I take a look? Oh, you don't need a reference book. The hammer and sickle is the communist party logo, and the other is the La Salle car company logo. They put it on all their automobiles. Should be made of gold at the prices they charge. You won't find many communists driving a LA Salle, I'll tell you that. Anything else?"

"Ahhhh. Maybe. If you were a rich person, and you could stay at any hotel in San Diego, where would you stay?"

From a pamphlet rack to her left, Miss Ellen took one and handed it to her. "Here's a list. The fancy ones are marked with an asterisk. Anything else?"

"Thank-you. Very much."

"You're welcome, Dearie."

But, before making the rounds, she had to 'gussy' up. She went to Dalton's third floor and asked for the consultant. "Do you remember me, Miss Lillian?" she asked. "I was in here about a week and a half ago for a widow's wardrobe."

"Mrs. Sanders. Of course, I remember. Did everything go well?"

The guest of honor was speechless and so was I, she wanted to say, but not many people would understand her sense of humor...except Sandy. Although she suspected Lillian might. "Yes, and I want to thank-you for not ridiculing my ignorance. Now I need a business woman's wardrobe, and evening clothes. Just a few pieces today, something a secretary might wear. No, more like a personal assistant. What do you suggest?"

"A haircut, shoulder length with a light perm, finger waves on the crown and soft curls all around."

Piper's hand went instinctively to her 2018 parted down the middle straight, and slightly curled at the ends hair-do. It was wash, dry, and go. "I don't have time to fuss."

"Hence, a perm. The hair salon is on the fourth floor. Talk to the stylist. But, since you're here, for daytime wear I suggest an off-white suit with a slightly bottom flare skirt and three-quarter sleeve bolero jacket, open toed Spectators, and matching bag. Not too large, of course. Striped stocking blouse and gloves. You should have a reliable watch, too."

"Can you put a collection together, while I'm on the fourth floor?"

Three hours later, Piper handed over a hundred-seventy-dollars for two pairs of shoes, hose, two suits, two dresses, slacks, a bathing suit, tennis shorts, hats, gloves, collars, two evening dresses, and four blouses, and had her boxes delivered. To go from useful and unremarkable to functional and fashionable was worth every cent. For the last lap of her investigational journey, she had to be appropriately dressed.

***

Her black arm-band stood stark against the creamy-white of her right sleeve, warning everyman, including Mitch Roberts, that she was still off-limits. Honnolore said nothing about her make-over when Piper entered the hall but gave her an approving nod of welcome from across the room. The Krasners were here again, and close by was a couple Piper hadn't seen before. She felt a tug at her elbow.

"Can I get a beautiful lady a drink?" It was Mitch. She'd know his purr anywhere.

He'd caught her staring, and if the visitors were people she should know, the question had to be diplomatic. She turned around. "You may, if you tell me what the occasion is."

"There's supposed to be something big brewing and they don't come much bigger than Alfred Blackledge right?" He disappeared and returned with two glasses lemonade punch.

"Are they staying with the Bauers?"

"Nope. Their suite at the Grant. I hear Harriet's parents stayed there on their honeymoon. No tennis court, but awash in nostalgia." He paused long enough to take a sip of punch. "But, you probably know what's on the agenda, judging by the way you traded bobby-pins for a bob."

"Let's just say I've every intention of moving up in the organization."

"Ahh, bold ambition. I like that in a woman. You wear it well."

"How long are they staying?"

"According to the Trib's society reporter, until June. But they'll be back in July for the dedication of the WPA County Adminis-tration Building. FDR's coming to do the honors. He's visiting the Trib, to see Beatty's murals, too."

"That's fantastic!" she said softly. "Does Cecil know?" Honnolore was waltzing the Blackledges towards them.

"Not yet. Carole told me ol' man Vance dictated a FYI memo to him about it today. He'll get it tomorrow."

"Alfred, Harriet, this is our own Mitch Roberts, and our dear Mrs. Sanders," Honnolore said as she linked arms with Piper.

"Call me Piper, please," she said and extended Harriet her hand.

"Oh, my Dear, we've kept you in our prayers every night since we got word." Harriet looked older than her husband, but was still trim, exuding calm consolation, as though she could hug people with words.

"Then you're responsible for the comfort I've received from everyone here at the Bund." She reached out to Mr. Blackledge. "And thank you so much for the roses."

He took her hand and kissed her fingertips. "Call me Alfred."

"You must bring Piper and Beatty to lunch one day next week, Mrs. Bauer. I understand you work, Piper."

"Wednesday and Thursdays are my days off."

"Then Thursday next it will be. Honnolore tells me you'll be leading a program for our young women."

"One day there will be no stigma attached to producing children for the *Fuhrer*, but until that time comes, I want to dedicate my efforts to ensuring the children are placed in homes that share the values of National Socialism."

"*Sie is das Juel des Vaterlandes*!" Alfred said, "You remind me so much of our daughter."

"I think this would be the time to make the announcement, Mr. Blackledge," Honnolore said. "Come with us, Dear," she said to Piper and they walked to the podium where Anatole was waiting. "It means, she's the Jewel of the Fatherland," Honnolore whispered.

"Everyone," Anatole began, "Mr. Alfred Blackledge has an announcement he'd like to make."

Alfred beamed at Piper and drew his wife to his side. "On behalf of the National Committee, I would like to invite all of you to the German-American Bund Convention in San Francisco this July thirtieth at the California Hotel! Heil Hitler!"

There was deafening applause and shouts of Here! Here! Alfred motion for silence, and continued, "One of your own, Mrs. Christopher Sanders has been nominated for special recognition ..." Before he could finish, there were more applause, and Alfred put his other arm around her, pulling her close. "Go ahead," he whispered, "they want to hear you."

She looked out at the faces of people who she believed never saw her as she served them hot food and cold drinks at the meetings. People who had more than once told her they were sorry she'd lost Sandy. People she'd talked to at the theater, the grocery store, and had invited to the hall. There were at least two dozen men in uniform, and two dozen young couples who had joined the ranks of the older people, who had worked so tirelessly to provide them with support and services they wouldn't have had through tough financial times. "The real credit belongs to those who showed me the way," she told the crowd. "The people who deserve recognition are the people who serve the *Fuhrer*, and they are, Honnolore and Anatole Bauer." She stood at attention, as she'd seen the servicemen do and gave the Bauer's the party salute accompanied by a forceful *Sieg Heil!*

She watched Honnolore count five and lower her eyes. Paying deference pays off, Mrs. Spurlock said once, and she was right. Even Mitch cast her a look of genuine respect as he stood, unnoticed, at the periphery of adoring believers. Most of them couldn't get to San Francisco, but they were welcome. They enjoyed food more, sang the songs louder, and left feeling more uplifted because of it too.

"It's a lot like church, ain't it?" Mitch said to her as they scraped dishes in the kitchen. As soon as Honnolore said good-bye to the last attendee, she'd be there, shooing him out to the hall soon enough.

"Yeah, but without the guilt and fear of hell. That's a plus." Piper had taken off her jacket and put on a bib apron tonight. Honnolore would have a fit if she played scullery maid in her new suit, but Piper refused to play the princess especially when Mitch was finally pitching in with clean-up. Maybe he'd taken Sandy as a role model.

"So, I take it you never met Blackledge before?"

Piper didn't miss a beat. "My boss is higher up the food chain," she said and filled the sink with hot, soapy water as he got a dishtowel from the closet.

"That sounds dangerous. Am I swimming with a shark?"

"I'd rather think of us playing ball on the same team, Mitch."

"Any chance of me hitting a home run?"

She remembered Carole's fluttering eyelashes the night she met Jim. "Well, it depends on how good a player you are," she said and nudged him with her shoulder.

"As fast as you can wash 'em, I'll dry 'em, Babe."

Was Honnolore purposely staying out of the kitchen? Probably. But it was alright if Mitch wanted to flirt with her. He'd given her the information she came for, and she didn't even have to ask him for it. She knew now where Edwina spent the last days of her life. Gunderson had given her information too. "Tell Captain Mike that Hitler is determined to protect the Germans in the Sudetenland."

Piper had never heard of the place.

***

Piper took the hotel brochure Miss Ellen had given her and drew a circle around the Grant Hotel an inch in diameter. Basically, two blocks in every direction. This, she calculated, was the maximum distance Edwina would have walked with a suitcase. Any further and she would have taken a cab. And somewhere in that area was a business or organization that had rental lockers. She drove down Fifth, past the Knickerbocker Hotel, to F Street, turned right at Front, and right again at B Street to Fourth. Her second pass was one block beyond the Grant, which took her E Street. She made a right and turn right on First. As soon as she crossed Broadway, she saw the only two places that Edwina might have gone: the Seven Seas Locker Club, that covered an entire block, and the Greyhound Bus Terminal. Both sold Traveler's Cheques, but only the Greyhound clerks would be accustomed to women coming in and out of the station.

She parked the Chevy and headed towards the station doors, her thoughts summersaulting inside her head. If Edwina wanted absolutely no paper trail, it was possible she'd simply stashed the cash. She went to locker number twenty-eight and slid the key in the slot. The door squeaked when she pulled it open, and inside was a box a little bigger than a man's shoe box, wrapped in brown paper and addressed to Alfred Blackledge, CEO of At-Pac Merchant Marine Builders.

It made sense. Before there was UPS or fed-Ex, Greyhound was the only insurable alternative to the Postal Service. All that was required was a declaration of the value of the package and a description of what was in it. Edwina could have said it was King Tut's teeth, and no one would have been the wiser. She didn't take cash to Chartman's and she didn't buy traveler's cheques. She kept the money at the Greyhound Station because she was going to ship it when she returned from Chartman's. Perhaps the freight window wasn't open when she brought in the box. Perhaps she was running late and had to get back to the hotel before Mitch arrived. It didn't matter. Nothing would bring her back. Hector had killed her for nothing.

Piper drove home, opened the package, and got more than she expected: One-hundred-twenty thousand dollars. How was it possible that meeting donations of ones and fives and silver coins were now neat stacks of hundred-dollar bills? Before her on the bed were twenty-four rubber-banded packs of fifty unused C-notes. If they were real, only a bank could have made the conversion which meant at least one bank in San Diego, there was a clerk loyal enough to the *Fuhrer* to launder money for the Bund.

She made another trip to Central Savings Bank and asked Miss Patterson to get her safe deposit box from the vault. Sandy had taken care of her. Hector Garza had made her rich. She laid her cell phone beside her cash stash. Maybe if she buried her past, she'd stop yearning for it.

Chapter XX

"Have you ever heard of the Lusitania?" Captain Mike asked Piper as they walked from the Cathedral steps down the portico that separated the school courtyard from the sidewalk. At the end was stone bench, for meditation Piper guessed.

"Never," she said.

"It was a passenger liner the Germans torpedoed in 1915. They warned Americans not to book passage because it also carried Canadian soldiers and supplies headed for the Western Front, but no one paid any attention because they believed no government would ever sink a ship carrying non-combatants. Over a hundred civilians died, and Wilson finally decided that America should rule the waves. Commercial shipping is a necessary target of a war machine if it's supplying your enemy and the German sabotage was rampant in America even though we were neutral: An ammunition dump in New York, chemical plants, munition factories, U-boat attacks off our coastal waters. Agitation for strikes."

"Jim and I told you there's going to be a war."

"I know it's inevitable and I hate it. The military and the politicians know. But the people don't want another war and will fight to keep out of the inevitable."

"What's your point, Captain McKnight?"

"I don't want you and Jim, and my daughter to hate me. Every one of the Bund members is a potential saboteur. When the Bund is outlawed, they'll all go underground and we'll lose track of them and their activities, unless you help us."

"That's what Jim told me. I can see that."

"Because Carole's my daughter, the Bund doesn't trust her, especially since the engagement's off. But you and Jim … their trust in you is more valuable to the war effort than your friendship with her. Do you understand?"

All too well. "Jim has to go to Germany, I have to sleep with Nazis, and Carole has to be a correspondent for the Trib and marry an ensign she doesn't love. I understand. What about Cecil Beatty? Does he have a role in this soap opera, now that Sandy's dead?"

McKnight pondered the question for a minute. "We'll find Sandy's killer, Piper. It may take a while, but we'll get him. There's so little to go on. One thing we know, Mitch's bullet is illegal in the U.S. It belongs to a German-made automatic 7.65 mm side-arm. If nothing else, we can arrest him at any time on a weapons charge. You see why we think you're valuable?"

He paused as though waiting for a sign he'd won her over. She didn't flinch. "Anti- German sentiment ran so high in the last war.," he said. "German aliens were subjected to harassment, vigilantism. Many of those people have found a hero in Hitler. Even naturalized German citizens and citizens of German descent were suspect. It'll be worse this time. To tell you the truth, I haven't given Beatty much thought. Maybe he can be your friend as long as he doesn't get in the way."

"You mean as long as other men don't think he's sleeping in Sandy's bed." She shot him disdainful daggers he returned with arrogance.

"Who you sleep with is your business. Your widow's role will only last for so long and it's not just any Nazi we want you to target, but one that Carole says is chasing you like a satyr in spring … Mitch Roberts."

"It's as easy to have a relationship with a bad guy as it is with good guy … sort of like it's as easy to love a rich guy as a poor one. I suppose if you're a whore, it makes sense."

McKnight lit up a Chesterfield. "And I though Carole was worldly wise. You don't bite your tongue, do you?"

"If powerful men didn't like to chase women, women wouldn't have any power at all. That doesn't change in eighty years, Captain McKnight. If it's any comfort."

He let a little laugh escape his lips. "It is, in a way. At least we're not the only generation of bastards to live on the planet. Seriously, I don't want you to despise America because I screwed up. I wish to God I could give you an answer as to *why* Sandy was killed, but I can't. Maybe there is no answer. Maybe it was a robbery gone bad by a deranged punk."

He didn't sound like he believed that and neither did she.

"Now I'm taking Carole and Jim away from you, too. God, what's next? Maybe you'll have to kill somebody the way kids all over America are going to have to." He took a handkerchief from his uniform pocket. It wasn't black like the one she carried, but it wiped away the same kind of sadness. "You all had such a fine and loving hearts and I broke them. During the last war, I never dreamed I'd become one of those incompetent officers who made ghastly mistakes with other peoples' lives, yet here I am, and war hasn't even been declared."

She could give him a small consolation. She could tell him Hector Garza killed her husband and justice had been swift and final. It was the same consolation she could give Alfred and Harriet Blackledge and Mr. and Mrs. Watson of El Paso, if she could trust them. But she was still angry at baby sellers and quacks who murdered helpless young girls and wanted to stop them. Most of all, she wanted to be free.

***

Thursday afternoon Jim tracked her down at Ocean beach, sitting in her car and eating a cone from Softee Freeze. "When all else fails, try the water," he said when she rolled down her window. "Can I join you?"

"Only if you're careful. The upholstery is still new."

He got in and felt the seat. "Beautiful. Celebrating or wallowing in misery?"

"Wondering. Josh is starting his second year as an Aztec. I wonder what his GPA is."

"I saw you talking to the Krasners at last night's meeting. Did they offer you a job?"

"Yep. Research assistant for the German-American Historical Society. I'll be photographing everything that happens in the city and surrounding environs. Sounds impressive, doesn't it? I'll get paid for spying. Seventy cents an hour." She threw a half-eaten cone out the window for the gulls, and they flocked to the car.

"When do you start?"

"As soon as I train my replacement for Mr. Marvin. I told them three months at least 'cause he's real picky."

"Is Cecil in the running?"

"It's an idea, but Mr. Marvin wants a pretty girl for the sailors to flirt with. Speaking of pretty girls …"

"Honnolore wanted to know the details. You're my cousin, you know."

It had to be painful if Jim didn't want to talk about the breakup.

"Since when?"

"Since she asked me if you'd come between me and Carole. I had to give her a reason why we were staying close friends."

"On Mama's side?" Piper said.

"Dad's side. She said she could tell right away we were related. Family resemblance."

"People see what they want to see."

"I'm going to Berlin right after the Frisco Convention. Six months language and fire arms training. I'm supposed to learn how to kill people."

"It shouldn't be hard if people are out to kill you. How did you pass a racial purity check with no birth certificate?"

"Believe it or not, we crow's-woods —Crenshaws —come from sterling stuff. We hail from Crawshaw-Booth in Lancashire, England, and there's not a Jew or a Slav in the entire genepool. Let's just say my contact contacted another contact and said my birth certificate doesn't exist because I'm somebody's bastard. There are places down south where the only birth records are sworn statements witnessed by a doctor. Not too hard to manufacture. The gov'ment just added my name to the Crenshaw family records in Virginia."

"How come it couldn't do that for me?"

"Won't do that for you, you mean. Cause you're a giiirrrl," he said and shoved her playfully.

"What's that got to do with it?"

"Nothing. There isn't any need unless you have to marry a German or join the SS. Uncle Sam likes to keep affidavit records to a minimum if possible. Don't worry, you're Anglo-Saxon."

"Well, that's certainly a load off my mind! she said never until now." He reached for her hand, and held it gently as they watched the ocean, always the same but with different waves.

"There are so many things I can't tell you Piper. Questions I can't answer. I'm sure the same goes for you. But I just want you to know, that we do have each other even if we started out as strangers. Our time. Our secrets. Someday, we'll share them."

Piper prayed the sunset would never come and they could stay together forever so she'd never be alone in this strange and dangerous time. What would it be like, she wondered too, if they did go back. Dorothy Gale was right about there being no place like home for a child, but she wasn't child anymore. And Jim … Jim seemed determined to be a hero as Carole said.

Tonight, she would find that journal she started months ago and never wrote in, and write what she knew about Edwina, Carla,

Sandy and the man who killed them. And after that, she'd think about the answer to Carole's question: What *was* she going to do, now that she solved the crimes and decided not to warn Cecil of his fate?

***

On July 27th, Piper signed papers at Central Savings Bank making her the owner of a three-bedroom sandstone house on Biona Drive in Kensington a block and a half away from Adams Avenue, and a four-plex apartment building half a mile away on Adams Avenue. She'd heard the government spiel on the coming housing needs when she and Mr. Marvin met with his lawyer, Irv Abrams, and Chief Petty Officer Grimes about converting the Goldstein building into Naval housing. "Income property," Grimes told them, "was the way to build wealth." She went house-hunting that afternoon.

"I don't suppose you'd like to live rent free in exchange for managing the apartments for me, would you?" she asked Carole as they did a walk-through. "They're two-bedroom units. You could have an office and when Jim returns, you'd have a nice place to … talk."

"Only if I can have a cat. Are you kidding me? I wouldn't mind it a bit!"

"It's settled, then."

Carole was staring at the wide kitchen windows that overlooked a small backyard. "Do you think Honnolore will make the curtains?" Piper laughed. "My dad says you're smart to put the place under government contract. It'll pay for itself," Carole continued.

"Yeah. That's true." The sad part was, eighty years later homelessness would still be a big problem. "The house has a studio apartment above the garage. I'm going to have Cecil help me landscape and keep up the place. He can drive Sandy's Chevy to and from the construction site. Did your dad tell you he's workin' construction on the airport expansion now?"

"Oh, wonderful. Another citizen enlisted in ONI."

"It's going to be a peoples' war, Carole. No getting around it. And we're close to an unguarded border. Your Dad's job is to recruit the best people he can get," Piper said in Captain Mike's defense. Maybe she'd forgiven him after all.

"There are plenty of Cecils in the world. He didn't have to trap Jim and my best friend too," Carole said. She had walked to the windows and was measuring them by stretching out her arms. "Six feet," she said. "The depth of a grave."

This was going to be a long, tough war.

Old news. New wounds.

www.ingramcontent.com/pod-product-compliance
Lightning Source LLC
Chambersburg PA
CBHW020904160726
47993CB00005B/1813